the
couple

Praise for

the
couple

'*The Couple* is the book I will say, from here on out, I wish
I'd written. The concept is genius and the writing is funny and
thought-provoking. I don't usually give books ratings but when
it's a 5 star, it's a 5 star'
CARRIE HOPE FLETCHER

'Hilarious'
IRISH SUNDAY INDEPENDENT

'Only Helly Acton could turn the world on its head and still
write the most relatable novel in human history. *The Couple* is
so good, I don't have words to define the goodness . . . I raced
through it in a day, loving every line and every page. I can't
recommend it highly enough'
LUCY VINE

'So clever, so thought-provoking, I loved it'
SOPHIE COUSENS

'*The Couple* is a fresh, funny, razor-sharp take on society's
views of relationships that will have you screaming "YES!" and
"OMG she's talking about me!" on every page. It's feminist, it's
provocative and it was a total joy to read'
HANNAH TOVEY

'A completely genius concept that shines a light on the often
archaic ways that society views relationships, or lack thereof.
I adore Helly's characters and the way she always manages to
write funny and soulful feminist fiction, that has the ability to
make us all stop and think. This book is not one to miss'
SARA-ELLA OZBEK

Helly Acton is a copywriter from London with past lives in Zimbabwe, the Middle East and Australia. She studied Law at King's College London before following a more creative path into advertising. At 26, Helly took a career break to travel in Africa and Asia, before landing in Sydney. Six years and one life-affirming break up later, she returned home and threw herself into online dating in the city. Helly uses this experience as a single woman in her early thirties – torn between settling down and savouring her independence – as a source of inspiration.

Helly currently lives in Berkshire with her husband, Chris, their little boy, Arlo, and their little dog, Milo. Sometimes, she gets their names mixed up.

🐦 @hellyacton
📷 @hellyactonauthor
📷 @sharingourshelves
#TheCouple

the
couple

Helly Acton

ZAFFRE

First published in the UK in 2021
This paperback edition published in 2022 by
ZAFFRE
An imprint of Bonnier Books UK
4th Floor, Victoria House, Bloomsbury Square,
London, England, WC1B 4DA
Owned by Bonnier Books
Sveavägen 56, Stockholm, Sweden

A CIP catalogue record for this book is
available from the British Library.

ISBN: 978–1–83877–386–1

Also available as an ebook and an audiobook

1 3 5 7 9 10 8 6 4 2

Typeset by Palimpsest Book Production Ltd, Falkirk, Stirlingshire
Printed and bound in Great Britain by Clays Ltd, Elcograf S.p.A.

Zaffre is an imprint of Bonnier Books UK
www.bonnierbooks.co.uk

For Chris

One

'OK, if I were wine, what would my label say?' Millie asks, reading the back of their bottle of red at their local, Buddies.

June taps her chin with her signature black fingernail. 'Soft at the start, but she'll leave you with a bitter aftertaste and a thumping headache.' She grins, proud of her creativity. 'OK, do me.'

'This old plonk is bold, complex and pairs well with a pungent cheese,' Millie quickly replies.

'Hmmm . . . pungent cheese.' June smiles, turning to the menu.

'Why are we drinking red anyway? It's July! We should be drinking white,' Millie protests.

'Because the only white I like has bubbles in it. And the only bubbles they have here is Cava.'

Millie can't imagine life without her pocket rocket pal, June Moon. Aged six, June moved in with Millie and her mum, the founder and CEO of Big, a large advertising agency. Now, both aged twenty-nine, they live five minutes away from each other, Millie a senior creative, June a solicitor. And, aged sixty-five, the two of them will retire together to a house by the sea. They've shared every milestone moment: their first day of school; their first period and the following freak-out; their last day of school; the time Millie cut her red curls into a bowl cut and wept when the other kids called her Willy; when June waxed her thick black eyebrows and wept when the other kids called her Loonie. Away from school, Millie protected June from the poison of her parents.

And June protects Millie from the pressure of her mother's expectations.

'OK, what do you want?' sighs Al holding a notepad, a pen in her mouth, appearing at their table looking like death warmed up. Before they can answer, she scooches onto the diner chair next to June and slowly lowers her forehead onto the tabletop, using the notepad as a pillow.

'Just . . . . write it down yourselves,' she moans, rolling the pen towards Millie without lifting her head.

'Al, do you think you should be working tonight?' asks June. 'You're a bit off-putting, to be honest. Like a living advert for sobriety.'

'Not living, I'm dead,' Al groans and blows her overgrown brown fringe away from her cheeks.

'Yeah, if anyone's dead, it's me,' June replies, unsympathetically. 'This is the first night I've left the office before midnight this month.'

'Oh please, you love being important,' Al replies.

June smiles, knowing Al's quite right.

'Should we wait?' Millie says, turning back to June.

'Yes! Why do they have to keep changing the menu? I'm barely past the starters,' June replies, running her smoky eyes down the menu before looking up. 'You read the menu before we got here, didn't you?'

'No!' Millie says, defensively. 'OK, yes.'

'Millie!' June cries. 'Reading the menu is part of the fun! Why do you always ruin it?'

'Do you know what ruins the fun?' Millie cries back. 'Panic-ordering and then regretting it.'

'But we aren't in a rush!' June shakes her head.

'Can you two stop talking so loudly?' Al whines, lifting her head up and slumping against the back of the chair.

'Al, can you give us a few minutes? We're still waiting for Ruth,' Millie asks.

'I'll send Jade over. I need to go home.' Al stands up. 'Thirsty Thursday is, hands down, the worst idea I've ever had.'

'You said that about Whisky Wednesday,' Millie points out.

'And Tequila Tuesday,' June helpfully adds.

'I hate my job,' Al moans.

'Go home!' June calls out, as Al drags herself back to the bar with sloth-level energy.

'Wait!' Al spins round and shouts, hushing the crowd. 'Do *not* order the frittata,' she says, bringing her hand up

3

to her mouth and gagging behind her palm. Jared the bar manager glares.

Millie turns back to the menu that she doesn't need. She's always been a planner. She's quite proud of it. Quietly, of course. She would hate to sound boastful. Others admire it too, but out loud and to her face, which triggers instant awkwardness. Criticism helps her improve, but compliments make her queasy. Millie blames her mum. Vivian's fed her too much praise over the years, and now the smell of it makes her feel sick. She isn't ungrateful, she knows her mum is proud and wants the best for her. And June.

'Sorry!' Ruth says breathlessly, plonking herself down and dropping a hundred shopping bags by her feet, before tightening her blonde ponytail and exhaling loudly. 'It's Sam's birthday on Saturday, and I couldn't decide what to get.'

'So, you got her . . . everything?' Millie replies.

'Well, there's a lot of pressure! It's the first birthday we're celebrating as a . . . *couple*.' Ruth looks around as she whispers the word; even after all these months she seems a bit shy saying it out loud. 'Do I get her something sentimental that she doesn't need, or something practical that she'll actually use?'

'So, what did you go for?'

'Books from the gallery where we met, and a load of stuff for our ski trip at the end of the year. Our first holiday together.'

'Ruth, please tell me *you* didn't read the menu beforehand, too?' June asks.

4

June always changes the subject when the conversation gets 'couply', and it makes Millie squirm. She's not used to this kind of chat either, but she tries to support Ruth's bold decision. When Millie points out that June avoids talking about it, she always gives the same explanation: 'What am I meant to say? When Ruth talks about Sam, all that's running through my head is "what the hell are you doing letting a relationship hold you back? You're smart, successful, beautiful. Why is someone like *you* in a couple? You're more than enough on your own. Probably five stars on Slide. Don't you get bored, being with one person?" But if I ever blurted that out, it would just make her feel bad.'

Being in a couple *is* different. And it *does* make people feel uncomfortable. They don't say it out loud, but you know they're quietly wondering what went wrong. When Ruth told Millie she was in a couple, Millie had to use every facial muscle to avoid looking shocked, or worse, pitying. But she's used to it now. Almost. Ruth talks about Sam all the time. Millie would hate to be in a couple, but Ruth seems happy. So who is she to judge?

'I didn't read the menu,' Ruth replies, pouring herself a glass of wine. 'But, and I'm taking a wild guess here, I'm going to have the mushroom burger with a side of coleslaw, polenta chips and a pistachio brownie to finish off.'

June moans dramatically.

'Sorry!' Ruth says. 'Sam says I'm a complete fun sponge at a restaurant.'

June shuts her eyes and starts to run her fingertip up and down the menu. 'OK, tell me when to stop!' she cries.

'STOP,' Millie and Ruth say in unison.

'One . . . small side salad for me,' June says, reading the result, and wrapping her sleek black bob behind her ear. 'Yeah. Don't tell me I don't know how to live!'

June has more reason than most to find couples uncomfortable. She was born in a couple-parent household. An unusual start to life, to say the least. Having two parents is rare, let alone as a couple; parents don't do relationships. Like everyone else, they know they don't last. June's parents were no exception; it turned sour. Very sour. June was the tiny casualty, constantly torn between the two. They weren't at war over their love for her, they were at war over their loathing for each other. Then her mum moved to China with work, and June was left with a father who'd pace around for hours ranting about his sorry situation. To escape, June started to spend all her time at Millie's house. 'Having two daughters wasn't in my life plan!' Vivian once joked, while nailing a 'June's Room' sign to the spare bedroom door. She'd promised June's mum, an old family friend, that she'd take care of her daughter. And she did, guiding her all the way through university and her training to become a solicitor.

'You see!' Millie says gleefully. 'What did I tell you? Bars aren't the place to take risks.'

'Well, according to you,' June replies slowly, 'neither are . . . shops, the park, the train, the office, the library, the cinema, the chemist, the lift, the bath, your home, a room full of cotton wool . . . Need I go on?'

'Millie Jones, the biggest risk you've ever taken is nicking a glug of someone's milk from the work fridge,' Ruth says.

'I replaced it the next day!' Millie cries.

'I once saw Millie crossing the road outside of the pedestrian crossing,' June brags, with mock awe.

'I would *never* do that.' Millie smiles.

'But that's why I love working with you,' Ruth continues. 'You're reliable, and honest to the core.'

Ruth is the chief creative officer at Slide, the world's fastest-growing strings-free sex app. She's also Millie's boss. But in reality, she's far more. She is Millie's work wife and career mentor. Ruth was one of Slide's founding hires, taken on as a creative intern when the app was a start-up. Ten years on, and a few months ago Slide was bought by Human, an American corporation employing 200,000 people globally and constantly hitting the headlines for lawsuits, innovative new products, tax evasion, insane working hours and generally being an evil giant. But they did give big bonuses and free breakfast on Fridays. And, with Ruth at the helm of their little creative team, even the move to Slide's state-of-the-art Battersea HQ didn't stop it from feeling like family.

When Al returns to take their orders, her demeanour has shifted. She stares at Millie with a twinkle in her eye and a big grin.

'DON'T,' Millie says sternly.

Al takes a deep breath. '*Happy bir*—' she sings, slowly and loudly.

'Shhh!' Millie hisses, sinking into her seat. 'OK, yes, it's my birthday. This is fact. Now, next subject please. I am happy to discuss anything else.'

'OK. Would you rather shave Uncle Derek's back or . . .' June suggests.

'. . . Adrian's teeny-tiny penis perm?' Ruth ends.

'But why?' Millie replies despondently.

The three of them stare at her in silence, waiting for an answer.

'Fine! Uncle Derek's back. Can we move on now, please?' Millie begs.

'OK, we're not moving on until we've given you this,' Ruth says, reaching into one of her bags and retrieving a large green box. When Millie sees what's on the outside, she grabs it and throws it under the table.

'Ruth!' she cries, as Al cracks up.

'What?' Ruth laughs. 'Don't think we haven't noticed that you haven't been getting much lately, Mils.'

'We thought you might be feeling a little . . . frustrated. And if anyone ever needed to let off some steam, it's you,' June adds with a smirk, lifting The Pear up to examine the back of the box. The Pear is a lifelike vibrator that went viral after appearing in fruit bowl pranks around the country this summer.

'Just because you two want to slide every night, doesn't mean I do! God, you lot really are Scum Chums,' Millie

8

says, referencing their group chat name and snatching the box back.

'I will never understand how such a prude is so brilliant at coming up with creative campaigns about sliding,' Ruth says.

Last week, Ruth told Millie that her pitch for the Slide Christmas campaign was the 'best idea she's ever seen' in front of the whole team. She knew full well it made Millie squirm. How was Millie supposed to respond? Agree, and she's cocky. Smile, and she's the smug teacher's pet. Slowly roll her chair away from the table out through the meeting room door and round the corner, and she's an HR alert. Millie chose a fake throat-clear and an unusually long sip of water until the conversation moved on and her cheeks cooled down.

'Have you teed up the other waiters for the cake and candles?' Ruth asks Al.

'If I catch so much as a whiff of a candle, I'm legging it to the loo and climbing out of the window,' Millie says.

'But it's your birthday, Mils!' June cries. 'You're twenty-nine! You might not want to celebrate your existence, but we do. And you've only got twelve months to go until the big three-oh. Why can't we do it properly for once?'

'Because you know I hate the attention! It's bad enough that next year's my thirtieth. Let me enjoy this one by celebrating it my way,' Millie replies.

'With no celebration at all?' Al asks.

'Yup.'

Praise and attention aren't the only things that make Millie's insides crawl. Her mind is a melting pot of panics. Imposter syndrome when she does well at work. Guilt about neglecting her mum. That choking fear of change. Losing control over a life she's so carefully curated. And these are just the main courses. For starters, there's an unlimited buffet of freak-outs. Running late. Running early. Running at all. The doorbell. Someone at work asking for 'a quick chat'. But watching her, you wouldn't guess. Millie keeps the lid on tight as she scuttles about her strictly organised routine.

'OK, fine. We won't mention the B-word again tonight, promise,' June says, lowering her glass.

'Thank you,' Millie replies.

'Happy p-irthday,' Al shout-whispers, retreating from the table.

Millie glowers at her.

'Talking about B-words, our new creative strategist starts on Monday,' Ruth says.

The two of them look at her, confused.

'Ben Evans. He's coming over from the Cardiff office,' she explains, then, when she sees that intel hasn't made things any clearer, 'His name starts with a B . . . Ben?'

'Is he fit?' June asks.

'I couldn't possibly say without looking unprofessional.'

'I'll take that as a yes,' June replies.

'He looks a bit like a pixie,' Ruth says. 'Big eyes, black hair. Pointy teeth.'

'Isn't that a vampire?' June asks.

'He's too cute to be a vampire. He's got freckles and dimples. Why have I never seen a vampire with freckles?'

'Because they disappear in a cloud of smoke in sunlight.'

'Ah, yes. Of course.'

'Wait, what are we talking about now?' Millie asks.

'Ben Evans,' Ruth says. 'You're going to hate him.'

'Hey, I don't hate anyone!' Millie replies.

'You hate Sasha,' June replies.

'OK, I strongly dislike one person. But why won't I like him?' Millie asks.

'Because he is your exact opposite. Utter chaos. He came in a day too early for our interview. And, when he went to shake my hand, he knocked his coffee all over the table. There's also a strong chance he'll offend someone in his first five minutes, because he doesn't seem to have a filter. But he's super smart, and knows the market inside out. I don't know – he's Marmite. You'll see what I mean on Monday.'

At the end of the night, feeling warm and fuzzy after three bottles, Millie and June wave goodbye to Ruth at the station.

'Same time next Friday, if I can get out of work early?' June shouts, swallowing a hiccup.

'I'll check with Sam. Should be fine,' Ruth shouts back, waving and blowing a kiss as she descends the escalator.

June shakes her head when she's out of sight. 'Thirty-five years old and asking for permission to hang out with her friends. God, I feel sorry for her. Actually, do I? She got herself into this mess.'

'I don't think she's asking for permission, is she?' Millie replies, moving her gift bag into her left arm and linking her right with June's. 'I think she's just checking they don't have anything else on.'

'But if they do, why do they have to go together? Sam has her own friends. Ruth has us. Why would Sam's plans mean she has to change hers? God, it's hard enough finding a space in my own calendar. My personal life hours are so precious.' June pauses. 'Do you honestly think she's OK, Millie? You know her better than I do. We haven't missed any cries for help or anything, have we? She isn't suddenly going to appear at work with half her hair shaved off, is she?'

'No!' Millie laughs. 'I know Ruth. And I know she's deliriously happy in her cosy little couple bubble.'

'Cosy? More like, claustrophobic. But OK. Whatever you say. Next thing you know they'll be living together and that'll be the last we see of her. I just can't believe anyone would be happier in a couple.'

'Well, you don't have to worry about it,' Millie replies. 'It's not like it'll ever happen to us.'

Two

Millie is on the bus, with her fingers trapped between a pole and the long greasy ponytail of a man leaning against it. She shifts her fingers to make her knuckle pointy and her presence quietly known. In doing so, she catches a few of his oily strands. He winces, scratches his scalp and spins round to glare at her through even greasier glasses.

'Sorry,' Millie mumbles. She doesn't mean it, but her auto-response is set to apologise. It's easier than arguing. She waits until Ponytail turns round before giving the back of his scraggy head a death stare. Millie wishes she stood up for herself more often. June seems to relish confrontation. If she were here, she'd bark at Ponytail to stop hogging the pole and invest in an industrial-strength shampoo. June's the type to shout into the bus carriage for people to squeeze up. Millie's the type to stretch her neck, throw a pleading look and hope they have the heart to make room.

Millie lives half an hour away from her desk. At 7.30 a.m.

she shuts her front door. At 7.35 she hops on the bus. At 7.45 she hops off the bus. At 7.47 she nods hello to Harry in reception. At 7.50 she joins the canteen queue. At 7.55 she steps into the lift clutching her carry cup of decaf oat milk flat white. At 8.00 she's in her chair and opening her emails.

After eight years of doing this every single working morning without fail, she doesn't expect this Monday to be any different. But it is.

It starts when the woman behind her in the canteen queue begins talking loudly about last night's episode of *Single Me Out!* The TV show is the new national obsession, where couples who want to split up attend decoupling sessions with life coach Doctor Alpha Joe, who guides them through their transition to single life. The couples live in separate flats for a month. Gradually, they see less and less of each other, and more of what life is like on their own. Millie and June have a watch party every Sunday. Last night, Ashley broke into his girlfriend Alice's room and tried to convince her to quit the show together. The episode ended on a cliffhanger, and the question on everyone's lips this morning is, *Will she or won't she?* Millie twists her neck in the direction of the conversation. After a few distracted minutes, she realises her coffee is late, which means she is.

'Timmy?' she asks the barista. 'Sorry to ask, is it almost ready?'

Timmy looks at the counter and picks up a carry cup covered in old cartoon stickers.

'This isn't yours?' he asks, looking confused.

'No.' She smiles.

'Then I'm guessing that bloke over there might have yours.' Timmy points behind her at a man with black hair, headphones and a backpack, also covered in old cartoon stickers, walking towards the lifts. 'And I'm guessing this is his.'

Millie takes the cartoon coffee cup and hurries towards Headphone Man, sticking her arms in between the lift doors just before they close. She hops into the lift and holds out the cup.

'Excuse me,' she pants. But the man is too focused on the notices at the back of the lift to hear her.

'Excuse me!' she says, louder, lifting her hand up to tap him on the shoulder. In that split second, he turns round and flinches, splashing his – no, her – coffee across his face.

He shoves the headphones back onto his neck and wipes his chin with his jacket sleeve.

'I'm so sorry!' Millie cries, scrambling for a tissue in her bag, doing a double take when she notices his eyes. Huge and green, framed by long, dark eyelashes so thick it looks like he's wearing eyeliner. His skin is ivory and covered in a mist of tiny freckles, which, contrasted against his jet-black hair, make him look sort of . . . magical.

'That's all right, bach,' he says cheerily in a broad Welsh accent, staring at her and flashing a quick smile that shows strong dimples and pointed white canines that Millie's instantly drawn to.

15

'I think that's my coffee.' She points at his hand. 'And I think this is yours?' She holds up his cartoon cup.

The man, who must be Ben, stares at her in silence like he's processing a complex calculation. After a few seconds, he darts his eyes down to his cup, then at hers in his hand.

'Oh jeez, I'm an idiot, here you go!' he cries. Definitely Welsh. Definitely Ben. 'But it's half gone now! Tell you what, I'll go back down and get you another.'

'No don't, honestly, it's fine,' she says, checking the time on the lift panel. 'It was my fault for being distracted in the queue.'

'You could drink mine? What's your poison?' he asks.

'Decaf oat milk flat white, no sugar,' she says, hating herself a little.

June always says she's so cringed by Millie choosing to drink 'warm, beige, mock-milk swill', that she refuses to stand with her when she orders it.

'Well, aren't you a wild one?' He laughs.

'You should see how I take my toast!' She leans in conspiratorially, smelling eucalyptus. 'Just butter,' she whispers.

'Stop it!' He chuckles. 'Well, I'm a triple-shot black Americano with three sugars. And Marmite an inch thick.'

'Well, aren't you a mad one? So, tell me, how old were you when you started drinking pure caffeine? Five?' she says, lifting up his cup and pointing at the stickers.

'Four, actually,' he replies. 'It was the only way to cope with those long nights, colouring in.'

16

They giggle as the lift button pings and the doors swoosh open.

'You work here too?' he asks, as they walk together towards the glass entrance doors.

'I do,' she says, smiling. 'I'm Millie. And you might want to pop in there first.' She points behind him to the men's loos and then at his chin.

He swivels on his heels. 'Ah, I really do. And I'm Ben. Ben Evans.'

Ben waves goodbye and walks straight into the women's loos, still holding her coffee.

'Trying to catch a fly?' Ruth says, when she sees Millie staring at Ben.

She and Millie are in the kitchen getting a coffee.

Millie snaps her mouth shut.

'So, first thoughts on your new desk neighbour?' Ruth continues. 'You look a bit shell-shocked!'

Ben, who's been put on the desk diagonally opposite Millie, is fidgeting with the height of his desk chair. It abruptly drops down and he disappears behind the screen.

'Well, I see what you mean about the chaos,' Millie remarks.

'He's kind of cute, though, if you fancy clowns,' Ruth suggests.

'Does anyone fancy clowns?' Millie asks.

'There must be someone with a clown fetish,' Ruth muses, blowing her tea. 'It would make a great Halloween special in *Slide Mag*. How about it?'

'No, thanks. The only thing creepier than a clown is a person with a clown fetish.'

'Fair enough,' Ruth shrugs.

Their office messenger dings on their phones and they groan in unison. Sasha has started a new company-wide thread called *Summer Par-tay*.

@sashah:

> Good morning, Sliders! I'm delighted to announce that this year's Summer Party theme is *drumroll*

@sashah:

> *My Secret Fetish*. Can't wait to celebrate with you all soon!

@bene:

> Amazing! Knew my clown suit would come in handy

Millie's mouth falls back open.

'What can I say?' Ruth laughs. 'My hunch is always right.'

Bruce and Millie don't have the easiest relationship, but they have made progress since he moved in. At first, he couldn't bear to be in the same room as her. Now, he reluctantly tolerates her. She can't decide which dynamic she preferred. At night-time, he sits in the dark under the hall table. In the daytime, he disappears into the building's abyss, only returning when he wants an easy feed. And, when he does, he pole dances around Millie's legs, making *meowsic*, as Al had once joked, scratching his ears and snatching her hand back just in time to avoid losing a fingertip.

When Bruce arrived on Millie's doorstep from the rescue centre six months ago, he came with a note.

Hi! I'm Bruce. I am part feral and I __must have__ personal space. Please __don't touch__ my underbelly or I will attack. I'm happiest when I'm __left alone__, but my eye socket needs disinfecting once a week. Wear goggles and thick gloves to __avoid injury__. I'm not purring, I'm growling. Be patient with me! I hope you love me as much as I should learn to love you, once you have __earned my trust__!

The note gave her mixed feelings.

Bruce's personal space is underneath the hall table by the front door, where he lies in wait for passing toes. Millie is surprised she still has any skin left on the tops of her feet. She didn't expect cat parenting to be this difficult, and has to frequently remind herself why she adopted him in the first place. *I didn't do this for the gratitude*, she whispered last week while wiping the blood from a fresh flesh wound. She did it to care for something. To give something back. She wanted another heart in her home. Yes, her fluffy feline flatmate is an angry little bastard, but she still loves him. He doesn't give her compliments or attention, and that's what she needs in a companion.

Tonight, Millie feels restless, as she lies on the sofa with her chin on her chest, staring at Bruce from across the room. Making small movements, she reaches for her phone and opens the camera. Sensing an imminent photo, Bruce scurries further back under the hall table until he completely disappears. Millie throws her phone down next to her. Then picks it up again and starts to search.

Unsurprisingly, Ben Evans is a popular name, but after a few dead-end clicks she finds a profile on a food blog that looks like it was designed at the dawn of the Internet. The About section has clip art and comic sans writing, written by him in the third person.

Ben Evans is currently studying Communications at Cardiff University. When he isn't playing word puzzles, this born-and-bred valleys boy indulges his passion for local produce and stokes the fire in his belly for regional Welsh fare. After he graduates, he will embark on a year-long giant taste test around the world. He's already drooling at the thought of fried spiders in Cambodia, fresh witchetty grubs in Australia and the occasional McDonald's when he's missing The 'Diff. Subscribe to the blog if you'd like to follow his travels!

Millie scrolls down the page. The only post he ever made was one entitled 'Goodbye Cardiff, hello Auckland!' with a picture of him at the airport, his backpack by his feet and a bib saying *boyeatsworld.org* around his neck. Millie leans forward and zooms in on a woman standing behind him with the same bib. As she does so, she accidentally likes the photo. She screams. Bruce bolts into the bedroom. After immediately unliking with shaky fingers, she stares unblinking across the room, listening to her thumping heart and wondering how possible it would be to resign from work, remove herself from the global grid and spend the rest of her days in a small cabin in Outer Mongolia.

21

Three

Something is the matter with Ruth. She barely muttered a word to Millie in the changing room this morning, and she hasn't glanced at her once during this yoga class. Not even when Darth Vader Woman made a sound like a deflating beach ball during Savasana.

'Is everything OK?' Millie asks, as they stroll in the sun along the river towards the office. 'You seem a bit distracted.'

'I'm fine,' Ruth says and sighs, folding her arms tightly.

'Well, that was convincing,' Millie replies. 'Are things OK with you and Sam?'

Ruth frowns. 'Why would you automatically think that something was wrong with me and Sam? I didn't realise you were a member of the couple pity party too.'

'I'm not!' Millie cries. 'But you usually talk about Sam non-stop. In superlatives. And you haven't mentioned her once today, even though it was her birthday dinner last night. I was expecting to hear the whole story in painfully granular detail.'

'God, am I that much of a bore?' Ruth replies, smirking.

'After your first dinner date, you described how she seasoned her food. So my answer is, yes! But it's OK. I'm not listening half the time,' Millie jokes.

'You're a good friend.'

'Yes, I'd love a coffee.'

Ruth sighs again. 'I'm sorry, Mils. I'm feeling a bit defensive about our relationship at the moment. Working here isn't helping. Plus, the chief executive orifice is being extra orifice-y right now.'

'You mean the managing directum?'

'I always forget the title change.'

'Just keep it simple. Adrian Masterbator.'

Adrian Master is the universally loathed founder of Slide. He has one fan in Sasha, the other senior creative on the team, who has him wrapped around her little talon and repeatedly pole-jumps over Ruth to go straight to the top.

'Honestly, Mils,' Ruth says, pausing outside the office. 'You're the only reason I stay here. This company is mad, and that man is maddening. I don't even know why he's still around! He got a massive payout when Human bought Slide. He never needs to work again.'

'All we can hope for is that he retires, he stuffs up or he chokes on his own bullshit,' Millie replies. 'Two out of three are quite possible. Now, coffee?'

'He's like runny dog shit on a new trainer.' Ruth stares into space. 'All stuck in the treads.'

'On second thoughts, maybe we should skip the coffee,' Millie decides.

'Nah, it's on me,' Ruth replies. 'For being a twat and thinking you were coming at me about Sam. I know you aren't like that. And you're right, I do want to tell you all about Sam's birthday meal, from beginning to end. It starts at the supermarket. They were out of celeriac. Total nightmare.'

Millie groans playfully as Ruth tugs her towards reception.

'Come on!' Ruth laughs. 'It's gripping, I promise.'

When Adrian leaves Slide, Ruth will take his place as managing director. And, with her reputation for award-winning work, there's a good chance that Millie will be made chief creative officer. It's a role she's been dreaming of since she was a kid, when her mum started framing all her drawings and telling her she'd be an award-winning creative one day.

The chance to land her dream job at London's coolest company isn't the only reason Millie stays: it's because she knows Slide. It's her home from home. Safe, comfortable, familiar. She loves her short commute, and how she could do it blindfolded. Sure, it has its challenges. But Millie's made a name for herself here, and she's trusted. More than that, she's respected. She'd never partake in self-promotion, but she has come up with some of Slide's most exciting creative campaigns.

'If I ever did quit Slide, it would have to be over a biggie,' Ruth whispers to her in the lift. 'And you know I'd drag you with me, right?'

'Promise?' Millie asks.

'Pinky,' Ruth swears.

When the lift door opens on the canteen floor, they come face to face with Adrian and Sasha.

'Morning, Ruth,' Adrian mutters through his puffy, spitty lips as he steps into the lift before giving them a chance to exit. As usual, he ignores Millie.

Just before the doors close, Sasha leans out and calls after them down the corridor. 'Millie! I tweaked that creative you did for the dirty talk widget. I know it wasn't my project, but I walked past and saw it on Skye's screen. Just felt it was a bit tame. No offence, babes! I think you'll love what I've done.'

Ben's already in the meeting room when Millie arrives.

'Am I late?' she asks.

Ben puts his phone down and sits up, gesturing to her to take a seat opposite him.

'Not at all, I was early. I'm terrible at timekeeping. Easily distracted,' he explains.

'What's this?' she says, smiling and nodding towards the stack of plain buttered toast on the table.

'That, Mildred Jones, is brain food,' he announces.

'Mildred?' she laughs. 'Yeah, that's not my name.'

'Mil . . . dew?' he asks.

'Very funny. It's Millabelle.'

'Well, that's a relief. Belle is a lot nicer than Dread when it comes to nicknames.'

'Or you could just call me Millie, like everyone else?'

'Did you know that *la poubelle* is French for bin?' he replies.

'I didn't.'

'Are you impressed that I know French?' he asks. 'I'm very sophisticated, you know.'

'I can tell. It's a shame you don't wear a bow tie.'

'Now there's an idea! Don't worry, I'll only call you Poubelle when I think your ideas stink. Anyway, I digress. It's a horrible habit of mine. The brew and toast is also an official apology for stealing your coffee yesterday. I mean, if you can even call it coffee. And a thank you for meeting with me. I know it's always tedious to explain what the current projects are to the newbie. We don't have to go into detail or anything. Basically, just tell me who to watch out for. Where to get the good snacks. Why Sasha seems to have taken an instant dislike to me.'

'Oh dear.' Millie smiles. 'What happened?'

'There was a desk situation. I accidentally sat at hers, and if looks could kill, I'd be six feet under right now. I mean, at least she wasn't sitting there at the time – I could have ended up on her lap!'

'Don't worry about Sasha,' Millie reassures him. 'She's

tricky. You have to take her with a pinch of salt. In her first week here, like, six years ago, she openly accused me of stealing her strawberry yoghurt from the fridge.'

A high-pitched laugh erupts from him, which makes Millie giggle.

'She even went to HR about it!' Millie laughs. 'To this day, she still thinks I did it. Then she started aggressively labelling her yoghurt pots "Sasha" in huge letters.'

'You shouldn't have told me that,' Ben says. 'Now all I can think of is stealing one later.'

'Don't! I'll get the blame again,' Millie cries.

Ben laughs. 'The perfect alibi for me! Come on, Belle,' he says, pushing the plate and cup towards her. 'Your butter's getting hard and your vegan cow sweat's growing skin.'

Millie has only known Ben for seventy-two hours, but he feels so familiar.

'So, Jones. Does that mean you're one of us? Welsh?' Ben asks, flashing his green eyes up from his screen.

She looks away. 'My mum's half Welsh. I guess that makes me a quarter?'

'A quarter marvellous!' he says, laughing. 'I mean, the other three quarters are a bitter disappointment, but I suppose it can't be helped. I am joking, by the way. Sorry. I talk utter rubbish most of the time, I'm afraid. Especially in the morning. My tongue tends to sprint until lunch. I have a theory that it's because I haven't spoken for eight hours, so I have all this stored-up energy that my tongue then needs to release, like a stretched rubber band.'

27

'I'm sure the crazy caffeine intake has nothing to do with it,' Millie says, laughing, tearing off a small corner of toast in an attempt to eat it elegantly in front of him.

'Me? Crazy caffeine intake? What on earth do you mean?' he asks, twitching one eye on purpose. 'Now, before we start, riddle me this, Belle. What is a unique biometric identifier that's six letters long?' he asks, taking out a newspaper folded to the crossword section.

Millie looks down at her toast as she thinks, taking a bite of the corner as quietly as she can. When she looks up, Ben is sticking his tongue out at her.

'Ah. Tongue!' She smiles.

'Yes! I was today years old when I learnt that. Isn't that mad?'

Ruth was wrong, Millie doesn't hate Ben. Far from it. She likes him. He's funny. Plus he gets bonus points for already pissing Sasha off. Yes, he's chaotic, but he's also comfortable. Mad, but cute. And when she sees a private message from him on the office messenger at 4 p.m. that day, her stomach clenches, weirdly.

@bene:
Belle

@milliej:
Hi

@bene:
Do you like puzzles?

@milliej:
I do

@bene:
Fancy a round of hangman?

@milliej:
OK

@bene:
Would you like some _ _ _

@milliej:
T

@bene:
T _ _

@milliej:
E

@bene:
TE _

@milliej:
A

@bene:
Wrong!

@milliej:
Really?!!

@bene:
Just kidding, yes, tea, would you like some?

@bene:
But only for you and me

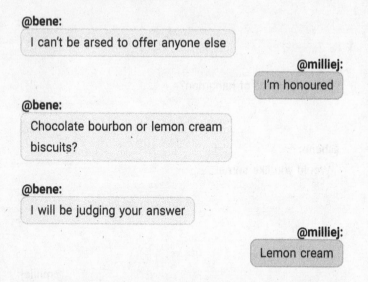

@bene:
I can't be arsed to offer anyone else

@milliej:
I'm honoured

@bene:
Chocolate bourbon or lemon cream
biscuits?

@bene:
I will be judging your answer

@milliej:
Lemon cream

Ben leans back at his desk and lets out a huge sigh. Ruth looks up, confused. Millie shrugs. She wants to start laughing, but she'd hate to spoil this little moment between them.

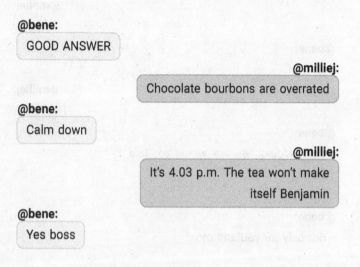

@bene:
GOOD ANSWER

@milliej:
Chocolate bourbons are overrated

@bene:
Calm down

@milliej:
It's 4.03 p.m. The tea won't make
itself Benjamin

@bene:
Yes boss

When Ben stands up from behind his desk, his face is dead straight. Millie squints at her screen, pretending to focus. She has the strange feeling that if she catches his eye, she'll blush.

●▬

'Looks like someone's made a new friend!' Ruth is smiling as Millie packs up her desk at the end of the day.

'Who?' Millie replies, knowing the answer.

'Ben! Obviously.'

'Hardly a friend.'

'Well, I didn't see him make anyone else a cup of tea.'

'Oh, that? He just owed me from earlier,' Millie fibs, and feels her cheeks flush. 'Staying much longer? Need me to stick around?' She changes the subject, pushing her chair under her desk.

'Nah. Got a catch-up with the Master-chist shortly. Go home! It's almost 8.30 p.m., and you should have left three hours ago. Get a life, you loser.'

'Nice. Thanks. What are you up to tonight, anyway?' Millie asks.

'I'm meeting Sam downstairs. Pantry's doing that Surprise Meal for One promo again. It's quite fun. Last time I got chicken satay. Yum.'

'How does that work when there are two of you? Don't you end up with different meals?' Millie asks.

'Well, we just get two of them and cross our fingers. But

yeah, it doesn't always work. When I got chicken satay, she got lentil stew that took about two hours to cook. But I waited, and we shared. That's what you have to do when you're a couple. It's a downside, admittedly. And bloody annoying. You'd think they could just do meals for two. Two people aren't necessarily a couple, anyway. They could be friends.'

'Ugh, stop. Sharing a plate of food is where I draw the line.'

'Well, that's probably why you could never be in a relationship. Want to hear something gross?'

'Go on.'

'Last night, we ate one piece of carrot cake with two forks.'

'Oh my god. You two are nuts,' Millie says.

'All the best people are, Mils,' Ruth replies. 'Might even drink a milkshake with two straws tonight!' she shouts, as Millie hurries away with her hands over her ears.

Three missed calls at midnight is never a good sign. Especially when Ruth knows that Millie is militant about her bedtime routine. At 10 p.m. she's in bed. At 10.30 she turns the light out. At 11 she's asleep with her phone on silent. Sometimes Millie worries that she might miss an emergency call, but that's never happened. Until now.

Four

It's been two hours, and Ruth still hasn't answered any of Millie's calls or texts. She's also set an out-of-office, with an auto message that says nothing about her whereabouts or return.

'Has anyone heard from Ruth this morning?' Millie asks around the creative hub.

Skye, the creative intern, shakes her head and shrugs. 'Do you want me to check her calendar?'

'Please,' Millie says, taking a seat at Ruth's chair and searching around her desk for clues. She's beginning to feel sick with guilt that she didn't pick up last night. Ruth was funny in the morning, but fine when Millie left the office. But she wouldn't call Millie in a medical emergency, she'd call Sam, or her family, or an ambulance.

It had to be something with Sam. Maybe Ruth didn't want to share her chicken satay again, Sam got mad and kicked Ruth out of her flat. Then Ruth locked herself out of her own flat and needed a place to stay, and now she's sitting frozen solid and her pale skin turned blue on a park chair – even thought it's summer – with her phone in her hand and Millie's number under her thumb. In years to come, Millie will engrave the chair with her friend's name and a pledge to keep phones at full volume.

'Nothing,' Skye says, interrupting Millie's daymare. 'In fact, there's nothing in her calendar for the rest of the week. Are you sure she didn't have annual leave booked?'

'Maybe,' Millie replies, knowing that she didn't.

Millie looks around to see if anyone's watching and nudges Ruth's mouse.

'Are you practising, or something?' Sasha coos, as she wanders slowly towards Ruth's desk while stirring a yoghurt pot. 'No offence, babe, but I don't think you're quite there yet.' Her baby voice sounds particularly high today. It makes Millie want to smack the yoghurt pot right out of her hands.

'Have you seen Ruth this morning?' Millie asks.

'Last time I saw her was yesterday. When you two were whispering about something in the kitchen, *as per usual*,' Sasha replies.

Behind Sasha, and in the distance, Millie sees a commotion. It's Ben, leaning face first against the reception door. She watches him whistle, steam up the glass and draw a sad face. It's the type of behaviour she'd expect from an eight-year-old, and normally she'd scoff at it, but she finds herself envying his childlike freedom from inhibition. He's unfiltered, as Ruth described. The opposite of Millie, as she also described. For as long as Millie can remember, she's felt the need to prove herself and please people. She'd love to be less like this, but she's twenty-nine years old. It is who she is. And, at this age, it's who she always will be. She can't change now.

'Can you believe Ruth hired that moron?' Sasha mutters to Skye with a mouth full of yoghurt, swivelling her chair and turning her back on the door. 'He's a sandwich short, if you ask me. He sat at my desk yesterday, when he could see that it's occupied. I mean, why would there be a framed picture of a dog on an empty desk?'

Millie hates that picture of Sasha's Italian greyhound, Lupo, dressed in a tiny tuxedo. He looks so depressed. If she dared to even try to dress Bruce in a tuxedo, she'd lose all her fingers and that would be fair enough.

'Ben's pretty smart, though,' says Skye. 'He helped me with one of Ruth's presentations yesterday.'

'If he's such a genius, why is he doing that?' Sasha jerks her thumb behind her.

Millie looks back at the door to see Ben softly banging his head against the glass. When he catches her staring at him, he puts his hands in begging mode and throws her a pleading look.

'Besides, why are you asking him for help, anyway? We're your line managers,' Sasha adds, briskly.

'Sorry,' Skye says. 'He saw me looking stressed and he offered.'

Millie wanders over to reception and opens the door, to a dramatic exhale from Ben.

'Thank you, Belle. You're a lifesaver.'

'Hardly,' she says, smiling.

'Quick question: does Sasha have impaired vision? Or has she been poked in both eyes recently?' he asks quietly.

'No?'

'Interesting. Anyway, Blackstone,' Ben says as they make their way together towards their desks.

'Sorry?' Millie asks.

'Blackstone. What is it?' he asks again.

'I don't know. Am I meant to?' she replies, wondering if he's teasing her again. 'Is that a riddle?'

Ben laughs as he takes out his phone and shows her his screen.

'I'm not a joke a minute, you know. I can be serious sometimes.' He smiles.

On his phone is a meeting that Millie has never seen before, called Project Blackstone: Confidential.

She shrugs. 'Don't think I'm in that one. Is Ruth?'

'Don't think so,' he says, squinting at his phone. 'You are in it, Belle! Project Blackstone is with you, me, Sasha, Margot and Adrian Master in G minus ten minutes.'

From the corner of her eye, Millie sees Sasha glance up from her screen.

'T,' Millie replies, correcting him.

'Tea? I would love some!' Ben grins.

She sighs, realising his mistake was a trick. 'Very clever,' she replies, as Ben drops his bag by his desk, takes a seat and looks around.

'Morning, everyone! Skye, always a pleasure. Sasha, have you had an eye test recently?' he says cheerily.

'What do you mean?' Sasha, unflinching at her screen, replies.

'Oh, I was just wondering why you walked past the door three times and didn't let me in,' he asks.

Everyone turns towards their screen, feeling uncomfortable but clearly eavesdropping.

'I'm sorry, Ben. I didn't see you,' she replies with an unconvincing smile.

'Hence my concern about the health of your peepers,' he replies.

Sasha scoffs.

'So, who watched *Single Me Out!* last night?' Ben says, and within seconds all chairs, bar Sasha's, turn to face him.

In the boardroom, Millie quietly searches for Sam's number in her mobile. Suddenly the door behind her swings open and bangs into the wall, making Millie jump in her seat.

'Woah! Sorry!' Ben says. 'I thought that door would be heavier.'

'And there I was thinking it was your massive guns,' Millie says, pushing his tea towards the chair opposite her.

'I mean, I'd say it was and then grunt like a wrestler, but we'd both know it was a lie,' he replies.

Ben takes the tea, nods his thanks and walks around the table, sitting down on the chair right next to her. Millie sees him staring at her left cheek for a few seconds and stifles a nervous giggle. She clears her throat and leans forward in her seat so she can't see him anymore, as she types a message to Sam.

Millie:

> Hey Sam, is everything OK? I got a few missed calls from Ruth last night and now I can't get hold of her. Is she coming in today? I'm getting a bit worried. Thanks, Millie.

Millie adds a kiss to the end of the message and then deletes it. Then adds it again. Then deletes it. She doesn't know Sam very well, so a kiss feels a bit overfamiliar. But she also knows Ruth wants them to be friends, so perhaps this could be a first step. She scolds herself for overthinking, as usual, adds the kiss, sends the message and leans back.

'You have freckles on your nose,' Ben states. 'Sorry for staring.'

'Well-observed,' Millie says, smiling, feeling flustered by his attention. 'I guess they tend to come with the territory when you're a redhead like me. What's your excuse?'

'I come from a family of redheads, you know,' he says. 'I'm just the black sheep.'

'Literally,' she says, glancing at his hair.

'Did your mates also play connect the dots on your face during a sleepover? And leave you with a small penis on the end of your nose for a week?'

'Surprisingly, they didn't,' Millie replies. 'But I wouldn't put it past them to do that to me now.'

'Look, I'll show you,' Ben says, taking her wrist with his warm hand and leaning towards her with a pen. She laughs and squirms away, quickly straightening up when Adrian bowls into the room, with Sasha and Margot, Slide's longest-serving strategist, hot on his heels. Shy, calm and polite – Margot is everything Sasha is not.

'What are you two doing?' Adrian booms, taking a loud and creaky seat at the top of the table and placing a small white box in front of him. 'You know my rule – if you're going to slide your colleagues, save it for after hours. And use the app.' He laughs loudly at his own joke.

Sasha joins in, even louder.

'I was only showing Millie how tiny my nib is,' Ben says, holding up his pen. 'See?'

Margot titters. Sasha scowls. Adrian chuckles. There's nothing he loves more than smutty banter.

Millie and Ben open their notepads and roll their chairs closer to the table at the same time.

'So, I have huge news for you four. Inside here,' Adrian says, tapping the little white box in front of him.

'What is it?' Ben asks.

'It's the biggest project you four will ever work on in your lifetimes. It's come all the way from Human in San Francisco. Prepare to have your minds blown.'

He opens the box, then leans back and puts his arms behind his head to reveal pit stains the size of a small pond. The rest of them lean forward. Inside the box is a tiny pink and white pill.

'This is Oxytoxin,' Adrian smirks. 'The world's first antidote for love.'

Five

The five of them stare wide-eyed at the tiny pill, like it's a miniature grenade in front of them.

'Sorry, what is it?' Margot eventually squeaks.

'Oxytoxin. The world's first antidote for love,' Adrian repeats, even louder. 'Do I need to say it a third time?'

'No,' poor Margot whispers.

'That sounds fucking amazing,' Sasha barks.

'How does it work?' Millie asks.

'What does it mean?' Ben adds.

'Who cares about how it works? That's for the lab nerds. All that matters is that it *does* work! Oxytoxin is a new hormone therapy from Human. You take two pills over a fortnight and it stops your glands from releasing the blend of hormones that creates the sensation of "being in love",' he says, with air quotes. 'To put it another way, it protects you from ever having your heart broken by preventing you from falling in love in the first place – no temptation to fuck your life up by being a "couple". And, if you already have a broken heart, it mends it. Boom.'

Adrian clicks on the meeting room screen remote.

'Meet Holly,' Adrian says, nodding towards a revolving image of a teenage girl. 'She's sixteen years old and she thinks she's *in love*.'

When Sasha tuts loudly, Ben shoots her a hard stare.

Holly's skull turns transparent to reveal a brain swarming with multicoloured lines, flowing and twisting over each other. 'Swirling around her young brain is a heavy blend of hormones that have a huge impact on how she behaves. Oestrogen, dopamine, serotonin, oxytocin, to name a few. Now, Holly was a good girl. Polite. Respectful. Top of the class. But since her hormones got fired up and she started hanging out with class rebel Dave, she's turned into a monster. Rude. Disrespectful. Bunking off school, getting bad marks and breaking all the rules. Most concerning for her parents is that her prospects are at risk. They thought they'd raised a prize-winning medic. Now they're worried they've raised hell. But, with one packet of Oxytoxin, they can help their daughter get back on track. Goodbye, Deadbeat Dave. Welcome back, Life Winner Holly.'

He clicks again. The next projection shows an adult man looking miserable.

'Imagine a world without heartbreak. Poor Eric here can't. He's thirty-five and for some reason his hormones are still raging like a horny teenager. He has a horrible habit of falling fast and hard in love with every man he meets. And when they inevitably don't feel the same way, he's crushed. But, with Oxytoxin, Eric can remove any risk of ever falling in love and deal with the horn the way normal people do – hooking up on Slide! The only regret he'll ever have is wishing he'd taken it sooner.'

Ben laughs. 'But being in love doesn't mean there's something wrong with you, does it?'

'Um, yeah, it does,' Sasha replies. 'It screams self-esteem issues.'

'I know someone from school who's in a couple,' Margot muses. 'Thinking about it, he was always a big clingy. And none of us talk to him anymore.'

'But it's not an actual illness,' Ben continues. 'Do you think every couple is sick? You *choose* to be in a couple. You don't choose to have cancer.'

'People *choose* to jump off bridges – it doesn't mean they're right in the head,' Sasha argues, cruelly.

'I don't *get* couples, but I'm with Ben,' Millie says, flashing a glare at Sasha when she isn't looking. 'Look at Ruth. She's in one. While I don't see the appeal of it, and I don't understand *why* she still chooses to be in a couple, I respect her choice. And there definitely isn't anything wrong with her.'

'Ah! You two might *think* that you choose to be in a couple,' Adrian responds, 'but the reality is, you don't. Our behaviour is largely dictated by how we are wired. How we act is in the hands of our hormones, and we can't control those without medical intervention. Can we?'

'But how we act can't *just* be hormonal,' Ben says. 'How we're raised must have something to do with it. Don't our parents have some kind of influence? People raised by couple parents, like me, might want to be in a couple. People raised by single parents might balk at the idea. That's not hormones, it's just what they know.'

'Conditioning can be so dangerous,' says Margot, shaking her head.

'I'm *so* sorry,' Sasha says, insincerely.

'For what?' Ben looks at her.

'That you were raised in couple household. Must have been tough. All those arguments. Being brought up to believe you're not enough on your own.'

'Who's to say they argued? I loved my childhood.' Ben stares at her, baffled and stung. 'Who were you raised by, wolves?'

Millie suppresses a giggle. Sasha turns back to Adrian, searching for backup.

'When I was fourteen,' Adrian explains, 'I thought I was in love with a girl on my football team. Michelle Barton. She was an absolute belter. For six months, Michelle Barton infiltrated my brain and overpowered my thoughts. Just the sight of her from across the field gave me instant stomach ache, so, I asked her out. She laughed in my face and then told everyone on the team that I was a freak. It took me a year to recover. If Oxytoxin had been around back then, I could've popped some pills and moved on with my life, instead of wasting a whole year feeling sorry for myself.

Better still, I could've taken it before meeting her and never felt that way in the first place. Love *is* an illness. Love can make you miserable. Love can push you over the edge.'

The four of them watch Adrian as he stares into space for a while.

Ben clears his throat. 'Look, I understand it can be a nightmare, but those feelings are part of being human. It's part of growing up. It's character-building. Avoiding it completely just seems like meddling. I mean, I can fall out with friends and family. Should I take a pill to stop me feeling anything? Should we all just become robots, to avoid the risk of going through any kind of emotional trauma?'

'Well, that's the brilliant thing about Oxytoxin,' Adrian replies. 'It's very precise. It doesn't stop us from feeling platonic love or sexual desire. It recognises that humans need to feel loved, and so it only disables romantic love. You can still love your friends and family. Your dog, cat, rabbit, hamster. In fact, you might even have *more* love for them after this. It also recognises our basic human need for sex, so it enables us to feel lust. Oxytoxin is going to prove to the world that being in a couple serves no purpose at all. I mean, we wouldn't be flogging it at Slide if it didn't, would we? Oxytoxin takers will still desire strings-free sex. And that's why the geniuses at Human have developed this.'

'Because,' Millie says slowly, 'if fewer people fall in love, it means more people are having one-night stands. It means more customers for Slide.'

'Exactly.'

'Isn't that clever?' Ben says, facetiously.

Actually, it's genius, Millie thinks. Of course, the pill isn't relevant to her. The closest she's ever come to falling in love was with a peanut butter, honey and banana cheesecake from Dairy Devils.

Millie thinks about Ruth and Sam, and how happy they've been. She thinks of the effort Ruth went to for Sam's birthday. The gifts, the ski holiday. If their relationship ended, Ruth would be devastated. Perhaps it has ended. Maybe that's what the missed calls were about. For all Millie knows, Sam could have ended it and Ruth could be sitting at home, sobbing her heart out. If Oxytoxin can prevent that kind of pain, it can only be a good thing, right? Millie glances at her phone. Still nothing.

'Personally, I can't imagine falling in love or being in a couple,' Millie says. 'And I don't think there's something wrong with people who are. I just feel sorry for them. They have to face so many challenges every day, and they've chosen to make their lives harder when their relationships are bound to break down anyway. And, if *Single Me Out!* is anything to go by, that kind of mental trauma is extremely painful. So, if this pill can help those who've had their hearts broken, that sounds . . . positive, right?'

'Why do you feel sorry for couples?' Ben turns to her.

Millie thinks back to when she found out about Sam. It took a few weeks for the shock to settle. And when it did, it left Millie with a permanent worry that Ruth was, deep down, unhappy, despite the smiles on the surface.

'I feel sorry for them for a few reasons. Emotionally, it's horrible to think that they can't be happy on their own. That they have to rely on someone else to feel complete. That they have zero independence. That they have to constantly check in with each other. Make joint decisions and agree on *every single thing*. Their children, if they have them. Their houses. Where they live. Their future. What to have for dinner! Practically, being in a couple sounds like a complete hassle, having to sacrifice time and share space and belongings. Financially, it's also way more expensive to be in a couple.'

'How?' Ben asks.

'In lots of ways, according to Ruth.'

Millie shifts in her seat. His visible disappointment makes her uncomfortable.

'Apparently, if she and Sam move in together,' Millie continues, 'their rent will double, and that's if they can find anywhere to rent at all. Loads of landlords refuse to rent to couples, because it doubles the rate of the wear and tear. I don't know, it just seems like everything is so much easier when you're single. But the worst of it is, what happens when they split up? What do they do with their shared stuff? Maybe sorry is the wrong word. Ruth hates people feeling sorry for her. Whenever anyone asks her if she's OK with being in a couple, she seems fine. Annoyed with the question, but fine.'

'Maybe she is,' Ben suggests. 'Fine. And annoyed.'

'Well, as far as I can see, love gives you brain fog. So that explains Ruth,' Adrian says.

On the one hand, a pill that stops people from experiencing romantic love feels like an evil act of tampering. On the other hand, a pill that prevents heartbreak and helps coupled individuals find focus and happiness alone, feels like an act of kindness. Is romantic love an illness? You get *lovesick*. You have a *crush*. You have your heart *broken*. You *fall* in love. Maybe it is. Maybe she's never thought of it that way. Why would she? Millie never thinks of romantic love at all.

'So how does it work?' Ben asks. 'You take a couple of pills and then you're sorted?'

'It's a two-dose course,' Adrian replies. 'The first pill in Week One to trigger the changes. The second pill in Week Two to complete them. After that, you're risk-free forever. For the rest of your life, you no longer have to worry about strange thoughts, stomach cramps, sweaty palms, ludicrous behaviour and poor judgement.'

'Well, that really does sound amazing,' Ben says, unconvincingly. 'So, what are the next steps?'

'I'm splitting you four up into two teams. Sasha and Margot, you're in Team One. Millie and Ben, you're in Team Two. In two weeks, I want to see some big campaign ideas from you about how we can launch this in the global market. Consider it a creative competition.'

'Brilliant,' Sasha says, tapping her pen against her teeth.

In one swift movement, Millie leans across the table, grabs the pen, breaks it in two and shoves both halves up Sasha's nostrils.

'Millie?' Adrian interrupts her.

'Sorry?'

'I said,' Adrian sighs, 'any questions?'

'What about Ruth?' Millie asks, thinking of a question just in time. 'What's her role in this?'

Adrian stares at Millie.

'I thought you'd know. Ruth quit Slide last night.'

Six

The news hits Millie like a sledgehammer straight to her chest.

'What do you mean, she quit Slide?' Millie asks, disbelievingly. 'She was fine last night!'

'Oh dear,' Sasha murmurs. 'You think you know someone, right, Millie? Aren't you guys meant to be like, *best friends*?'

Millie ignores her. Probably better than punching her.

'I'm not sure,' Adrian replies. 'Perhaps our creative differences finally caught up with us. Perhaps Ruth feels like she's taken the team as far as she can. I do know that she told me, in no uncertain terms, that when she walked out the door, she wasn't coming back.'

'But something must have triggered her,' Millie says softly.

'Are you OK?' Ben asks.

Millie nods. Her voice might tremble if she speaks. How could Ruth leave without even letting her know?

'Ben, Margot, I need to have a word with Millie and Sasha alone,' Adrian says.

Millie watches as they leave the room. On the other side of the glass wall, Ben does a mug and a thumbs up signal. Millie nods slowly, still in shock.

'Look, I didn't fire her,' Adrian continues. 'She chose to walk out. Well, storm out, I suppose.' He chuckles. 'But that's not why I asked you to stay behind. I asked you to stay because with Ruth gone, we have no chief creative officer. We need one. And I think you both have the potential to fill her shoes.'

Millie Jones, Chief Creative Officer.

When Millie was ten years old, she made business cards with this very title on them and handed them out to her mother's advertising colleagues at the door of the agency Christmas party, telling them she was in charge of the decorations that year. She can't believe that her entire purpose, the reason she has poured her life into this place, is now within reach. Millie's heart races when she thinks of the look on her mum's face if she were to get the title. Vivian will be like a puppy in a park, running around yapping to all her friends. Then she'll swiftly move on to a discussion about how the role will give Millie solid experience for taking the next step in her career: starting her own advertising agency. Her mum isn't the type to celebrate scoring a goal for long – her eye is always on the next prize.

Just as the corners of her mouth start to lift, Millie pictures Ruth. How could she be a good friend and yet step into Ruth's shoes when she should still be wearing them? It would feel like Millie was yanking them off her.

'Millie?' Adrian interrupts her thoughts again. 'Did you hear me? I'm putting both you and Sasha forward for Ruth's role. I thought you'd be pleased.'

'I, for one, am truly, Adrian, thank you,' Sasha replies, beaming sycophantically.

'Sorry, I am pleased,' Millie says. 'Delighted, actually. It's just a lot to process.'

'Good. Now listen, you're strong candidates, but you're not certainties. You both have an excellent work ethic and you're dedicated to the cause. You have unique strengths which fall in your favour. Millie, you're a people person. You're inspiring. The juniors flock around you like you're a mother hen. Sasha, you're more of a board member type. You inspire in a different way. Millie's a good cop, you're a bad. And both management approaches have their virtues. The juniors listen to you, Sasha, because they know they'll get that signature dagger stare if they don't.'

Sasha smiles smugly.

'Millie, my biggest concern with you is that you're overly cautious and you care too much about what other people think,' Adrian continues. 'Leaders need to take risks, face criticism and tackle confrontation head-on, especially when it comes to handling hot potatoes like Oxytoxin. We need someone who will defend what we do here, no matter what challenges we face in the media or elsewhere. I can't have another Ruth. Another quitter. I need someone with commercial smarts and a smattering of ruthlessness. Ha! Ruthless. I guess we're all Ruth-less now, aren't we?' He grins. 'Sasha, my biggest concern with you is likeability.'

Sasha's repugnant grin morphs into a frown.

'We need a charmer. Someone who can win the critics over. This pill will literally be a difficult one for many to swallow, so we need a softer touch than the blows you're known to deliver.'

'Well, I'll be sure to dial up the charm then,' Sasha replies.

'So, is there an interview process? Do we have to present to the board?' Millie asks.

'This Oxytoxin pitch *is* your interview process. We'll be judging you both on how you lead the project, work with your team, and ultimately on the strength of your campaign ideas. The winner, and the new chief creative officer, will be announced at the summer party.'

'May the best creative win!' Sasha sings, clapping her hands.

Millie didn't want a promotion by default. She wanted to earn it, with Ruth handing over the reins. Millie had imagined the moment a thousand times. Ruth would take her to lunch at Regina's On the River and order an expensive bottle of champagne. Then she'd lean forward and announce in a whisper that it was finally happening: Adrian was stepping out and they were stepping up. Instead, Ruth has abandoned her and Millie's here, stuck with Adrian, who's tapping through Slide in front of them now and grunting when he gets a match. Gross. Millie pictures Ruth at home, looking miserable. Of course, she might not be. She wasn't happy about being here yesterday. Maybe she's at Regina's On the River with Sam, toasting her swift exit.

After the meeting, Millie heads to the office kitchen, leaning back on the counter as she blows the steam from the top of the tea that Ben has left for her. It came with a sticky note saying *I'm excited to get crea-**tea**-ve with you.* It's made her smile, when smiling is the last thing she feels like doing in the wake of Ruth's walkout.

She's worked all her life for this position. She's been the brains behind their biggest campaigns. She's spoken at conferences when no one else would, despite wanting to crawl into a hole each time. She deserves this promotion, and she's allowed to feel proud of it. Isn't she? Besides, Ruth's the one who left without a word. Ruth's the one who broke their pinky promise – that she'd take Millie with her if she left. Millie imagines what her mum will say when she finds out.

You don't owe her anything.

You owe yourself everything.

Millie's ears prick up when she hears whispers in the print room.

'Did you hear? Adrian fired Ruth. Huge argument, apparently. Something about her being in a couple and so a poor Slide spokesperson,' Voice One says.

'Why wouldn't she just give up the partner?' Voice Two replies.

'Beats me. I mean, being in a couple is weird enough, but to choose that over a career here? That's full-blown bananas.'

'What are you two talking about?' Millie says loudly, her heart thumping as she walks round the corner with her arms folded. The two creative interns pause in shock.

'Haven't you got work to do? If I find out that you're spreading rumours about someone in this office, there will be a formal warning.'

As Millie watches them slink away, their comments replay in her head. How *could* Ruth throw away everything she's worked so hard for here? She was one position away from the top. How could she sacrifice her career and change the whole course of her life just for a relationship, if that's what it was?

Millie's phone beeps.

It's a message from Ruth.

Ruth:

Can you talk?

●──

After checking under the stalls, Millie dials Ruth's number.

'So, I'm guessing you know by now,' Ruth answers. 'I'm officially an ex-Slider. God, it feels good to say that.'

'Well, it doesn't feel good to hear it! What happened? And where have you been all morning?' Millie cries, feeling hurt that Ruth could be so glib about something so huge. 'You can't leave me hanging with three missed calls and then just disappear off the face of the earth. I was worried!'

'Sorry, Mils. That was a bit insensitive. I'm still on a bit of a high.'

'OK, well, I'm glad you're smiling and not weeping into a bottle of tequila,' Millie replies begrudgingly, still struggling with processing it all. Truthfully, she'd rather Ruth *was* weeping into a bottle of tequila. Maybe it would make her feel less like chopped liver.

'I mean, tequila is on the cards for later, but it's definitely more of a fiesta situation,' Ruth replies.

'I'm not sure I'm quite ready to celebrate being left on my tod with Sasha, but give me time.'

'Again, I'm sorry.'

'Can you tell me what actually happened? Adrian wasn't specific,' Millie asks. 'And he's hardly a trustworthy source.'

'You know I've been feeling like I don't belong there for a while. And Adrian's treated me like an outcast ever since he found out I was in a couple. Constantly questioning the credibility of my professional opinion on single matters because of my personal relationship status. Bringing it up at every board meeting. Repeatedly asking me to explain myself, so they could understand couples better, like I was some kind of guinea pig. Then, in our catch-up last night, he dropped the biggie. I told you, Mils, if I ever quit it would have to be over a biggie.'

You also said you'd take me with you, thinks Millie.

'Oxytoxin,' Millie replies.

'That's the one.'

'It's pretty massive.'

56

'It's pretty bloody vile, too, don't you think?' Ruth says.

'Mmm,' Millie replies, noncommittally. Now's not the time to get into a moral debate.

'That was the last straw,' Ruth continues. 'I told him I wanted nothing to do with a pill that makes couples like me and Sam feel like there's something wrong with them. I don't want to make anyone feel that their way of life is something to fear or be fixed. It's so insulting. I can take teasing, but this is going too far. How many times do I have to tell people that being in a couple is a choice, not an affliction? There's nothing wrong with us. I could break up with Sam tomorrow if I wanted to. Get back on Slide. Be like everybody else. But I don't want to. I'm happy just the way I am. And I can't work somewhere that believes otherwise. Slide used to pride itself on being open-minded. Now it's part of Human, and on an anti-couple agenda. And that means it's time for this couple type to jump ship.'

'I get it,' Millie says. 'I just hate that you were pushed.'

'Yeah, me too. But really, he did me a favour. I'm just sorry I couldn't get hold of you before he did.'

'Did you get my messages this morning?' Millie asks.

'Not until lunch, sorry. I had my phone on silent and I slept until midday – it was bliss! Hope you weren't too worried,' Ruth says.

'I think I'll recover,' Millie replies. 'But I do need to go and call off the search party. So, deadbeat, what are you doing for the rest of the day? Back to bed?'

'This deadbeat is going for a long walk in the sun on the

heath, followed by a Perfect for One feast. Sam's on a work trip. Millie, I can't tell you how much freer I feel to be out of there.' Ruth sighs.

'It's so weird to think of you not being here. Promise you're OK? You've been at Slide forever.'

'I guess Sam's my forever now,' Ruth replies.

Millie flinches at 'forever'. Being in couple is weird enough, but being with someone *forever* sounds utterly bonkers. She ends the call with conflicted feelings. Relieved that Ruth is OK, but hurt that she didn't try harder to contact Millie to let her know. Frightened for her friend about all the emotion she's investing in her relationship with Sam. Thrilled about the chance to land her dream job, but guilty about dancing on her friend's workplace grave. Concerned about how Ruth will feel about Millie staying at Slide to work on something that goes against all her values, her way of life. Then again, Ruth didn't ask Millie to go with her, like she promised.

Millie exits the toilet cubicle and stands up straight in the mirror. Ruth has made it loud and clear that her personal life is more important. Millie's truth is that her professional life comes first. Her career is her Number One. Staring at her reflection, she makes a silent pledge to throw herself into the pitch, land the job, achieve her life's dream and become chief creative officer by her thirtieth birthday.

Millie picks up her Perfect for One meal delivery, swings open her front door and scurries quickly through the hall.

'Ha!'

She turns round, seeing Bruce's paw stuck in the rug.

It retracts slowly.

She places her laptop on the kitchen counter, clicks on tonight's catch-up episode of *Single Me Out!* and starts to chop the half of a pepper that came in her Panang Curry Kit.

'What?' she says, when she sees Bruce staring at her from the kitchen door. 'It's research.'

'Tonight on *Single Me Out!*,' the narrator starts, 'we follow Ashley as he leaves the retreat and dines out alone for the first time in five years. How does he feel about Alice's rejection? Will they keep in touch? And will he stay single?'

The camera zooms in on Ashley at Steaks and Cakes.

'Yeah, feeling pretty good, actually. Alice is a vegan, so this is a real treat for me. Do you know if she's watching?' he says, stuffing a large piece of sirloin into his mouth.

'Also on tonight's show: Alice takes a leap and joins Slide to see what she's been missing!'

The camera closes in on Alice zooming in on a bare six-pack, then cuts to her talking to camera.

'What am I most looking forward to in my future? I suppose having my own space again,' she says.

Millie winces at the thought of someone else living here. A guy in her flat, being near her the whole time and watching what she's doing. His feet up on her coffee table. His boxers on her floor in her bedroom. Smelly man things strewn across the bathroom and a scattering of beard hair stuck to the sink. Only having half the bed to herself. The snoring. Being forced to find something on TV that they both want to watch. Having to offer someone else a cup of tea the whole time. Asking for a bite of her cheesecake. Who could bear it?

Wandering over to the sofa with her laptop in her left hand and the curry in her right, she places both on the coffee table before curling up on the sofa and reaching for her phone.

Ruth and June were right – Millie hasn't had a slide in months. She hovers her finger over the app and toys with the idea of having a look now. After a few seconds, she lowers her hand. Now isn't the time to find a slide for the night. Not when she needs to focus on the pitch. Not when she's had a curry.

Her phone buzzes in her hand, making her jump, but when she sees who it is, she finds herself unexpectedly grinning broadly.

Ben:

Team Ashley or Team Alice?

He must have looked for her number on his emails.

Seven

At 6 a.m. on the dot, Millie sits up, throws her duvet off and swings her feet over the side of the bed before placing them firmly on the floor. Right foot first, then left, and never the reverse. 'Starting off on the right foot' has been a superstition that she's held ever since her mother had mentioned how important it was. As a child she thought it was meant literally, and though she now knows it's not, it remains an important part of her routine. She realises it's irrational, but Millie is convinced that if she doesn't start her day on her right foot, it will be awful.

At her dressing table, she runs a brush through her hair, starting from her left temple and moving over to her right, making sure not to miss a single strand before placing her headband on.

Thursday's jogging outfit is all black. Mixing colours makes Millie feel messy, as does wearing something unplanned. Every Sunday evening, she prepares her wardrobe based on three things: weather, meetings, evening plans. Then she organises her cupboard accordingly. It saves her at least ten minutes a day, which really adds up over time. She learnt the trick, as she did most of them, from her mum. She doesn't understand how people like Al can leave the decision to the last minute. It makes her shudder just thinking about it.

There's a lot to do before leaving for work at 7.30 a.m. sharp, so Millie divides the time into manageable fifteen-minute blocks. It's the only way she can tick it all off.

06.00–06.15	*Drink hot lemon, get dressed*
06.15–06.30	*Run to the park*
06.30–06.45	*Run around the park*
06.45–07.00	*Run back home*
07.00–07.30	*Shower, get dressed, hair, make-up*
07.25–07.30	*Attempt a goodbye with Bruce, leave home*

Millie's running route takes her round the big pond in Battersea Park, where people sit on chairs and dangle their toes over the water. On Saturday mornings, Millie and June like to drag two chairs together and snack on cheese toasties while the ducks float close by in hope. As Millie turns the corner towards their favourite spot, the morning sun hits and she feels the sweat start to bead on her forehead. She takes a long, slow breath.

'*Shit!*' she whispers, stopping abruptly when she sees a familiar face eating a bap by the water. Ben. The last person she'd expect to see so early in the morning, and the last person she wants to run into, for professional reasons, of course, with her bee-stung cheeks, blotchy skin and a wheezing chest that makes her sound like a chain-smoker. She doesn't want their new strategist to see her as a sweaty mess in skintight clothes that leave little to the imagination. She quickly searches for the nearest hedge.

'Millie?'

Ugh.

Millie pats her cheeks with her sleeves, checks the time on her phone and turns round.

'Well, you've put me to shame. The last time I ran was away from an extremely amorous dog. Just over there, last week.' Ben points towards the river and grins.

'I just fancied a quickie to blow away the cobwebs,' she pants.

'Excuse me?' He stares at her, amused.

'Yeah, that came out wrong,' she says, laughing. 'How come you're here so early?'

'I couldn't sleep. I still have my pyjamas on under my coat.' He shakes his ankles.

'Cosy.' She smiles, wondering how he isn't sweltering in this heat.

'So, do you live near here, then?' he asks.

'Over there, on the other side,' Millie pants, pointing in the direction of her flat.

'Ah! I'm right there.' He points in the opposite direction to the red-brick mansion block on the corner. 'Hold on, that might explain it. Were you outside my window last night? I heard someone screech an insufferable rendition of "Nothing Compares 2 Me" and then vomit into the bushes after the high note.'

'That *was* me! What did you think?' She laughs.

'A for effort. D for delivery,' he replies. 'I mean, next time, just call me?'

'That's how we welcome people to the area. You'll learn our London traditions soon enough.'

'In Cardiff we screech "I'll Never Fall In Love".'

'Tom Jones!'

'The Welsh king himself.'

They smile and stare at each other for a borderline-toe-curling few seconds of silence.

'OK, don't be alarmed,' Ben whispers, making Millie instantly panic. 'But I think you're being watched. Look slowly to the left, and don't make any sudden movements.'

Millie frowns and turns her head towards the pond to see a goose eyeballing her from the water's edge.

'That's another thing you've got to watch out for, Ben,' she whispers. 'Goose gangs.'

'Would you say it's a few bad eggs, ruining it for the rest of us?' he asks, seriously.

'You've cracked it,' she replies, grinning. 'I should go. See you at work?'

'Oh, I see how it is. Every human for themselves. Go on then, save yourself. I'll see you in there, if I survive.' He shakes his head, looking at the goose.

'Run, Ben, run! Save yourself!' she shouts as she starts jogging backwards, feeling self-conscious about him watching her run from behind.

He salutes her from afar, his thick black hair shimmering in the morning sun. She wonders if he's still watching her as she turns the corner.

Millie stares at the tiles in front of her as the hot water gushes over her shoulders. She replays yesterday's events in her head and tries to imagine her worries washing down the plughole. Ruth saying Oxytoxin is vile. Adrian saying she's too cautious. He's right to be worried. She is young, wary and cares what people think. But she can't change who she is. Millie will never be someone who takes big risks – certainly not without weighing up the consequences first. So, why did Adrian bother asking her, if he thinks she's so likely to fail? He must see something in her. If she can't change herself, she'll just have to change his mind and convince him that you don't have to be ruthless to be ambitious for the role. And that she shouldn't get black marks for weighing up the risks before making a decision. That she can be her own style of chief creative officer *and* make Oxytoxin a global game changer. One with her name on it.

Back in her bedroom and seated at her dressing table, she opens a drawer and removes a small purple velvet pouch. She carefully wiggles her finger into the gap to prise it open, tips it upside down into her left palm and examines the glossy black pendant. Nan's onyx necklace. Nancy was her mum's best friend from childhood. Vivian's June. She was effectively a co-parent, although they never made it official. Lacing it through her fingers in contemplation, she takes both ends and clasps it at the back of her neck, admiring it glistening in her reflection. Millie moves to stand up again, but hesitates for a second time. Finally, she reaches for a bottle of perfume that sits, mostly decoratively, on top of her dressing table and sprays herself three times across her neck. It's 7.27 a.m. and, for the first time in as long as she can remember, she's in danger of running late.

'Well, of *course* they want you to be the new chief creative officer, Millie, there's no one better suited to that role than you! You've been there long enough. You've won them enough awards,' Vivian's voice shrieks down Millie's phone on the bus. 'You could have done it five years ago with your eyes closed. I'll stock the fridge with champagne for Sunday.'

'It's not definite, Mum. There's someone else in the running who has a good chance too.'

'You do know what this means, don't you?' Vivian asks. 'I've got a fifty-fifty chance of being made chief creative officer at Slide?'

'No. It means you're one step closer to starting your own agency.'

'Mum, can we just handle this first?' Millie laughs through the clamped feeling in her chest which she always gets when Vivian talks about her future.

'Well, you're almost thirty, Millabelle. Time is ticking. You don't want to leave it too late. No one wants a washed-out CCO, I promise you. They want fresh young meat with a finger on the pulse.'

'Ew.'

'It's true! I should know. I'm sniffing out fresh meat all the time at Big.'

'Yuck, Mum. Anyway, I'll see you on Sunday.'

'I'm actually quite astounded, Millie.'

'That they're considering me?' Millie asks, having a sudden crisis of confidence as she reaches forward to press the stop bell.

'That Ruth's walked! That she's choosing this "relation-ship" over her career.' Even down the phone Millie can hear the judgemental air quotes. 'She always seemed so together. Independent. In control. I just can't imagine it. It's tragic, really.'

'She isn't dead, Mum.'

'Well, she's dead to me.'

'Mum!'

'I'm joking, Millabelle, don't be so sensitive! You know you can't be sensitive as a CCO, don't you? You need to be tough, fearless. Brave.'

'Some people would think Ruth is brave, to prioritise her personal life over her professional one.'

'There's a fine line between courage and crazy. As long as you don't get any funny ideas. I mean, I know you looked up to her. Good grief.' Vivian laughs. 'Can you imagine if you were in a couple? I'd feel sick with worry. Promise me right now, Millie, that you'll never ruin your life for a relationship.'

'Mum, chill out.'

'I know, I know. You're far too rational to ever find yourself in that situation,' Vivian replies.

Millie glances at her screen when she feels her phone vibrate against her ear.

Ben Evans has shared a photo

'Mum, I have to go,' she says.

'Chat later. I'm so proud of you, my perfect girl.'

Millie rings off and immediately opens the attachment, bursting out laughing, quickly covering her mouth in case people stare.

Ben:

I need an ambulance

In the photo, Ben is lying on the grass with his bap bag over his face.

68

Millie:

I've got GOOSEbumps!

Ben:

Stop ducking around and call the old bill!

Millie:

Calm down, that goose just needs a bit of dough for some quack

Ben:

Worst. Neighbour. EVER

Millie:

I'll make you an apology tea when you're in

Eight

The four friends stare out of the window across the twinkling city lights at dusk, their foreheads shiny and their chests heaving. They turn to each other with a look so shook you'd think they'd just escaped from prison. Sam gave Ruth tickets to a Spin for your Supper experience on Tower Bridge for tonight. Millie regretted it the second she was forced to sit at the front of the class. In any other class – like still life or flower arranging – the front would be proud-teacher's-pet Millie's go-to spot. Not when she's in literal spitting distance of the instructor, who was definitely out for revenge on someone.

'Do you think Sam's trying to tell you something?' Millie pants, slumping at the table with shaky legs.

'Now I do,' Ruth replies, frowning. 'But what's she trying to say?'

'Has she made you take out life insurance recently?' Al wheezes.

'I think I nudged that instructor on Slide last week,' June comments out of the blue. 'If that's how she spins, imagine what she's like in bed.' She exhales dramatically. 'Intense.'

'Still, please thank Sam for the freebie,' Millie says. 'Remind me again – why isn't she here?'

'Yes, why *didn't* your girlfriend want to be tortured in a dark basement for an hour before indulging in a delicious feast of . . . watercress soup?' Al asks, turning the menu over. 'Where is the booze on this menu? I need a pint of Pinot after that.'

'It's a health café,' June explains. 'Booze-free.'

'I did not sign up for this,' Al groans.

'Sam isn't here because this is me time. Us time. I don't want my relationship to encroach on my friendships,' Ruth answers. 'I think it's healthy to have our own lives, our own space. Look, just because we're together, it doesn't mean we need to actually *be* together all the time. We don't need to be in each other's pockets. Especially with you three. It's awkward being the only couple at a table full of singles.'

Ruth catches Millie's eye. It's June that's the problem. Millie's had dinner with Ruth and Sam a few times, and it's been mostly fine. Admittedly, she didn't love it when Sam spoon-fed Ruth a taste of her starter. She didn't know where to look.

'Besides,' Ruth continues, 'if we want to socialise as a couple, we tend to go out with our couple friends.'

'What the actual?' Al says. 'You have other friends? You

71

know *other* couples? Do you guys sit around playing board games for four and laughing at how boring us singles are?'

'Well, you've clearly been spying on us because that's exactly what we do,' Ruth replies. 'But we also have dinner every few weeks. Go to couples' bars. Talk about couple problems.'

'Like how the hell you're going to split things when you eventually break up?' June suggests.

'Oi! Don't talk about that. And no . . .' Ruth replies. 'Like how we wish people would stop asking us if we're single yet or telling us not to worry because it won't be forever. Saying our time will come, it'll happen for us one day. Or the latest and greatest, which is – have you thought about signing up for *Single Me Out!*?'

'I'll tell my mum to stop texting you,' Millie replies.

'Yeah, can you?' Ruth laughs.

'Have you had any thoughts about what you'll do now?' June asks. 'Recruiters must be queuing up to place the ex-chief creative officer of Slide.'

'I think I'm going to take an indefinite career break,' Ruth replies, and shrugs.

'Yay! Welcome to the club, friend.' Al lifts her empty glass. 'Finally, someone to hang out with during the day. Taking a career break was the best decision I ever made.'

'Hold on,' June says, laughing, turning to Al. 'What career are you on a break from? You've been working at Buddies since you left uni! And working is stretching it, to be honest . . .'

'Rude,' Al replies indignantly. 'My journalism! It's on hold.'

The three of them stare at her blankly.

'My blog?'

'Ah, yes, Lond-ON!' Millie cries.

'It must have been tough writing all those posts,' June mutters. 'How many did you do in the end?'

'Five,' Al states. 'They were long!'

'Well, I do hope you've finally recovered from all that hard labour,' June asks, placing her hand on Al's with fake concern.

The idea of a career break brings Millie out in a cold sweat. Millie's work is her whole purpose, her identity, and the reason she bothers getting out of bed every day. Nothing fulfils Millie more than getting her work done, and getting it done well. Being unemployed as a fully capable adult and having to rely on another person for money makes her want to vomit. How can Ruth hack it?

'What are you going to do every day?' Millie asks.

'I don't know. I might get some hobbies.'

'Like crochet?' June suggests.

'Topiary?' Millie adds.

'I tried slam poetry last year,' says Al. 'It was fucking awful. How about craft beer brewing?'

'No,' Ruth states.

'We could just stare out of the window together, waiting for someone to walk past?' Al suggests.

'Like dogs? OK, fine. So, there's a risk I'll go stir-crazy

after a while. But even trainspotting would be better than working on Oxytoxin,' Ruth says, firmly.

Millie was hoping to avoid the elephant in the room. There's no denying it's an awkward situation. Ruth has left Slide because of Oxytoxin. Millie has stayed at Slide to lead the Oxytoxin campaign. On top of that, Millie could end up with Ruth's job. Then again, Ruth promised they'd leave together, and she hasn't mentioned that since she walked out.

'Remind me why we don't like Oxytoxin?' Al asks, once the waiter has taken their order.

'Because telling people to take Oxytoxin is telling them that being in a couple is wrong. Undesirable. Unhealthy. When it isn't, it's a *normal* choice, obviously,' Millie responds, although she isn't totally convinced of that herself.

'St Bridget's Day is bad enough,' Ruth adds. 'Making us feel like shit every 2nd February when we get nothing through the post that celebrates us, too. Rubbing our faces in it with cards, chocolates and cuddly toys,' Ruth adds. 'Oxytoxin takes it to another level. And they aren't launching it because they care about people's well-being. They don't want to save people from heartbreak – they want everyone to be single, so they can get their numbers up on Slide.'

'But regardless of their intentions,' June says, 'isn't taking Oxytoxin a choice too? No one is being forced to take it.'

'By creating the pill in the first place, they're suggesting couples need to be cured. Do you two think I need to be cured? Do I look sick? Do I look unhappy? Actually, don't answer that right now, not after that class.'

'You and Sam might have a healthy and happy relationship, but there will be some people who are in a couple for the wrong reasons, who are struggling to end it and who need help,' Millie says.

'OK, but they aren't just aiming Oxytoxin at couples. They're aiming Oxytoxin at single people as well, telling them to take it as a preventative measure so they can ensure they never fall in love and risk ending up in a couple or having their hearts broken. And I worry they'll feel pressured to take it. By their parents, their other single friends, society in general. Would you take it?'

'I can't imagine I'd ever need to,' June replies. 'But I'm sorry, Ruth, I do see the positives. If my parents had taken Oxytoxin, back in the day, perhaps they wouldn't have had such a stormy relationship and messy exit. Maybe it would have saved me a few sleepless nights when I was little, listening to them screaming at each other.'

Millie puts her hand on June's arm.

Ruth sighs. 'OK, I see what you mean. Maybe in special cases, then. But you'd hope in situations like that that therapy would work, and medical intervention would be a last resort.'

'They tried therapy, but it didn't help. I think the problem was that they always had very intense feelings towards each other. It started off with fireworks, then it went to the dark side. Dad was jealous of Mum's career, and how much time she spent at the office. Mum was jealous of Dad's friends, of how much time he spent with them. Neither of them was willing to accept any wrongdoing, or relent. Sad, really. Looking back, they just wanted to have more time for each other. But neither would compromise or sacrifice – the same reason I'd never be in a relationship. I love being single, and I would never give any of it up for someone else. But it's just who I am, Ruth. I promise I respect you for being able to achieve that same kind of happiness with Sam.'

Ruth smiles at June. 'Thanks. And look, I can see where you're coming from, too. I've been single all my life until now, don't forget.'

'So go on,' Al says. 'Give us the elevator pitch. Why should we buy that you're happier being in a couple than being single, despite all the known drawbacks?'

Ruth laughs. 'OK . . .' she says tentatively. 'Well, it's comforting to have someone to cuddle up to in bed. My slides were always in and out – pun intended. Sam makes me a cup of tea every morning. And she does this cute thing where she sends me a tea emoji if she isn't there.'

June stares at her deadpan and slowly sticks a finger down her throat.

'You asked!' Ruth cries.

'I'm kidding,' June says. 'So basically you're saying that being in a couple is like owning a Teasmade? I like having my whole bed to myself. The Pear is cuddly at the right angle.'

'June, please, stop,' Millie says, covering her face.

76

'But please continue to tell us poor singletons what we're missing out on,' June concludes.

'OK, well, there's the obvious, like having someone I fancy to look at all the time. Honestly, I've seen her smile a thousand times and I still get butterflies when she turns up at my door. It isn't just that I fancy her, it's like I'm drawn to her.'

'Is that where "attractive" comes from?' Al asks.

June shrugs.

'I can't describe it,' Ruth continues. 'Because I know I'd never felt it before now, so I suspect you guys won't have either. I also like having someone to cook a meal for me, someone to cook a meal *for*. Someone to talk to on tap, and to have adventures with on a whim. But there are also the invisible benefits, which I never expected. I feel like I can be myself around her. I mean, I wasn't myself at first, I was on my best behaviour. But now that we're a year in, I'm OK with her seeing every side of me. She knows my good, bad and ugly, and she's still here. I don't have to hide anything.'

'Do you bite your toenails in front of her?' Al asks.

'No!'

'I'm also calling that out a bit, Ruthy. Because I can be myself at home, too . . .' June interjects. 'And it doesn't take me a year to get there.'

'Don't we make you feel at home?' Millie asks, more sympathetically, giving June a warning glance.

'You do, but it's just different with her. Not better, not

77

worse. It's more intimate. Plus, although I feel confident that you three love me, I'd never subject you to an hour of pillow talk at midnight about my fears, hopes and dreams.'

'Well, that's a relief,' June replies.

'Sam and I are teammates. We've got each other's back. If I need help with something, I know she'll be there to lift the load, and me likewise. She makes me feel safe. She looks after me, and I look after her.'

'That's funny,' June replies. 'You are literally describing the relationship I have with myself.'

'Ha ha,' Ruth says. 'Look, I get it. You're convinced that because I'm in a couple I must be unhappy. But I promise you, I'm not. The idea of not being with Sam makes my heart so sore, I can't tell you. I know this sounds weird, but sometimes I'll be walking down the street and I have a daymare that she's died in a freak accident. And the idea of her not being here makes me feel like sobbing on the spot.'

'Wow, being in a couple sounds fantastic,' June says with zero emotion. 'I'm really missing out.'

'From falling in love to falling apart, eh?' Al adds. 'If collapsing at the idea of being apart isn't love, I don't know what is.'

'Aren't you worried that you're a bit too dependent on her for your happiness?' Millie asks.

'And now your finances,' adds June, directly.

'Maybe a bit, but I can't help how I feel,' Ruth says.

'Oxytoxin could,' Al points out.

'I suppose that's why I reacted so strongly to it. The very idea of me not having feelings for her, or her not having feelings for me made me fly into a panic. She's my love partner, my best friend and my family rolled into one. She's my jackpot lottery win.'

'But . . .' June says, cautiously.

'But what?' Ruth replies.

'But . . . she's also a curse, if just being with her is causing you to panic in the first place.'

'Yeah, but the positives outweigh the panics,' Ruth says.

'Did you have a Sam-shaped hole in your life before you met her?' Millie asks. 'Did you think your life needed improving, and would be improved by being in a relationship?'

'Not at all. These feelings just came out of nowhere. I didn't plan it.'

Millie smiles. But underneath the smile is a huge sense of unease at Ruth's vulnerability. If she's rolling all her relationships into one and having panic attacks imagining life without her, how will she cope when they break up? Relationships don't last. Everyone knows that. So, when it inevitably comes crashing down, Millie will just have to be there to help Ruth pick up the pieces. Maybe even with a packet of Oxytoxin.

'Fancy a burger chaser?' Millie asks, as she and June wave goodbye to Al and Ruth at the station.

'I'd love to, but I've got a slide in an hour who I need to freshen up for,' June replies. 'I don't think sweaty, smelly and sticky will do wonders for my rating.'

'What are you at now?' Millie asks.

'I've gone up to 3.8! I'm quite pleased with that. My slide last week was extremely grateful. It was off-putting at first, but hey, at least it paid off in stars. What's yours? When were you even on it last?'

'No idea. The last time I signed in was a month ago. Think I was at three. It went down after I fell asleep on that guy's chest.'

'Before you slid?' June asks.

'Yep. Like, as soon as we got into bed.'

'Well, that'll do it.'

'I was working late, and tired,' Millie explains. 'I didn't even get time to explain myself. I found a note on my side table the next morning saying, 'Don't worry, I won't charge you for my taxi ride over here.'

'Three is pretty dismal, Mils. If you don't do something about that soon, you'll start to match with the dregs.'

'Is it wrong that I don't care, though?' Millie says.

'I take it someone's been spending time with The Pear?' June laughs.

'No, I haven't! I'm happy just as I am right now. I'm getting more satisfaction from my new puzzle book subscription.'

'Millie, I love you,' June says. 'But you need a slide.'

Nine

One pinch of salt, two squirts of hot sauce and three twists of pepper. Millie worked out the perfect seasoning combination for the canteen's poached egg and avocado sourdough toast a couple of years ago. She polishes her knife and fork with a paper napkin and stares at her breakfast with a deep sense of satisfaction, as she always does at her favourite table for one by the window every Friday morning at 10 a.m. Poised to cut her first corner, she pauses when she hears the familiar fast clack of heels approach her from behind. Her jaw clenches. Seconds later, her view of the river is blocked by a Sasha-shaped silhouette.

'Ew, what's that?' Sasha says with a scrunched-up nose.

'Good morning to you,' Millie replies.

'Hon, no. Trust me, you don't want to eat *canteen* eggs,' Sasha says, scraping the chair from the adjacent table and sitting down with a thud. She folds her arms and wraps her long legs around each other like snakes.

'Well, I've eaten them for the last eight years, and I think I'm fine,' Millie replies, cutting through to the bottom of the toast aggressively.

'OK, well, you do you. Where have you been? We have so much to talk about!' Sasha hisses, leaning forward.

'At my desk?' Millie replies.

'I didn't even see you there. You're quieter than Margot the mouse these days. Are you OK?'

'I'm fine. Why wouldn't I be?' Millie replies.

'I thought you might be feeling lonely without work wifey. You know you can always talk to me, don't you?' Sasha says.

'About?' Millie asks.

'Well, first of all, Oxytoxin! How stoked are you? I mean, Ruth leaving is a shocker and all, but talk about a silver lining, right? Chief creative officer. The dream! And we'll get to be CCO on the biggest pill launch since, I don't know, the pill? I hate that we're going to be competing against each other, though. I wish we could be joint CCOs. You know, like the good cop, bad cop situation Adrian talked about. But I guess someone needs to be in charge, don't they?'

Millie nods her head slowly and takes a long sip of water.

'My best friend is in a couple,' Sasha continues. 'Well, ex-best friend. She turned into such a bore that I froze her out. She stopped answering her messages, her phone, started flaking on nights out, the usual.'

Millie wonders who really did the freezing.

'And if she did ever bother, she'd bring along her parasitic twin of a boyfriend, who'd spend all night stroking her arm and asking if she was OK. It was *so* annoying. Is Ruth like that? They probably all are. I do miss her. Not Ruth, obviously. Tara, the ex-bestie. I'm half tempted to invite her out for a drink and put an Oxytoxin in her prosecco while she isn't looking.'

'How are things going with the summer party?' Millie asks, changing the subject.

'Honestly, Millie, I thought it would be a good way to get to know people better. But the more I get to know people, the more I hate people. I wish I'd never stuck my hand up for it. Do you know how many complaints I've had about the theme? Fuck me, if you don't want people to know your fetish, make one up, it's not that hard! We work at one of the coolest companies in the world, but you wouldn't think so speaking to some of these nerds. Most people here have the imaginative capacity of a lobotomised pigeon.'

'So, what are you going as?' Millie gets a word in.

'A leather-clad dominatrix, of course!' Sasha laughs. 'I just need to find someone to pair up with who's willing to wear a lead and a pair of handcuffs. Are you up for it?'

'No.'

'Imagine if I could get Adrian to do it! That would be wild. Have you thought about your outfit? Wait! Let me guess . . .'

Sasha squints at her for an uncomfortably long time, and Millie despairs about how cold her eggs must be by now.

'A geography teacher,' Sasha finally says.

'No.'

'A file on the server that needs reorganising?'

Millie stares at her blankly.

'An old leather book with a musty smell?'

'Yes!' Millie replies with false enthusiasm.

The truth is, Millie hasn't a clue what she'll go as. She doesn't have a fetish. She's always liked it slow, simple and, most important of all – silent. Two people in a totally intimate moment. No toys, no talk, no role play. Definitely no feet. Does it make her a bore? Maybe. But she isn't going to pretend to be someone else. She tried sex talk with her last slide and ended up telling him that he had a filthy little bishop, which ended the session abruptly. The truth is Millie just isn't Slide material. All the top Sliders are kinky, and Millie is about as kinky as a ninety-year-old nun.

'Oh god, it must be something *filthy* if you're not willing to even tell me!' Sasha giggles, then, sensing Millie isn't going to give anything away, she moves on. 'Anyway, I'm sorry you've been lumped with that clown for the pitch,' Sasha says, nodding towards the toast station behind Millie. Millie turns round to see Ben staring at the menu, swaying backwards and forwards on his white trainers, which have a visible hole in the side. He turns his gaze towards the window and the sunlight illuminates his face. He spots them, breaks out into a big, dimpled smile, and waves. Millie's stomach flips.

Save me, Millie thinks.

As if he can hear her thoughts, Ben's hand wave rotates into a hand gesture for Millie to join him. Millie throws her fork down with a clatter on her plate, stands up and glides across the canteen to his side. Hand in hand, they leave, turning heads as they go. At the door, Millie takes one last look behind her and lifts her middle finger up to Sasha, who's mouthing something aggressively . . .

'Are you listening to me or what?' Sasha says.

Millie blinks a little, confused by the daydream and hoping her cheeks aren't red.

'What did you say?' she asks Sasha.

'I said, why does he dress like he's sixteen?' Sasha whispers. 'I mean, have some self-respect. And what's his obsession with puzzles? How are we supposed to take a man-child seriously? I don't know what Ruth was thinking when she hired him for the London office. Maybe it was her last "fuck you" to Adrian and this place.'

'Maybe she was hiring him for how he thinks, rather than how he dresses. I mean, what he looks like doesn't matter. I'd never hire someone who looked like they spent more time on their wardrobe than their work.'

'First impressions are everything, Millie. And he looks like he doesn't give a crap about what people think. Tell you what, if I'm made CCO, I'm going to bring in a dress code. Don't worry, you'll be fine. I'd describe your style as . . . comfortable, not controversial. Plus, you wear the same thing every week. Hold on, apart from that necklace!

Is that new? Millie Jones, are you trying to impress someone?' Sasha laughs.

Millie grabs hold of the stone around her neck.

'No, I just found it yesterday. It belonged to a friend,' she says.

'No offence, babes, but I'm not sure a necklace is going to impress him!' Sasha smirks.

Millie blushes and darts her eyes towards Ben. 'I'm not trying to impress him!' she rasps.

'What?' Sasha frowns, following Millie's eyes. 'No, you dickhead, I meant Adrian.'

'Oh.' Millie exhales, dropping the necklace and wondering why her mind went there.

'Anyway, I'm surprised you're leaping to Ben's defence,' Sasha continues. 'I can't imagine a worse match, to be honest. I thought you'd hate him. He's all over the place. You're more of an always-in-the-same-place type.'

'I don't hate anyone,' Millie replies.

'Everyone hates someone, Millie. Oh, shit on a kitten, he's coming over here.'

'Greetings, desk associates!' Ben says. 'That looks good,' he nods at Millie's toast, which has gone hard.

'It was going to be,' Millie sighs.

'Mine's a sausage and 'shroom. With extra sausage. And 'shroom.' He smiles, holding it up proudly.

'Good choice! But you've made a fatal error.' Millie shakes her head.

'What?' he replies, looking worried.

'Extra butter.'

'Bollocks! I knew there was something.'

Millie reaches into her bag and removes a plastic wallet. It's full of salt, pepper and hot sauce sachets. She happens to have some extra butter pats in there today too.

'You're such a fucking geek,' Sasha scoffs.

'Millie Jones, you're my angel!' Ben cries, as Millie hands him one, her heart leaping.

'So, Ben, are you still going as a clown to the summer party?' Sasha smiles.

'I guess so. It's the only fancy dress outfit I've got,' he replies. 'I dressed up as a clown for my niece's birthday last year.'

'Cute,' Millie says.

'Not really, actually,' Ben says, grimacing. 'By the time I realised I'd accidentally ordered an *evil* clown suit with a blood-squirting nose, it was too late. The theme went from circus to screamfest very fast, let me tell you.'

'Evil clown fetish! Love it,' Sasha replies.

'I don't actually have a fetish. The truth is, I should probably come wrapped in my weighted blanket, with a cup of tea.' He shrugs.

Sasha unfolds her legs and stands up straight, towering over him in her six-inch heels.

'My god, maybe you two *do* make a dream team,' she says.

'May the best one win!' Ben smiles, slipping behind her and taking her seat.

'Isn't she a saint?' he says, when she's out of earshot. 'This morning, she was kind enough to make sure that all my paperwork was back on my side of the table, and not a millimetre inch over on hers. I'm guessing she didn't want me to lose anything. *So* kind.'

'Very considerate,' Millie agrees, managing to match his mock-straight face.

'I'm glad you're here,' Ben says. 'Because I've had a brilliant plan for the Oxytoxin pitch, and I've been dying to tell you. I was going to text you last night, but it was a bit late. I didn't want to message you about work during your evening. I was worried you'd think I was some kind of text pest.'

'I definitely would have,' Millie replies.

'Well, I am, so you'd better watch out,' he says, opening the butter pat. 'I've got quick fingers and no friends in this city, so I have plenty of time on my hands. If you're not careful, I might start texting you some hangman puzzles in the middle of the night.'

'Is that a threat or a promise?' Millie asks.

'It's a guarantee,' he says, smiling.

'So, what's this brilliant plan?' Millie asks, pushing her plate to the side and leaning forward.

Ben leans forward too, and suddenly they're in their own little bubble at the table.

'Do you like trains?' he asks.

Millie frowns at him, confused.

'Don't worry, I'm not asking you to visit the London

Transport Museum with me, although something tells me you'd love it, because I reckon you might be a secret nerd, like me. I mean, do you enjoy trains as a method of getting from A to B?'

'I do,' Millie says with caution. 'Depending on where B is.'

'Well, then it's settled. I realise we've only known each other for a week, Belle, but we're going on a little trip together. Just two days, you and me. Leaving on Wednesday.'

'This Wednesday?' She laughs, her palms going clammy. On the one hand, the idea of being alone with Ben for two days makes her insides fizz with excitement. On the other, a trip requires planning ahead: tickets, wardrobe, a cat-sitter for Bruce. The last one walked out on her. How is she supposed to organise it all for Wednesday?

'Yes, Wednesday. It's not like we've got anything else on, is it?' Ben smiles, taking a big bite of his sausage sandwich. An entire sausage falls out the other side of the bread and lands on the table. He picks it up and squashes it back in.

'I guess not,' Millie says, her heart pounding, but her face suggesting otherwise. 'But why?'

'It's a research trip for the pitch. I'll tell you all about it on the way there,' he says, smiling.

'And where exactly is *there*?' she asks.

'That's a surprise too,' he replies. 'Trust me, Belle.'

To Millie's amazement, she does.

Ten

'Introducing our new chief creative officer, Millie Jones! Millie Jones, CCO, a few words about your appointment, if you will?' June shouts across the table, when Millie returns from the toilet.

'Hi, everyone. Wow, what an honour. I'd like to start by thanking Ruth. If it wasn't for her, I wouldn't be standing here tonight. Well, I mean, because she taught me so much. Not because she resigned. Bleurgh, sorry.' Millie grimaces. 'It's a good thing she isn't here yet, she'd kill me.'

'Incredible,' Al says, putting their bottle of Merlot down and giving a slow handclap. 'My favourite bit was when you made everyone feel awkward in the first five seconds of the speech. Now that's talent.'

'How can I do this job if I can't even accept it?' Millie replies.

'Just keep it simple. All you need to say is four things.

Thanks. I'm excited. I'll do my best. Sasha, you're fired,' Al says, backing away from the table.

'This is stupid. I don't even know if I'll get it.'

'Like you won't get it,' June says, and rolls her eyes. 'You're the shooiest of shoo-ins. Have you decided what you're going as yet? What *is* your secret fetish? Your desk organiser? Your microfibre cleaning cloth?'

'Soft furnishings!' cries Al.

'I see you two are being especially troll-like tonight,' Millie says.

June's phone lights up with a Slide request.

'Do you know what I wish?' June says, staring at the picture and clicking the 'Maybe Later' button. 'I wish they'd invent Oxytoxin for cheesy fries.'

'I wish they'd invent Oxytoxin for Merlot,' Al says, standing up and pushing her notepad into her apron. 'No, actually, I don't, I take that back.'

'Obsession, yearning, butterflies, stomach cramps,' June says, picking at the crumbs on an empty plate of cheesy fries in front of her. 'It's all there. That sounds like love if you ask me. Or at least, that's how they describe it on *Single Me Out!*'

'Maybe you've got stomach cramps because you've just finished your fries and now almost mine?' Millie says, drawing her plate towards her.

'You snooze, you lose, Mils. How do you not know that by now? It's been twenty-four years!'

Millie smacks June's wandering hand away from her plate.

91

'Anyone watching you two would think *you're* an old bickering couple,' Al says, laughing.

'I guess we kind of are, aren't we?' June replies.

'When we move into the house by the sea, you'd better not complain about the heating all the time,' June says. 'I'm telling you now, the temperature is fine!'

'It is *not* fine, there's a draught!' Millie says in a shaky voice.

'Put a bloody jumper on!'

'Do you have to have the volume *so* loud?!'

'Shut your toothless trap, you old tart!'

They burst into laughter.

'Yes! Tune!' June shouts, swaying to 'I Will Always Love Me' as Millie waves at Al for another bottle. 'Mils!' June throws her eyes open. 'We need to start thinking of your thirtieth playlist!'

'Um, no we don't, it's almost a year away!' Millie responds.

'You've already done it, haven't you?' June's face falls flat.

'No,' Millie says, pouring June a glass of water, avoiding her glare. 'OK, fine, yes.'

June frowns at her, and then suddenly breaks into dramatic lip-syncing at the song's peak, as Millie texts Ruth.

Millie:

At Buddies. Are you coming hot stuff? x

'Karaoke!' June cries, slamming both hands on the table. 'Tonight! Al!' she shouts across the bar. 'Karaoke later!'

'Hell, yeah!' Al shouts back.

'Oh, go on, Mils, it's Saturday night and we haven't done karaoke in ages!' June pleads. 'And my vocal cords are all warmed up now. Is Ruth on her way? She'll be up for it. Although she'll probably have to *check with Sam* first.'

Millie looks at her phone and shrugs.

'She's not coming.' June sighs. 'She never comes out anymore.'

'She was out with us last week!' Millie laughs.

'OK, but you have to admit, she isn't coming out as much,' June says. 'I give it another six months until she gets too cosy at home with Sam and stops coming out completely.'

'That'll never happen. You heard what she said the other night after spin. She's determined for her and Sam to lead their own lives. She'll keep on coming out.'

'But with Sam in her life, she has to split her time even more. It's inevitable that she's going to see less of us. Plus she's not in town for work anymore – she's at home making dinner for her *girlfriend*. We've got to accept that Sam is her priority now. Not work, not us. Not family. Look at *Single Me Out!* Ashley and Alice did the same thing. Us singles pay the price when a friend falls in love and leaves us behind.'

Millie thinks back to the *Single Me Out!* episode when Ashley's mum was interviewed for the show. You could see how conflicted she was between wanting them to be happy and worrying that they couldn't possibly be. Ashley's mum was adamant that she'd done something wrong in raising him to make him feel like he wasn't good enough to be on his own. Alice's co-parent dads refused to be interviewed at all – clearly they didn't approve.

'Maybe they close off from the people around them because they're uncomfortable. They know that people can't relate to them. They know everyone's whispering behind their backs. I guess that's why Ruth and Sam have couple friends and go to couples' bars, because it's easier to hang out with people who've made the same life choices, who have to deal with the same issues. I mean, would you go out with a bunch of couples? Or throuples?'

'No, I'd feel like a total random.'

'Maybe they'd be jealous.'

'Yeah!' June says, holding up her phone to Millie's face to reveal a close-up dick pic.

Millie shuts her eyes quickly.

'Oh Mils, such a sensitive little soul, aren't you? It's just a willy wearing a sombrero!'

It isn't the first time June has teased her about being a *sensitive little soul*, and Millie can't deny there's a grain of truth. But after the millionth time, it feels like a dig. The way June says it makes her feel like she's small and silly. To keep the peace, Millie is happy to continue sidestepping these sideswipes, instead of tackling them head-on. Unlike June, confrontation isn't her thing.

'Why do you *want* to see a willy in a sombrero?' Millie asks. 'Penises aren't exactly oil paintings, are they?'

'Um, I beg to differ,' June says. 'But if they bother you so much, how about this?'

June holds another one of her Slide matches up. It's a naked woman doing the splits on a paddleboard and winking at the camera.

'That's more impressive than a sombrero,' Millie comments.

'Woah!' cries a new but distinctive deep voice next to them.

Millie spins round to see Ben standing next to her, shielding his face from June's phone.

'Um, sorry, can we help you?' June says, bristling.

'June, this is Ben!' Millie quickly adds, surprised to find herself grinning.

Ben smiles that perfectly imperfect dimpled smile and stretches his hand out across the table.

'Lovely to meet you,' Ben says. June shakes his hand with a confused frown.

'Ben's from work – he just joined us last week from the Cardiff office.'

June's forehead relaxes, and she raises her glass. 'Ah, I see. Sorry, I thought you were just a nosy creep.'

'Hey, I might be a creep, but I'm not nosy, I promise,' Ben replies, laughing.

'Welcome!' says Al, appearing as if by magic at their table. 'And who is this?'

'This is Ben from Millie's office,' June says. 'And, apparently, your neighbourhood creep.'

'I've just moved here from Cardiff,' Ben says. 'I live round the corner on Prince of Wales Drive.'

'How apt,' Millie smiles, and he grins back at her.

It might be her imagination, but it feels like there's a moment between them. Why her imagination would go there is a mystery.

'Well, I see you're fitting in already, finding the coolest spot to hang on a Friday night,' June interrupts loudly.

'Indeed! And only five minutes from my flat, too,' he says, sitting down at their table. June glances at Millie and frowns for a second, before smiling at him again. Millie immediately notices that he's changed outfits since work earlier. He looks more polished than he does during the day, and he smells of eucalyptus again. It's delicious.

'Anyone fancy a top-up?' Al asks, staring at him.

'Aperol Spritz for me, please,' Ben asks. 'How about you two?'

'All good, thanks,' June says, pointing at their bottle, looking at Millie, amused by his order.

'Oh, I'm sorry – two seconds,' Ben says, getting up from the table and putting his phone to his ear.

'He's cute,' Al comments, winking at Millie as she tucks her pen behind her ear.

'Is he joining us?' June asks in a stage whisper, leaning across the table.

'I don't know!' Millie hisses, and shrugs. When she fluffs her hair, June lifts an eyebrow.

Ben sits back down and grins at them both.

'Cheers for the invite!' he says.

'Who are you here with?' Millie says at the same time.

Ben's face falls.

'Wait, what?' June says.

'Amazing,' Al comments.

'I'm here with you. You invited me!' He laughs awkwardly, staring into Millie's eyes so closely that she could count his eyelashes. The entire right-hand side of his body is pressed against her left. It feels familiar, warm and firm. Millie has a brief thought that she could sit here for hours, just being next to him. She strokes her neck to hide the heat rash moving up it.

'Did I? I mean, don't get me wrong, it's great that you're here. But I don't remember inviting you,' Millie says.

'This is all a bit cringe,' Al says quietly.

'Not being a dick, but aren't you supposed to be getting the drinks?' June laughs. Al sticks her middle finger up at her and leaves the table.

Millie is certain she didn't invite Ben because if she had, she'd have washed her hair and bought chewing gum. And maybe wouldn't have drunk quite so much.

'Well, this is extremely awkward,' he says, picking up his phone and scrolling the screen.

'No, it's not, at all! We're so pleased you're here!' Millie cries. 'Aren't we, June?'

'Of course!' June replies.

Ben lifts his screen to show Millie.

Millie Jones:

At Buddies. Are you coming hot stuff? x

A few hours later, Millie and Ben are walking the circumference of the pond in Battersea Park, which is lit up silver by a bright full moon. Shortly after Ben arrived, June abandoned the idea of karaoke and arranged to meet the splits woman from earlier.

'I mean, I don't know what's more humiliating. Sending a message by mistake like that to me,' Ben says, 'or boldly assuming that I am *hot stuff*?'

'We're both as bad as each other,' Millie laughs.

'June didn't leave because of me, did she?' Ben says. 'Did I crash your party?'

'Not at all! She's obsessed with getting her Slide rating up at the moment. She was probably delighted, so she didn't have to feel guilty about leaving me on my own.'

'Good. I thought our lengthy debate about what's harder – sudoku or cryptic crosswords – might have sent her packing.'

'Talking of packing, are you *still* not going to tell me where we're going on Wednesday?' Millie asks. 'I need to plan my wardrobe!'

'Millabelle Jones, you don't need to plan a thing. We're going away for two nights, not two weeks. I promise we won't be changing climates. Just wear what you normally wear. You always look nice,' he says. 'I mean, fine. You wear clothes.'

'Thanks.' Millie smiles, squealing silently inside at the compliment. 'Sasha described my style as "comfortable" the other day.'

'She's a peach, isn't she?' Ben says, laughing.

'Wait, we've gone past your flat.'

'I'm walking you home!' he cries.

'You really don't have to, it's not far. I'll be OK.'

'I'm not being nice, I'm being horrible. I want to know where you live. I told you, I'm the neighbourhood creep, it's part of my job. The other parts being . . . lurking behind trees and telling women to smile as they walk past.'

She giggles. 'Well, you just be careful on the way back. There could be a goose with a flick knife hiding in the shadows.'

'Nah, Goose Springsteen and I are best mates now,' Ben explains.

'This is me,' Millie says with a heavy heart when they reach her steps. She has a fleeting wish that she lived further away. She isn't ready to say goodbye. Ben stays on the bottom step, watching her walk up. As she turns around, he salutes her goodbye.

'It was a pleasure to be of service, ma'am,' he says, walking backwards. 'I will see you in the canteen queue on Monday morning at 7.50 a.m.'

Suddenly, Ben dashes up the steps, two at a time. He wraps his arms around Millie, leans her back until her bag touches the floor and kisses her passionately on the lips.

She kisses him back even harder, the scent of eucalyptus and Aperol swirling around them.

'Millie? You there?' Ben says from the bottom step, looking at her quizzically.

'Yup, sorry, was just thinking of something. I'll be there!' she calls out, unlocking the door and pushing it open. Monday feels like ages away.

'Remember to pack your hiking boots!' he shouts, smiling.

'What? I don't have hiking boots!' she cries, standing in the doorway.

'I mean, your snorkel!'

'Ben!'

'Just kidding. But don't say I didn't warn you to bring your wellies,' he chuckles, turning away and disappearing round the corner. She hears him shout, 'Wear something comfortable!' in the distance.

Inside her quiet flat, Millie turns round and falls back-first onto her bed, still in her coat. She feels the blood rush to her head, and the room starts to spin. But it's not the booze, it's Ben. Millie gets the same feeling every time he's near her. What is it? She closes her eyes and sees his eyes staring back at her, his long eyelashes casting a subtle shadow over his freckles. In her head, she watches him walk backwards down the street. His bottom lip catches underneath his pointy tooth when he smiles. She can't explain why she finds this quirk so attractive, she just does. Her heart races just thinking about it.

It's called a crush, Millie. You'll get over it.

A hot ray of sunlight wakes Millie up. She blinks a few times, confused, and twists her head away from the source. She forgot to shut her curtains, and she's still lying on her bedcovers in her coat and outfit from last night, with her phone in her hand. Never a good sign. She rubs her dry eyes, smudging her mascara further, and looks at her last few messages.

Millie:

Did you get home safely? Xxx

She must have been drunker than she thought last night, and feels mortified by the kisses and suggestive tone of her text messages.

Ben:

I did, thank you. And thanks for not making me feel like a total arse for coming along in the first place.

Millie:

My mistake. Glad I made it xxx

Ben:

_ _ /,_ _ _ _ _ / _ _ / _ / _ _ _ _ _ _ _ / _ _ _ _ _ _ x

Millie must have fallen asleep after that. At least the message was returned. What's she supposed to do with this hangman puzzle now? Leaving it unanswered is awkward. But in the sober light of day, it's too weird to start guessing the letters now. She opts for a subject change.

Millie:

Hey! Sorry, I was so tired last night, I fell asleep the moment I hit the pillow. I call it a wine down. Hope you manage to get out and see some of the sights while it's sunny. I'm going to

Millie stops and deletes the entire message. There's no need for an essay.

Millie:

Sorry, fell asleep! Have a good Sunday. See you at work tomorrow x

She deletes the kiss and clicks send.

Eleven

Vivian's hallway is a family shrine, and it always takes Millie at least five minutes to make it past the first few steps. The wall is a sea of Millie and June photos, certificates, medals and paintings. There's always something new to look at with every visit. Today, it's a framed programme from a prep school play, where nine-year-old Millie was the lead. Millie rolls her eyes and steps forward to her favourite photo of her and Nan at Christmas.

Millie loved cuddling up to Nan on Christmas Eve, snacking on sugared almonds and listening to her stories about growing up with Vivian.

Millie moves along and sighs when she sees the photo of her and June's graduation lunch on the river. The bucket hat phase. Millie has begged her mum on multiple occasions to burn the evidence, but there she still is, in all her awkward student glory. She remembers the lunch like it was yesterday. It was the week before June joined her first law firm and

Millie joined Slide, a little-known start-up that had secured millions in seed funding and was set to take the sex business by storm. Millie recalls trying to keep a straight face as she explained it to Vivian and Nan, while June's shoulders shuddered in silent giggles beside her.

'It's a new company called Slide,' Millie said. 'I'm starting off as a creative intern but hoping to make my way up to chief creative officer one day.'

'Hoping? Expecting, Millie. A first-class student like you doesn't need to rely on hope. You'll be a chief creative officer and June will be made partner by the time you're both thirty, I guarantee it,' Vivian replied.

'What's Slide?' Nan asked.

'It's a website for people to find other people to meet up and have . . . get . . . be intimate with. For a night. Nothing more. Just one night of . . . passion,' Millie explained.

'Are you trying to say *have sex*?' Nan said in her signature no-nonsense style. 'Spit it out, Millie. Your mum and I might look ancient, but we aren't dinosaurs. Well, I'm not, anyway.'

'Yes. Sex. Then you can rate them afterwards, which makes it easier to find someone compatible next time,' June added.

'Bloody hell, that's fantastic. That would have saved me a world of wasted time and effort,' Nan responded.

'Well, there aren't any age restrictions,' June said. 'Let's sign you both up now!'

'Yeah, can we *not*?' Millie replied.

'I'd rather poke myself in both eyes, thank you,' Vivian

said. 'I'm delighted those days are done. The only one-night stand I want is with a good book and a glass of Dom.'

'Now that's a ménage à trois I can get behind,' Nan replied. 'Or should I say from behind?'

'Ew, Nan!' Millie cried.

The four women burst out laughing.

Chief creative officer by thirty.

Millie stares at the photo and smiles, thinking how close she is to accomplishing her – and her mother's – dream. But the smile fades when a horrible realisation hits her. What comes after that? If she does win the pitch, what is there left to strive for? She'll still have at least thirty years of work to go. Her mother has always encouraged her to start her own agency, with a promise to back her financially. But Millie's fear of risk followed by failure outweighs her ambition.

'Millie, for the last time, I am *not* removing the graduation lunch picture!' Vivian shouts from somewhere inside the flat. 'It was *your* choice to wear a bucket hat, so don't punish *me* for it.'

Millie follows the voice into the kitchen and finds her mum opening a bottle of champagne. As she does with every visit, she makes a beeline for her mum's fridge, which is a treasure trove of craving fixes. Who it feeds is a mystery; Vivian eats like a squirrel on a fast and is the same size as one, too. Millie suspects her mother runs entirely on nervous – no, angry – energy.

'None for me, thanks, Mum,' Millie says, chewing on a

slice of brie. After last night's antics, the smell of champagne is making her quietly gag.

'Nonsense!' Vivian insists, pouring a second glass. 'We have things to celebrate.'

'Not really, I haven't even got the job yet!' Millie says, checking her phone. It's blank.

The front door slams.

'Hello, fam!' June chirps as she swans into the kitchen, stealing the glass from Vivian and a piece of camembert from Millie. 'Yum, thanks. Such service! Are you hung-over, Mils?'

Millie glares at June with wide eyes and narrow lips. She hates it when June talks about hangovers in front of her mum. Vivian likes her wine but would never let herself lose control, and she expects the same of Millie, too.

'Millie!' Vivian cries. 'What are you doing, wasting your time getting drunk?'

'Why?' Millie mouths at June.

'Losing control is not a good look,' Vivian continues. 'How many times do I have to tell you two that? And don't get me started on the effect it has on your motivation levels the next day. Everyone knows the most successful people don't drink beyond their limits. Your limit should be two.'

'Two bottles?' June asks.

Vivian glares at her.

'Magnums?'

'Mum, how do you know what my limit is?' Millie says.

'Because you and I are the same, and two is my limit,'

Vivian insists, before looking June up and down. 'June's limit is three.'

'Yesss,' June fist-pumps, and walks into the living room.

'Thanks for that,' Millie says, following her.

'How was the rest of your night with Brian?' June asks.

Brian? June is spiky today. Either her slide didn't live up to her rating, she's hung-over or Millie has done something to upset her. Sometimes June has to be handled with care. It isn't surprising, considering her shitty early start in life. When Millie gets tired of treading on eggshells around her, she has to remind herself that June must still suffer from abandonment anxiety and a fear of being unloved – despite all her bravado and confidence.

'You know his name is Ben,' Millie corrects her. 'And yeah, fine, we didn't stay that late.'

'Really?' June frowns. 'Because you texted me a picture at 1.30 a.m.'

'Did I?'

'Wow,' June says, laughing, taking out her phone and holding up a picture. 'I knew you were tipsy, but I didn't realise you were blackout drunk.'

Millie leans forward and squints. It's an arty picture of her and Ben posing by the lake. The message reads 'Millie and Ben: Pond Life'. Then she has a flashback. As they passed the pond, they decided it would be funny to create an album cover to launch the start of a new friendship. Millie starts giggling.

'Yeah, hilarious, Mils!' June laughs, but with an edge.

'Extra funny after the tenth one, when I was right in the middle of things with Erica!'

'Sorry!' Millie grimaces. 'We didn't ruin the moment, did we?'

June stares at her across the sofa then breaks into a childlike smile. 'Hell no, I still got a four!'

'A four what?' Vivian asks, wandering through with the cheese platter that Millie has been picking at from the fridge.

'Nothing, Viv,' June says.

'You two peas in a pod with your secrets. Just like Nan and I,' Vivian says, and smiles. 'I miss her. Now, Millie, tell me about this new role. More money? More responsibility? Will you learn more about how the company runs day-to-day?' Vivian speaks at the speed of light.

'I'm guessing yes to all the above,' Millie says.

'You need to find out these details, Millabelle. It's important. Being a chief creative officer isn't just about the big ideas and the fun stuff. You need to know the commercial side of the business. Especially with your ambitions for your own agency.'

'Your ambitions,' Millie says under her breath.

'Millie doesn't even know if she's got the job yet,' June says, coming to Millie's rescue. 'Perhaps we should just take things one step at a time. We don't always have to plan things ten years in advance.'

'Five years,' Vivian corrects her, automatically, 'and of course she'll get it, why wouldn't she get it?'

'I know, she's a shoo-in, right?' June replies.

'It's a competitive pitch,' Millie replies. 'I'm up against another creative at work. On the Oxytoxin project I told you about.'

'Oh yes, remind me again. It's some kind of pill that's meant to stop people falling in love or something, isn't it?'

'Two pills, two weeks and it's game over,' Millie says, checking her phone again.

'More like level up, if you ask me,' June interjects.

'Incredible, if it works.' Vivian sips her champagne. 'I suppose it will be a godsend for people who can't control their emotions. I don't see it being particularly relevant to any of *us*. But I'm sure it could help a lot of people find true happiness with themselves.'

'Have you ever had a boyfriend, Mum?' Millie asks, pushing her phone back into her pocket, aware of June watching her from the other side of the sofa. There's still no message from Ben, which is making her feel a bit sick. Was she a twat last night?

Her mum sniggers. 'No, of course not! It's not in my DNA. Our DNA. The only "love at first sight" moment I've ever had was when I saw you for the first time. This tiny little doll of a girl with a shock of bright red hair. I've never felt anything like it. In that moment I remember looking at you and thinking, "It's you and me, baby. Together, we're going to conquer the world". Then along came June, and our tiny team of two turned into a triple threat!'

'Careful, Mum, you might shed a tear,' Millie smiles.

'Oh please, it's a statement of fact, not emotion,' Vivian scoffs.

'You didn't know Millie's donor, did you?' June probes, as she has a habit of doing.

'No way. Traditional anonymous-donor-and-implant route. And with Nan living down the road, she was your honorary co-parent. Who needs to fall in love when you have your friends by your side?'

'Amen!' Millie sings.

'Who needs a boyfriend, when you can have a toyfriend?' June says with a comedy wink.

'My friend Mandy had a boyfriend,' Vivian continues. 'Poor Mandy. She had so much spark to her. Her big dream was to start a gluten-free bakery. Brilliant idea! But the more Jasper became a part of her life, the longer she put it off. She got too comfortable in the relationship, and the Bakerfree dream eventually fizzled out. When I asked her about it, she said that she didn't have the time or headspace anymore. That she was happy in her relationship, and she didn't want anything to get in the way, or eat into the time she wanted to spend with Jasper.'

The story reminds Millie of Ruth, and the way she's been acting these past few months. Before she met Sam, Ruth used to talk all the time about taking over Slide. She had grand ideas for how the business could operate differently, expand into different relationship areas, diversify with sex toys and events. When Sam came on the scene, those conversations dried up. But the truth is, Millie can't put that all on Sam, because at the same time, Slide was bought by Human and the possibility of Ruth having any control became more remote.

'How do you know it was the relationship that made Mandy give up, though?' Millie asks. 'Maybe Jasper saved her from making a big mistake. She can't have been that attached to her dreams for her to toss them aside so easily, surely? Maybe she wasn't as ambitious as you thought she was.'

'No,' Vivian says, shaking her head. 'But I knew Mandy well, and for a long time. She could have achieved so much more with her life if she'd just stayed single.'

'Nan's parents were a couple, weren't they?' June asks. 'Weren't they happy?'

'Look closer at the photos,' Vivian replies. 'Nan's mother has the dull eyes of a stuffed and mounted cat. The eyes of someone whose life has not panned out the way she hoped it would. But she made her choice. We are the product of our own choices, girls, and the architects of our lives. It's up to us to make sure that no one ever gets in the way of that.'

'Perhaps I should take an Oxytoxin?' Millie teases.

'I don't think any of us needs to do that, sweetheart,' her mum says, then: 'Do you?' She looks worried.

'Ummm,' Millie teases.

'Don't you dare. At your age, well, at any age, you two have far more important things to focus on.'

111

Ben:

> So I lost my phone, and my marbles
> last night

Ben:

> It was in the fridge

Ben:

> Next to some glazed ham that looks like
> it's been mauled by a ravenous bear

Ben:

> Still haven't found the marbles though

'Oi, why do you keep checking your phone?' June asks Millie, when they're in the lift on the way down from lunch at Vivian's.

'Emails,' Millie replies with a half-fib and a hidden smile. 'The next couple of weeks are going to be crammed with this pitch. Think I need to work tonight.'

'What about *Single Me Out!*?' June looks crestfallen. 'I thought you were coming over?'

'Sorry, I can't. Rain check for Friday? Highlights and takeout?'

June nods and the lift fills with silence for a few seconds.

'Do you like him?' she asks.

'Who?' Millie asks.

'Brian.'

'You mean Ben? Yeah, he's cool, why do you ask?'

'I mean *like* him, like him. I don't know. Last night, you were . . . different in front of him. The main reason I left was because I felt like a bit of a spare wheel. I couldn't get a word in edgeways with your riveting puzzle chat. So much for karaoke.'

'I thought you left because of Erica?' Millie asks.

'There was that, too, but I wouldn't normally dump you for a slide, you know that. I just think I saw something between you and Ben, that's all. Maybe just be a bit careful. When you're on the cusp of being promoted, the last thing you want is an office scandal.'

'June, there's nothing there, I promise. I need him for this pitch and we just get on, that's all. He's funny. You'd like him if you got to know him.'

'He is funny. And his face? Just your type,' June says, and smiles with raised eyebrows.

Twelve

To: Millie Jones
From: Ben Evans
Re: The Trip

Bonjour Belle!

Nope, sorry, it's not Paris. But I have left you a little clue below. Activating Serious Ben Mode now: I've found four subjects with different romantic relationship experiences who are willing to be interviewed. Non-Disclosure Agreements are already signed. I think it'll give us some useful insights to come up with a kick-ass angle for the pitch. Hope you agree. You in? You're in. She's in everyone *screams across the office, everyone cheers*

B

PS Here's your one-word clue:

_ _ _ _ _ _ _ _ _ _ _ _ _ _-_ _
_ _-_ _

To: Ben Evans
From: Millie Jones
Re: Re: The Trip
I'm in.
How is that one word?
E?

To: Millie Jones
From: Ben Evans
Re: Re: Re: The Trip
_ _ _ _ _ _ _ _ _ _ _ _ - _ _ _ _ _ _ _ _ _ _ e _ _ _ _ _ _ _ _ _ _
_ _ - _

Millie stares at Ben across the desks, pretending to be unamused. Her screen pings.

@bene:

> has anyone ever told you that you have a wonderful smile

@milliej:

> haha

@milliej:

> FAKE CLUES

@bene:

> how dare you!

@milliej:

> U

Ben pauses typing, smiles, opens his notepad and starts drawing something on the paper. When he lifts it up, it's a single line, depicting the bottom of the hangman gallows. He stares at Millie and makes a slicing motion with his finger across his neck.

Millie sees Sasha watching them in her peripheral vision, and quickly turns back to her screen to open the attachment from Ben's first email.

Confidential

Interviewee One:
Deion Matthews
Age:
16
Family:
Parent, Daniel Matthews

Notes:
Deion was a star pupil, but he is now falling behind at school. His father suspects his poor marks are the result of being in a romantic relationship with his classmate, Michaela, but he won't admit to anything. Daniel is worried that he won't excel in his exams and qualify for a top university. He's going to waste Daniel's time, effort and money, end up abandoning his dreams, ruining his future and regretting everything when he's older.

Campaign Angle:
Secure Their Future.

Millie feels instant empathy with Deion. Vivian might have put pressure on Millie at that age, but she was never that forceful. She just wanted the best for Millie. She was practical. And pushy. Wasn't she? Then again, romance was never a risk for Millie. Like all her school friends, the idea of having a partner was laughable. Her mother has never had to worry about her.

When Millie opens up the next attachment, she sees a woman in a pink shellsuit looking bereft.

Confidential

Interviewee Two:
Ginny Hodgson
Age:
70
Family:
N/a

Notes:
Ginny and her ex-partner Gareth were in a relationship for thirty years. Last year, Ginny walked in on Gareth sliding two women in the garden shed. Gareth has since confessed to sliding all over the shop and has left her to lead a single life. Ginny still loves Gareth and misses him constantly — her home and life are filled with reminders of him, they have many mutual friends and her heart breaks every time she sees him at a social event. It's become so humiliating and hard for her to watch that she no longer sees their

friends. If she could stamp out her lingering feelings for Gareth, she could rekindle her friendships and move on with her life (without having to sell all of her possessions) as a confident, happy, single woman.

Campaign Angle:
No More Pain.

Taking Oxytoxin to heal a broken heart like this is the most positive argument yet for the antidote. Millie would love nothing more than to help Ginny's invisible wounds heal and rediscover how to be happily single, like almost everyone else. If Ruth and Sam ever break up, taking Oxytoxin might be just the tonic.

Confidential

Interviewee Three:
Thandi Nkosi
Age:
53
Family:
None

Notes:
Thandi is the CEO of a marketing consultancy. On the surface, she is a professional success story. Underneath, she's a personal crisis. She started her business straight out of university and has grown it to be one of the region's leading agencies, with a string of big clients in its portfolio.

But she's been secretly in love with Simone, her business partner, for 20 years. While she has managed to hide it, her feelings can be all-consuming, and she struggles to cope at times. She just wants to get rid of the weight of them so she can focus on work.

Campaign Angle:
Stay Focused.

This too is convincing. If, in some alternate universe, Millie did fall in love with someone, losing focus on her work would be her biggest concern. She stares at Thandi's photograph in admiration before moving on to two cherry-cheeked people in white, balancing a young girl on a Shetland pony between them.

Confidential

Interviewee Four:
Betty and Marius Rogers
Age:
36 and 38
Family:
Lily, daughter, 6 years old

Notes:
Betty and Marius met at work ten years ago, where they *'felt an instant spark the moment they set eyes on each other'*. They ignored the comments and concerns from parents and friends and eventually formalised their 'couple' status,

regardless of the social and financial implications of doing so. Recent tax incentives for single people to stay single along with the pre-existing financial benefits of singledom are making them question whether they should split up for the sake of their daughter – to give her a more stable financial future.

Campaign Angle:
Avoid the Stress.

One of Oxytoxin's great perks is helping people to avoid falling in love in the first place. Dodging that love bullet. Millie realises she needs to clue up on the financial implications of being in a couple before the pitch. It could be a huge pull. Ruth's moaned a few times about what it might cost for her and Sam to live together with double occupancy fees, but Millie has never paid attention to the details. All she can think of is the pain of paying for large-order charges on food deliveries and missing out on solo dining deals. She briefly thinks of calling Ruth, but decides against it. Ruth is so perturbed by this pill; it would be unfair of Millie to ask her to participate. What's more, she hasn't heard from Ruth since the spin class. She was a no-show on Friday, and she's been offline all weekend. Millie glances over at Ruth's empty desk. Old desk. Her chest swells as she imagines herself sitting there, with the best view of the floor, taking delivery of a fresh new batch of business cards.

Her screen pings again.

@bene:

lunch?

@milliej:

yes

@bene:

sorry, I meant to send that to someone else

@bene:

cringe for you

@milliej:

ha ha

@bene:

today's lunch special: a taste of your own medicine

@milliej:

O

@bene:

```
_ _ _ _ _ _ _ _ _ _ _ _ _ _ _ - _ _ _ _ _ _ _ _ _ _ o _ e _
_ _ _ _ _ _ _ _ _ o _ - _ _ _ _ _ _ _ _ _ _ _ _ _ o
_ o _ o _ o _ _
```

@milliej:

oh ffs

@bene:

```
_ _ _ _ f _ _ _ _ _ _ _ _ _ - _ _ _ _ _ _ _ _ _ o _ e _ _
_ _ _ _ _ _ _ _ _ o _ - _ _ _ _ _ _ _ s _ _ _ _ o _
o _ o _ o _ _
```

@milliej:

I didn't mean that!

Millie grabs them a spot for two by the window while Ben fetches their food. It's a Monday, which means Millie orders the Asian chicken salad with a side of miso and mango juice. When Ben returns, he has ordered the same thing. If Millie was June, she'd flip out. The only thing that annoys June more than Millie reading the menu before they get to the restaurant is someone ordering the same thing as her.

'You're not one of those people who hates ordering the same food, are you?' he asks, as if reading her mind.

'Not at all,' Millie says. 'I say order what you enjoy.'

'Well, you can have my miso and mango juice. Not a big fan of either,' Ben says.

'That's half the meal! Why did you order it?' Millie asks, laughing.

'I don't know, it just seemed easier and faster! I had Sasha breathing down my neck in the queue and I panicked. Is my neck red? I'm pretty sure there was fire coming out of her mouth,' he says, spinning round.

Millie slathers her hands with sanitiser, then gives the same treatment to her knife and fork.

Ben sits down, picks a piece of broccoli off the top of his salad and pops it in his mouth, as he puts his notepad and pen on the table.

'Go on then,' he says. 'Know where we're going yet?'

'Is this like a trick place? A place that doesn't actually exist, and you're going to turn around and tell me that it's my imagination?'

'I'm not that much of a knob. And frankly, if you can't guess it, I'm insulted.'

'Why?' Millie laughs.

'You'll see.'

Suddenly Millie has a mental breakthrough. She watched a documentary on it last year. It was the longest place name in Wales, and there is no way she's going to remember how it's spelt or how to pronounce it.

'I know where you mean!' She laughs. 'As *if* I could ever spell it, Ben Evans. This is a total trick!'

'And why not? It's very simple, really.'

'OK, if it's that simple, why don't you try it?'

'Llanfairpwll-gwyngyllgogerychwyrndrob-wllllantysiliogogogoch. Easy!' He shrugs. 'Now you try. Where are we going?'

Millie smiles. 'Wales?'

'OK, that's cheating. Yes, we're going to the motherland. Sadly, not to Llanfairpwll-gwyngyllgogerychwyrndrob-wllllantysiliogogogoch specifically.'

'Now you're just showing off.'

'I am not! If I wanted to show off, I would have said we were going to Taumatawhakatangihangakoauauotamateaturipukakapikimaungahoronukupokaiwhenuakitanatahu.'

'That's not even a place,' Millie replies.

'It is! It's in New Zealand. I went with my girlfriend a few years ago.'

Millie's chest clamps up instantly.

123

Ben has a *girlfriend*.

And for some strange reason, it bothers her.

Bruce is being uncharacteristically affectionate this evening, not that Millie is complaining. She dare not move an inch in case she scares him away from his current position on the far edge of the sofa. The warm black fluff of his bottom is keeping her left toes, and her heart, warm.

Ben's casual announcement that he has a girlfriend earlier has left her feeling queasy. Most of all, she's irritated by her reaction. Why does she care that he has a girlfriend? It shouldn't matter to her in the slightest.

What are these feelings? When he walks into a room, her stomach does somersaults. When he sends her a message, she squeals inside and wants to reply immediately, which is kind of pathetic. When he looks into her eyes, her cheeks go hot and she has to look away in case he sees. Does she want something to happen between them? Does she want him to come knocking on her hotel door in the night and grab her in a passionate embrace before stumbling back across the hotel room and falling backwards onto the bed together and sliding all night long? Maybe. OK, yes. It can't be anything more than a crush. A stupid crush that she will never act on. Still, she wishes she didn't feel an ache at the thought of his girlfriend. She wishes she had the energy to eat something. She wishes she would stop trying to find his girlfriend online, which she's been doing since she got home an hour ago. Ben's girlfriend does bother her. But it's only because it proves Sasha right. He's . . . odd. And perhaps partnering with him in the pitch will put her on the back foot. If he's in a relationship, he can't be objective.

A message appears on her screen as she's scrolling through his blog for the billionth time, startling her and sending Bruce flying off the sofa.

Ben:

> Want to work from mine tomorrow? I've
> bought some fancy biscuits just for the
> occasion x

Millie might get to meet the mystery girlfriend in person. She scrolls through their messages, trying to find clues from the first time he messaged her. Then she sees his message from last Friday night.

Ben:

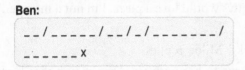

Whatever he was trying to tell her, she'll never find out. Like these feelings of jealousy, pain and longing, Millie will have to park it and move on.

Thirteen

'Breaking park rules, I see!' Millie says as she scrapes a chair up to Ben, who is sitting with a bag of seeds next to a large sign that says DON'T FEED THE DUCKS. It's 8.30 a.m., and she's feeling out of sorts about this routine-switch. She'd normally be at her desk filing her first email by now, not at the pond watching Ben throw seeds into the water, creating tiny duck tornadoes.

'Well, I can't sit here and enjoy my toast knowing how much these little guys would love a piece. I'm not a monster,' he cries.

'Just a maverick,' Millie replies.

'I like it!' He turns to her with wide green eyes that look especially bright against the water this morning. Millie turns her gaze away quickly.

'I got you a decaf oat milk flat white and a croissant from the stand at the front gate,' he says, leaning underneath his chair and bringing up the goods.

'You remembered,' Millie says.

'It was a memorable first meeting.' He smiles.

'Plus, it was only a couple of weeks ago,' Millie replies.

'Is that all?' he says. 'I feel like I've known you for two years, not two weeks.'

Millie feels the same way, but she'd never come out and say it.

'Time goes so slowly when you're bored witless,' he says, staring across the water.

'Oi!' Millie says, nudging his shoulder, wishing she'd said something wittier.

'Shall we walk and talk?' Ben asks, standing up and looking down at her, his face half silhouetted by the sunlight as he offers her his hand. She takes it and stands, releasing herself from his grip quickly. She can't bear to feel his skin against hers. It's not because he has warts and blisters; he doesn't. It's because his palm is so soft and warm, she's in danger of holding it up to her cheek.

Millie and Ben wander through the park towards his flat as if they're moving in slow motion. Morning runners speed past them, tutting as they go, irritated by the space that two people are taking up on the path. Several times, Millie has tried to navigate them to the side, but ends up awkwardly walking into Ben as she does.

'Don't worry, Belle, they can run past us. Lone runners don't have exclusive rights to these roads. But thank you for keeping me warm by sidling up to me, anyway.' He smiles at her. She keeps her eyes ahead.

'So, now we've established that it's only been two weeks, and that we don't know each other at all, how about a quick-fire quiz? Five questions each, as fast as we can,' Ben says.

'Anything to break this cringe-level-ten silence between us,' Millie teases.

He laughs that unashamedly high-pitched giggle that gives her flutters.

'You first.' She smiles.

'OK, question one. Dogs, cats, fish or hamsters?' he asks.

'Cats! I have one called Bruce.'

'What? How did I not know this, and why haven't we met?' Ben cries.

'He hates everyone, including me.'

'I have a trick to make cats love me.'

'Please share, because I'd like to finally feel safe in my own home.'

'I smear my hands in bacon dripping. That's why my hands are so soft and salty. Here, fancy a lick?' he says, holding them up to her face. She laughs and ducks. If only he knew what she'd been thinking a moment ago.

'OK, question two. Do you have a family?'

'I do. It's small. Mum, me and June.'

'Question three. What the hell – June is your sister?'

'Sort of. Not by blood. She came to live with Mum and me when we were little. My mum's best friend was around then, too. Nan. Short for Nancy,' she says.

'Question four. Do you know anything about your dad? Is he around?' Ben asks.

'Nope, a donor. Anonymous. Standard,' Millie says, surprised to hear him use the word 'dad', then remembering he grew up with two parents. Single parents aren't the norm for him, like they are for most people.

Millie sometimes wonders how her life – how she – might have been different if she'd known her donor. Her mum's Type A personality has been her biggest influence. Nan and June helped to dilute it to some extent to provide Millie with a bit of balance.

'Mum spent holidays in Wales as a kid, you know.'

'Good woman! Question five. Where?'

'Tenby?'

'I know it well,' he says, smiling. 'We used to go fishing at Tenby on our holidays. Shrimply the best.'

Millie giggles.

When they leave the park, Ben points her towards the end of the road and the red-brick mansion block he'd shown her before. Millie starts walking towards it, then she realises she's on her own. Ben's already crossed the traffic and is waving at her from the other side. She points and mouths towards the lights. He nods and smiles.

When Millie catches up to him, after crossing the road at the right place, he giggles at her. 'OK, final question: are you telling me off in your head for not crossing the road at the traffic lights?'

'Um, your questions are up, my friend. It's my turn now,' Millie replies.

'Fair enough, I said five and I, for one, would never break the rules.' Ben puts his hands up in defeat.

'OK: question one. Are you close to your family?'

'You could say that,' he says. 'Although it's hard to be close when it's so massive.'

'Question two. How big is your family?'

Ben laughs. 'Village big, literally. We all live in the same village. One family. Grandparents, parents, five sisters, cousins, aunts, uncles, niblings, four dogs, three cats and the occasional hiker who we adopt for a few days. Don't worry, my sisters aren't my aunts too, in case you're worried.'

'Wow,' Millie says.

'My parents have been together for almost forty years now,' he says, turning to her and smiling as they reach the bottom step.

Oxytoxin must have hit a raw nerve for someone with couple parents and a girlfriend. Millie is starting to feel a bit sick about meeting her. Maybe it's just the croissant.

'Good for them,' Millie states with a sure nod, hoping she sounds more convincing to Ben than she is to herself.

Ben scrambles around in his pockets, seemingly retrieving random things which he then places in Millie's hand: a boiled sweet, paper receipts and several individual keys. It has to be past 9 a.m. now.

'It's OK to think my couple parents are odd,' Ben continues. 'They are to most people, but I'm used to being told that. School was harsh. I decided that if I made the jokes first, the bullies would have nothing left. It's why I don't take things too seriously.'

'Question three,' Millie says. 'Do you have to empty your pockets every time you reach your front door?'

'Yes,' he says, pulling at his pockets so hard that Millie thinks his jeans might fall down.

'Question four. Wouldn't it be easier *not* to carry all this stuff?'

'Nah, I've got the hang of it, see?' he says, pulling out a small key without a key ring. 'It only adds a few extra minutes to my day.'

They walk down the stairs towards a basement flat, the steps covered in a mass of multicoloured cactuses and half-melted candles.

'Question five. Is your girlfriend at home, and does she mind us working here?'

Ben frowns at her. 'First, that was two questions, so . . . naughty. And second, what girlfriend?'

Ben doesn't have a girlfriend. He *had* a girlfriend, five years ago. They met at university, they went travelling together, and she wanted to stay in Australia when he wanted to return to his family. It must have been the woman in the photo behind him, the one in his blog. Millie feels ten pounds lighter than she did a few hours ago, and annoyed with herself at the same time. Perhaps she's relieved that she doesn't have another Ruth situation on her hands. Or that she doesn't have to share him with anyone. Of course, he's only a friend. But he's *her* friend.

Millie wanders through Ben's flat, soaking up the photos, pictures, frames, blankets, maps, books, notepads and trinkets. If her mum's photo wall is a sea of family memories, these walls are the five oceans. Normally the clutter would make Millie feel like she's covered in ants. But there's a warmth to Ben's flat that is definitely lacking in hers, and she finds herself feeling relaxed. She checks her phone: 9.04 a.m. The feeling is fleeting.

'Ben, we'd better start!' she calls out, stepping over a pile of papers and hearing a crash from the kitchen.

'Bollocks! Three-second rule,' Ben cries to himself, before appearing with two mugs of tea and a plate of broken lemon creams. Millie doesn't ask.

'Deconstructed lemon creams? They're the latest thing in confectionery.'

'Maybe later,' Millie says, and smiles.

'I'm not a hoarder, promise,' he says. 'I just haven't got round to sorting it all out. I wanted to get the photos up first. Look, this is me on the first day of my taste trip.' He points at a framed photo on the coffee table beside her. Millie picks it up and smiles. It's the picture from his blog.

'At uni I had this dream to travel the world tasting crazy foods and writing about it on a blog called Boy Eats World. Good idea. Terrible name.'

'But you did go, didn't you?' Millie asks with a straight

face, as if she hadn't studied his blog so many times that she could probably recite it word for word. She opens her laptop, hinting.

'I did, but it didn't last very long. We started in New Zealand, went to Australia and then my mum got ill. I wanted to come back, Sarah wanted to stay. So, we said our goodbyes on Bondi, and that's the last time I ever saw her.'

'Any regrets?' Millie asks.

'Regrets? No! I don't believe in them, Belle. I hope you don't either. Regrets are pointless and mistakes are lessons. My break-up taught me a lot about how I want to live my life. How important my family is to me. How I bloody hate oysters, and no, a different sauce won't magically change my mind.'

'Fluey phlegm bombs.'

'Thank you!'

They both laugh.

'It sounds cheesy,' he continues, 'but I want my life to be as colourful as possible. With different shades, dark and light. I want to see them all. Don't get me wrong, I was gutted when Sarah and I broke up. It was a dark time, and for ages I worried that I'd made a terrible mistake, but I saw the light after a few months. And I certainly didn't need a pill to fix me. Time healed me just fine.'

Millie stares at him from across the top of her screen.

'Perhaps some people aren't capable of fixing themselves alone,' she says. 'Maybe they need the help.'

'I know. I'm lucky I'm not wired that way. Perhaps Oxytoxin, in those cases, can truly help someone who's properly heartbroken,' he replies.

Millie's ringtone shatters the peace of the moment and June's face lights up Millie's screen. It's Movie Tuesday and she'll want to know about the cinema tonight. Millie puts her phone on silent and lets it ring out. She can't say what time they'll finish work, but at this rate, it will be late. Millie looks at the clock and swallows her unease. It's 9.32 and all she's done is open her laptop and type in her password.

Millie:

Just in a meeting, will call at lunch x

June:

Cool – we'll need to book tix by 2 x

June:

They're showing some of the classics.
What about seeing *Life, Actually*?

Millie:

Yep, keen. Will let you know by then x

Millie gets home at 7 p.m. after a day of brainstorming, strategising and snacking on too much takeout from Battered Sea. She looks around her flat, at its blank white walls and bare shelves, bar a couple of candles. What felt clean and ordered just this morning now feels cold and empty in comparison to Ben's cornucopia of curios and memories. Millie hangs her bag on the hook, leaps across the hallway to avoid the claw and opens her photo drawer. She takes out a framed photo of her and June, and tests it on the wall.

Shit!

She scrambles through her pocket to find her phone and dials June's number, but there's no answer. She tries again: the same.

Millie:

> I'm so sorry! Swamped today and forgot to call you. Such a lemon xxxxx

June:

> No worries, I can't answer now, with a slide x

Sliding on a Tuesday? That's a first even for June, Millie thinks, as she takes out her toolbox and rummages around for picture nails in the small drawer.

Fourteen

It's Wednesday morning. The train doors are going to close in three minutes and Ben still isn't here. Millie paces the platform at Paddington, pinching the skin on her top lip with her teeth and squeezing her fist so hard into her palm that her skin might break.

This is the final call for passengers travelling to Cardiff on platform three. The train will depart in two minutes.

She lowers her head and mindlessly kicks her pointed nude flats at the concrete floor beneath them. Closing her eyes, she counts down from ten in her head and convinces herself that he'll be here when she opens them. Three . . . two . . . one. Still no sign of him.

The truth is, Ben being late isn't the only thing troubling Millie this morning. What's churning her insides is how she

136

forgot to call June yesterday. She's never forgotten to call her back ever, even on her busiest days.

Passengers are reminded that they have thirty seconds before the train doors close.

Suddenly a strong hand clamps her left wrist and pulls her towards the flashing doors. It takes seconds for Ben to hoist Millie up the carriage steps and towards him, squeezing her tightly in a locked embrace as the doors slam shut behind them. He grips her close, holding her head against his chest, and apologises repeatedly into her left ear, his words getting lost in the tannoy above. His chest smells of him – eucalyptus – and feels warm and firm as it rises up and down. His heart is thudding against her flushed cheek, and his short, minty exhales are tickling her hair, giving her goosebumps.

'You know,' he pants, 'this is actually how we greet each other in Wales. So it's a good thing we're getting some practice.'

Millie feels frustrated by his recklessness and humiliated by the drama of this public embrace. Even so, she doesn't want him to let go. She just wishes the other passengers would disappear. Or stop staring.

'We're not in Wales yet,' she says, her words muffled by his shirt.

Millie counts down for five seconds before pushing herself out of his arms and dusting her cheeks off. She glances at his pale blue shirt to check she hasn't left half her make-up behind.

'Yeah, I made that up,' Ben says. 'We slap each other as hard as we can on our backs instead. It's an old and painful tradition,' he replies, putting his hands gently on both her shoulders. 'I am sorry, Belle,' he says, seeming genuine. 'I had a terrible night's sleep. Let me make it up to you. Peace Pastry? Mates Again Mimosa?' he asks, taking her bag from her and putting it on the top shelf with his. His chest expands in front of her and she takes a step back, tightening her scarf to cover the neck on her skin, which is pink. It's a reaction, all right, but not an allergic one.

'Thanks. I think we're this way,' she says, signalling down the aisle with a nod.

She wonders where his eyes are wandering as she walks ahead of him, smoothing down the back of her hair to detangle it from the chaos of a few moments ago.

'Much better,' Ben whispers from behind.

'You have toothpaste on your face,' she says, casually. He doesn't. She glances at the window reflection and sees him frantically wiping his mouth on his sleeve.

━━

'My gut told me that you'd like banana muffins,' says Ben, taking his seat fifteen minutes later.

'Didn't I tell you that yesterday?' she replies, squinting at him.

138

'That too,' he says.

'So, why did you sleep badly? You weren't worried about this, were you?' Millie asks. She can't imagine Ben worrying about anything.

'Nah, this'll be a breeze. I slept badly because I went on a date last night.'

Millie, surprised by this admission, takes a long sip of her coffee, burning her lip in the process but hiding it well. She pictures Ben laughing with someone across a table. Kissing them in the cab home. Is that what happens on a date? She hasn't a clue. No one dates. Millie manages to squeeze a word out through her winded lungs.

'Oh?'

Millie, a master at mimicking being fine when she's far from it, opens her laptop and pretends to focus on her screen, which is just a blank document. All she can think of is him stumbling through his flat with his date attached to his face. The flat where they'd spent all day together, just the two of them. Sure, they were working, but it had felt special. Their own private little bubble, now popped by some stranger. And not even a slide. An actual date. Who goes on dates? Not only that, Millie missed her cinema trip with June because she was with him. Funny how his plans with a random date worked out and hers with her bestie didn't. Most of all, why does she feel so pissed off about it?

Stop. Being. Weird.

She glances up and sees him staring out the window as

the countryside flies by in one long blue and green blur. His profile is so handsome she has a weird urge to outline it with her finger. She wonders what the date looked like. If the photo of Sarah is anything to go by, blonde and tall. The opposite of red-headed, short Millie. His head moves and she looks back down again and starts to type. Well, pretend to, at least.

jasdfpiojasdflj.

sdflkjo asdflkjof lskkjf! slkfjojsdfljsdf asdfoiasdflksdf

'It was a shocker,' Ben says eventually. Imaginary applause erupts in Millie's head and she pauses. 'That's why I slept badly.'

'I'm so sorry. What happened?' she comments, feeling absolutely delighted.

'Well, first up, I was late. I blame you for that, by the way.' He lifts his eyebrows.

'You were the one who secretly ordered dessert!' Millie protests.

'You were the one dropping major hints that we should order dessert!' he says, and laughs.

'"Dairy Devils cheesecake is nice" is hardly a hint,' she replies. 'Besides, you didn't tell me you had a date, otherwise I'd have left earlier.'

Why *didn't* he tell her he had a date? In the entire ten hours they spent together, he didn't mention it once.

'Well, anyway, I was ten minutes late, so she was already

prickly when I met her outside the station. Then she looked like she'd seen a ghost when I suggested we have a drink at the pub. Then it took a total nosedive when I told her about my family and Sarah. Turns out, she didn't realise it was a date. She thought we were just meeting at the station to go straight back to mine. You should have seen the look on her face. Like she was physically repulsed by this information. I mean, I get it. It's weird for some people, but don't treat me like a leper. Anyway, I thought we'd got past it until she polished off her third glass of red and started going on about how her anonymous donor dad found her when she was little and tried to force a relationship on her, which left her with lifelong emotional scars. It was intense.'

He shakes his head and leans on the table, closer to Millie.

'You know, I'm sad for her that she had a hard time,' he says, seriously. 'But I think people should be free to be in a couple without fear of judgement or scorn. My parents aren't selfish, they're in love. It just happened naturally. Or unnaturally, as some people might view it. Sarah and I didn't actively decide to go against the grain and be a couple.'

'Of course, I mean, who would do that?' Millie adds, starting to wonder if Ben still has feelings for Sarah. This isn't the first time she's come up in conversation.

'Exactly. Sarah and I met working at a coffee shop. We clicked, spent time together, then spent more time together until we realised we preferred being together over being apart. It just felt right.'

141

Millie clenches her jaw at the description, which feels a little too close to home.

'My mates even tried an intervention!' He laughs. 'But I think they just missed me. I don't know, Millie. We're all conditioned to think that being single is the right path. That we can't possibly be happy if we aren't living our lives alone, cooking for one, caring for no one's needs but our own. We grow up, get a flat, get a job, have meaningless sex on tap, grow old. Everyone's on the same path. It's depressing, isn't it? Where's the colour in that?'

'But where's the colour in going home to the same person every night? Arguing about what to have for supper or whose turn it is to take the bins out sounds a bit bleak to me,' Millie says, smiling.

'Touché,' Ben says, and grins. 'Let's just agree that everyone should do what the hell they like without judgement.'

'So, are you going to see her again?' Millie laughs nervously, hoping not.

'I hope not! My mate Owen set us up – she's his cousin. He must have known what her story is, the absolute prat. Anyway, her attitude stank, and it just kept me up all night thinking how horrible humans can be when they face the unfamiliar. What really does my head in is that I'm letting it affect me. I shouldn't give a toss. I never normally do. I don't care what people think of me.'

Millie could see that, from when they'd first met, Ben had always done the unexpected, from feeding ducks to

142

chatting about puzzles in the pub. She can see the appeal, but it was completely opposite to how she lived her life.

'I've spent my life defending my parents – not that I'd tell them that,' Ben continued. 'They'd be mortified if they knew how hard it's been. Anyway, I shouldn't moan. I was lucky. My childhood was really happy, and I have my parents to thank for that.'

'I get it,' Millie says. 'We should all care less about how others live their lives and focus on what makes *us* feel fulfilled.' Feeling in that moment that she should do the same.

Like many people, Millie has spent her life worrying about what people think of her. And now, with the pitch, she's more worried than ever. Perhaps it's time she took a lesson from the Book of Ben and cared less. What she can't remove from her mind is that he *knew* he was going on a date. Does that mean he *is* looking to be a couple?

Millie feels Ben's legs shift under the table and press against hers. She isn't sure if he knows he's doing it, but either way, she doesn't want to move an inch. She closes her laptop, looks out of the window and catches his eyes in her reflection.

'I wondered when you were going to stop pretending to work.' He smiles at her, and nudges her knees with his.

Fifteen

'Here we are,' says Ben, as he parks the hire car outside a smart Victorian terrace in Whitchurch. It's an expensive-looking street. 'Someone's doing alright for themselves, aren't they? I'm starving. Would it be unprofessional to ask him for a spot of lunch? Bet you his fridge is full of fancy food like . . . lobster.'

'Unprofessional and messy,' Millie laughs.

A man with a moustache answers the door in a black polo neck, which is odd for August, cream chinos and pristine white slippers. He hides a strained smirk as he turns, gesturing for Millie and Ben to enter.

'Hello, I'm Daniel,' he says calmly. 'Do you mind?'

In the hall, he points at Millie's shoes and then towards a shelf of white slippers. Millie hesitates, wondering who's worn them before her. Ben removes his shoes on the hessian rug by the front door, revealing mismatched socks.

The three of them glide across a hallway of sparkling

white tiles, stopping at a cabinet filled with trophies. It reminds Millie of the one her mum has at home for her and June. Originally it was in the lounge, but Millie and June convinced Vivian to retire it to the box room. Talking about their achievements was tedious and boastful, and it made them feel mortified in front of visitors.

'I adopted Deion when he was two years old. And he's been winning awards since he was three,' Daniel explains. 'Across the board, too. Academic work, sports, music. He's always been advanced. I suppose that's what every parent says, but I guess I've got the proof!'

'Congratulations,' Millie comments.

'Thank you. You know, I've invested so much in Deion,' Daniel continues. 'Time and money, emotion. I want to give him every opportunity to achieve his full potential. And, up until recently, he has. You name it, Deion has mastered it. Under-eighteens Welsh chess champion three years in a row, top of his mathematics class. He's achieved grade eight in the violin, he's fluent in four languages, captain of the first in rugby, and his poetry could melt a heart of stone.'

A look of disappointment washes over Daniel's face.

'Let's move into the dining room, shall we?' he says.

Millie stops at a wall of identically framed photographs of the family from over the years. Daniel and Deion are wearing matching black polo necks. She's never seen a baby in a polo neck. How could he breathe? Deion's expression matches his dad's. Neither of them is smiling in any of the pictures.

145

'Isn't he flawless?' Daniel whispers.

'He certainly is,' Millie says softly. 'It looks like you've done a wonderful job.'

'Well, I've tried my best. The best that money can buy, I suppose.'

'Have you ever had anyone else in your lives?' Ben asks directly.

Daniel instantly stiffens.

'No, it's always been just the two of us.'

Millie nudges Ben as they follow him into the dining room. They take seats on chairs as hard as concrete at a glass table so polished that the ceiling light is blinding in the reflection, and Millie is afraid to touch it.

'I'm Ben,' he says, reaching his hand out. 'The strategist. It's my job to ask difficult, sometimes uncomfortable questions.'

'I'm a waver,' Daniel says, looking at Ben's hand, which retracts into a thumbs up.

'Millie, creative.' Millie waves.

'So, where would you like to begin?' Daniel asks, the strained smile appearing again.

'Let's start with why you'd be interested in a product like Oxytoxin?' Millie asks.

Daniel lets out a sigh and looks up. 'Sorry, I get very emotional about it.'

Millie and Ben glance at each other briefly. Daniel is showing as much emotion as the vase with a single white rose stem behind him.

'As I was saying in the hallway,' Daniel begins, 'Deion has been a dream. Quiet, kind, respectful. I've put thousands into his education and extracurricular activities to ensure he makes the most of what he was born with. The best schools, holiday schools, teachers, tutors. Not that he needed it,' adds Daniel, defensively. 'I just didn't want him to waste hours on TV shows or computer games. Although he is a very good coder. I sent him to a special camp to learn earlier this summer. I guess you could call code his fifth fluent language!'

'Well, it certainly sounds like you got your money's worth,' Ben states. 'He sounds like a dream child,' he adds quickly, seeing Millie's wide-eyed stare.

'Up until a few months ago, he was,' Daniel sighs. 'My investment was paying off. For me and him, obviously. I mean, you saw all the trophies. He is a remarkable child, and I've given him everything to ensure he excels in the one life he has.'

'What happened a few months ago?' Ben asks.

'It all started one Saturday, just before term ended in July, when he didn't get up for violin practice,' Daniel says, a shadow forming over his face. 'Deion gets up at five thirty every day – weekends included – for violin practice, and has done since he was five years old,' he explains.

Ben clears his throat. 'That seems awfully young.'

'It's the only way to compete in this day and age!' Daniel raises his voice at Ben's disapproval. 'That's why he's won so many national awards. But that Saturday, last month, he didn't come down. I went up, and he was still asleep. I tried to wake him, and he refused to get up. Just like that. He said he wasn't going to practice, that he was tired. He even shouted at me, which isn't like him at all. It was all very out of character.'

'And what's happened since?' Millie asks gently.

'He hasn't played the violin. His marks at the end of term were down. And he wasn't picked to play at the last game before the summer holidays. He's basically throwing all the money I spent on his instrument, classes, extra classes, down the drain,' Daniel states. 'Honestly, sometimes I wonder if it's possible to sue your own child!'

'How do you conclude that Oxytoxin might be the solution?' Ben asks. 'What does that have to do with being what sounds like a typical rebellious teenager?'

'Deion is not typical!' Daniel exclaims, his face contorted. 'He's special! And he's not rebellious, he's unwell.'

Ben keeps his hard gaze.

'Ben didn't mean it like that,' Millie says, trying to steer them away from a confrontation.

'Actually, Millie, I did.' Ben turns to her with a look she hasn't seen before, or wants to see again. 'I'm sure Deion is a very special and talented boy,' Ben continues. 'But it would be unusual for him not to go through some hormonal ups and downs at this age. Isn't that all it is? I mean, teenagers are supposed to rebel a little. That's what makes them human. It's just hormones.'

'Well, of course it is!' Daniel exclaims. 'I know it's bleeding hormones, I mean, that's why you're here, isn't it?

I want to get these hormones under control. That's what Oxytoxin does, does it not?'

Ben sighs and leans back. 'I suppose. But what has Deion's behaviour got to do with romantic relationships? Those are the hormones it suppresses. Not idleness, if that's the problem we have here.'

'Well,' Daniel says quietly, before clearing his throat and shifting in his seat uncomfortably.

'A month ago I had a call from Deion's extra maths teacher who he sees every Friday night during term time. He told me that Deion had missed three maths lessons in a row. So, I confiscated his phone and went through his messages. It turns out he's been seeing a girl in the park after school. That's where he was going every Friday night.'

'Ah, Michaela,' Ben comments.

'I never liked the look of this Michaela!' Daniel exclaims. 'I've seen her stare at Deion at the school gates. Reeks of trouble.'

'Can we speak with Deion?' Millie asks.

'Of course,' Daniel says, before screaming a deafening 'Deion!' into the air.

Deion appears at the dining room door a few minutes later. Black polo neck, black chinos, white slippers.

'You could have put a brush through your hair. We have company!' Daniel says.

Deion rolls his eyes and U-turns out of the room.

'Deion, mate,' Ben calls after him. 'Fancy a private chat, just us three?'

Daniel looks to Millie for an explanation.

'He might open up a bit more,' she says, guessing Ben's tactic.

Deion hesitates and nods, looking utterly miserable as he walks slowly up the stairs.

Sitting down on crisp white bed sheets in a room that looks more like a hospital ward than a teenager's bedroom, Deion releases a loud sigh and hunches his shoulders in defeat. 'My dad is such a control freak. He's the problem, not me. I've done everything he's asked. I study hard, I get good marks, I go to rugby. It's not my fault. I can't help how I feel about Michaela. And I don't want some pill to control how I feel about her either.'

Deion leans back against his pillows.

'I like how she makes me feel, and who I am when I'm with her. Or when I see her face at the school gates. Or when a message from her appears on my screen. It's exciting. I'm still getting good marks. They might not be the best marks in the class anymore, but I don't care. Michaela makes me happy. Isn't that the most important thing? Not that he gives a slide about that. All he cares about is that he gets his money's worth. I'm not a bloody stocks and shares account, I'm a human being. And I'm almost sixteen years old. I'm just counting down the days until my birthday. Michaela and I are planning to run away.

Maybe go to Europe. I don't care where we go, as long as we're together. Fuck university. Fuck my dad, and fuck these black polo necks. Making me look like a muppet since I was in nappies.'

'Sounds like you've got it all worked out, mate,' Ben says, smiling. 'You guys should check out Barcelona. That's pretty cool. Too hot for polo necks, as well.'

Deion's face softens. 'Yeah, well, maybe we will. But we're choosing where we go ourselves.'

'Of course. You're in charge, buddy.'

'I don't want to take a fucking crazy pill,' he says, sounding nervous.

'You're sixteen, Deion. Your dad can't *actually* force you to take anything, you know. But you can't tell him I said that. Promise?'

Deion's eyes soften. 'Only if you don't tell him I'm going to run away with Michaela.'

Ben holds out his hand and they shake. Millie watches, feeling torn. Deion is so close to finishing his school career on a high. To throw away twelve years of hard work and good marks for what is, realistically, a temporary crush, does seem like such a waste. He doesn't have long to go; he should stick it out.

'Tell you what, though,' Ben says, and sits on the bed. 'I wouldn't leave at sixteen. You know, you won't even be able to drink or anything. It'll be dead boring. Why not finish school, get some money in your pocket and then go travelling? Start saving now and you could go further than

Barcelona. That's what I did. I banked the exams to give myself options, worked for a while and then we took off.'

'Who did you go travelling with?' Deion looks inspired.

'My girlfriend,' Ben answers. 'We were totally, madly, stupidly in love with each other. We were until we were twenty-five. Then, in what felt like a heartbeat, everything came crashing down and suddenly we were totally, madly, stupidly, *out* of love with each other. But that's OK. Heartbreak feels like it will last forever, but it passes.'

'Do you regret it?' asks Deion, mesmerised by this tale.

'Not for one second,' Ben replies firmly.

That night, as Millie lies between the stiff covers of her sparse hotel room bed staring up at the ceiling, she thinks of Ben on the other side of the wall. There's only few inches between their heads. She reaches her hand up and lays it flat against the cool plaster. Suddenly, she feels three knocks underneath it. Smiling, she gives three knocks back.

Half an hour later, as Millie is flicking through the channels, there's another three soft knocks. Only this time it's not on the wall, it's on her hotel room door.

Sixteen

Millie lifts the cover from the room service tray in the hotel passage and finds a whole cheesecake on a plate. She wheels it into her room before anyone sees and sits back down on her bed, staring at it. A note on the lid says 'Happy Hump Day'. She puts the note to one side, takes a photo and sends it to Ben.

Millie:

Did you do this?

Ben:

Do you mind? I'm sleeping. And I'd never say anything as cheesy as Happy Hump Day.

Millie:

How did you know it said that?

153

Ben:

Well played.

Millie:

Do you have a fork?

Ben:

Fork yeah! Never without one.

Five minutes later, Millie and Ben are sitting cross-legged next to each other on her hotel bed, with the cheesecake in front of them and *Single Me Out!* highlights running in the background on mute. 'For research purposes!' Millie had joked earlier, when Ben had protested.

'Is there a reason why all the interviews are in Wales?' Millie teases him.

'Well, firstly,' Ben says, leaning back, 'It's God's country. And secondly, I don't have any connections in London, so I had to use the ones I had. They're all back home.'

'I guess it's nice to see where you come from,' Millie replies, wincing inside afterwards. She shouldn't be so interested in his personal life.

'And I've already seen where you come from, so it's only fair.' He smiles.

They both reach for the cheesecake at the same time. Ben knocks her spoon away with his and holds one arm in front of her so she can't reach the plate. After some jostling, Millie giggles and gives up.

'Belle! Please. I'm trying to be professional here, and you're making it hard. Let's talk about Deion. He's hardly a candidate for a story about Oxytoxin, is he?' Ben says, after swallowing a large mouthful and pushing the cheesecake in front of her.

'He might be a candidate for a story on kids who kill their parents,' Millie replies.

'Poor guy,' Ben mutters.

'Although on paper, I suppose he's a success,' Millie continues. 'I mean, all those trophies, awards, skills. It certainly puts my mum's shrine to shame,' she says. 'He's done well.'

'He's done well to not explode with a dad like that, pushing him to be perfect.'

Millie spoons another blob of cheesecake into her mouth and thinks of her mum and the pressure she's felt all her life to be perfect. To never stop achieving. The difference is, in Millie's case, she and Vivian always felt like they were a team. It was never Millie versus her mum. It was always Millie and her mum versus the world. Her mum never treated her like an investment. She treated Millie like a champion, who never put a foot wrong. She feels a sudden surge of gratitude and love.

'I suppose, in a case like that, we'd need to aim the campaign at the parents,' Millie says.

'I think we need to avoid this angle. Kids are off the table, in my book,' Ben says determinedly.

Ben is right. Millie isn't going to argue. Oxytoxin for kids feels far too dark. It would create headlines for all the wrong reasons. And Millie would never want to put her name to a pill that manipulated children without their understanding or consent.

'So, what's your definition of success, if it isn't a cabinet filled with trophies?' Millie asks.

'A cabinet filled with cheese.'

'No, seriously,' Millie says, spooning some topping into her mouth.

'I don't know . . . happiness,' he says simply.

'OK. And what's your definition of happiness?'

'Adventure, freedom, family, friends,' Ben replies, scraping his spoon around the empty plate. 'And cheesecake. Here, you have the last bit, I insist.'

Millie holds the last piece of cheesecake up in the air with her spoon. 'To cheesecake.'

Like a crocodile that's been lying in wait, Ben lurches forward and grabs the spoon between his lips. Millie's mouth falls open as she stares at her empty hand.

'You need to work on your reflexes, Belle,' Ben smirks.

The next morning, Millie and Ben are standing in Ginny Hodgson's living room, staring at a large portrait of Ginny and Gareth hanging on the wall and bathed in the early light pouring in from the window. Her modern flat, overlooking Cardiff Bay, doesn't suit the old dark wood furniture. It doesn't suit Ginny, Millie thinks.

'That's Gareth, obviously,' Ginny says. 'Handsome devil, isn't he? He's always turned heads.'

'He . . . sure is,' says Millie, staring at the gold chain around Gareth's neck. It's big enough to anchor a ship.

'You must think it's odd to keep it up there.' Ginny sighs. 'I just can't bring myself to take it down. I don't have anything else. Gareth has been, or at least was, my entire life for thirty years.'

'You could cover his face with a picture of the cat,' Ben suggests, looking amused.

Ginny giggles.

'Or a calendar?'

'I don't have a calendar. What's the point of having a calendar when you don't have anything to put on it?'

Millie's heart bleeds for this little speck of a woman, who speaks so softly she can barely be heard over the rain outside.

'Well, if you ask me, that might all change for you!' Ben chirps. 'And the more you put on it, the better you'll feel.'

Ginny breaks into a broad, beaming smile on hearing this, and Millie could hug Ben for bringing it out in her.

'I hope so,' Ginny replies.

'Or perhaps even a huge mirror, so you can stare at your reflection every day and be reminded that you don't need Gareth to make you happy. You can make you happy. Piss off, Gareth. Say it with me, Ginny!'

'Piss off, Gareth!' she squeaks.

'Louder, Ginny!' Ben says, laughing.

'PISS OFF, GARETH!' Ginny shouts.

'Ginny!' Ben shouts. 'With that kind of attitude, perhaps you don't need a pill after all!'

Ginny's so enthralled by Ben that Millie's sure she can see actual heart shapes in her eyes.

'Can we have a seat?' he asks, nodding towards the dining room table that's shoved up against the wall in her tiny sitting room.

'Please do,' Ginny says. 'I'm sorry there isn't much space. Gareth told me it wasn't fair for me to stay in the house. So we sold it all and split everything fifty-fifty. I lost so much of the furniture I loved, but I've managed to keep a few bits and bobs.'

'Bloody hell,' Ben says, shaking his head. 'No worries, Ginny, this is fine. You have a lovely home.'

'So, Ginny,' Millie says, flipping open her notebook. 'Do you want to start from the beginning? And then tell us why you want to take Oxytoxin?'

'Yes,' Ginny says. 'I guess where we begin is thirty years ago. Gareth and I were both forty when we met down the pool hall in our local village. I was the manager there, and he was new to the area. He challenged me to a game, I beat him, and he wasn't like the other men. He was chuffed to bits for me. A true gent. That's the thing about Gareth, he always was a true gent. And he loved me, I know he did. That's what makes this whole situation so hard to swallow, so hard to overcome. It was unusual to meet someone who was so interested in having a relationship, and it took a lot to persuade me. I wasn't keen at all, and I thought it very strange of him to ask in the first place. But I guess it gave him a certain charm. We were the only couple in the village. People used to talk behind our backs all the time. *What's wrong with them?* Wendy, my best friend, would constantly ask me, 'When are you two going to break up?' My mum would comment, 'Don't worry, you'll find yourself soon.' Fast-forward thirty years, and we still hadn't. I was so proud to prove them wrong. I thought that we'd beat the odds and we'd be together forever. And then, the shed happened.'

'How did it feel?' Ben asks.

'When I saw them through the window, my entire world crumbled. I've never felt pain like it. Searing. In that moment, I knew Gareth was gone. I knew we were finished and the whole future I was counting on was wiped out. There would be no more *us*. I was on my own. I hadn't planned to be on my own, and here we are. I'm so glad we decided not to have kids, otherwise their hearts might have broken too. I just . . . don't feel like I can cope. I wasn't the one who wanted this relationship in the first place, so being shoved out of it feels like a right kick in the teeth.'

And that's the problem with relationships, Millie thinks. You become so reliant on one other person that you forget how to rely on yourself. You're convinced you can't be happy alone. That's what she fears for Ruth.

'But that's not the worst part,' Ginny continues. 'The worst part is that I'm still in love with him. I can't stop thinking about him. This portrait is one of the only things I have left of our lives together. I still have the crockery from the first house we bought. He hated it! Hates it, I mean. I can't bring myself to get rid of it, even though my heart breaks just looking at it. I can't even bear to wear my perfume anymore, and I've been wearing it for twenty-five years! It was a gift from him at a happier time, and I've never worn anything else since. I don't want to find a new perfume! Anyway, those happy memories are filling my head with unhappy thoughts. And seeing him at our social clubs going home with other women, remembering how it used to be me by his side, and only me, it's just . . . it's like a thousand knives stabbing me in the gut. And it's not just the humiliation of it all. It's that I miss him. I really miss him.'

Ben takes a tissue packet out of his jacket pocket and hands them to her. She whispers thank you and starts to quietly cry into her hands.

'I'm so sorry, Ginny,' Millie says. 'It sounds so tough. I wouldn't wish it on anyone.'

'That's OK,' Ginny sniffs, lifting her head and blinking away the tears. 'I'm just glad there's a light at the end of the tunnel with this new pill of yours. It's the first time I've seen a light in over a year.'

'Well, I really hope we can help,' Millie says, looking at Ben.

Ben nods. 'Me too, Ginny.'

'If I could take a pill that makes me stop loving him, then all this pain would disappear. I could move on with my life. Start going to my clubs again. Steer clear of relationships and be happy on my own. I know I can be happy on my own, I was before I met him, after all. I just don't have the strength to do it by myself. I've tried, and nothing works.'

'Would meeting someone else help? Perhaps take your mind off him?'

'Oh, no! I've learnt the hard way why couples aren't right. I don't want to risk another situation like this, Ben. That's why I think Oxytoxin is my only choice. I feel like it could be a cure, and prevent me from making such a stupid mistake ever again.'

'Don't forget you had thirty years of happiness together. Perhaps you could find the same happiness with someone else, if you're the relationship type.'

'The only relationship I want is with me,' Ginny concludes, playing with the heart-shaped locket on her chest, engraved with G & G.

'OK, I get it now,' Ben says, shutting the car door. 'I feel for the poor woman.'

'So Oxytoxin is not totally evil?' Millie asks, turning her head round to reverse.

'In certain, very specific situations, Oxytoxin can be good,' Ben states. 'Although there's still a chance she'll regret it. She was happy as a couple for thirty years. She could find that again.'

'You heard what she said. She wants to find herself again, and I think that's pretty damn great.'

Millie turns the radio on.

'Fitting,' Ben comments, nodding when 'Love Me Like I Do' fills the car.

'I'm actually excited for her to take Oxytoxin and see how much happier she can be flying solo,' Millie says. 'Good riddance to Gareth. And good riddance to relationships.'

'Bad relationships,' Ben says. 'Not *all* relationships, surely?'

'I suppose,' Millie says.

'Millie Jones, don't tell me you're a member of the anti-couple brigade as well?' Ben scoffs, as he stares out of the window at an approaching storm cloud looming over Cardiff.

'I'm not anti-couples,' Millie says. 'One of my best friends is in a relationship. I'm just . . . cautious of them. Personally, I'd never be in one. I just can't for the life of me see the appeal.'

'Never? That's a long time,' Ben comments.

'So is forever,' Millie counters. 'Taking care of me takes up enough of my time, I can't imagine doing it for two. Way too much hard work. Way too much drama. Way too much heartache.'

'Yeah, but with the right person it doesn't feel like hard work or drama. With the right person, you aren't adding to the load, you're sharing it.'

'Don't get me started on sharing,' Millie says.

'What do you mean?' Ben laughs.

'Sharing everything with someone else? Sliding nightmare, if you ask me,' Millie explains.

'Well, with all the siblings I grew up with I guess I'm used to it,' Ben replies. 'I didn't have my own bedroom until I was eighteen, at uni. And at mealtimes, I had to guard my food with a pointed fork.'

'Yup, not for me,' Millie laughs. 'It was hard enough sharing that cheesecake with you. And it ended badly for me.'

'I'm honoured. Of course, sometimes it is nice to share,' Ben says. 'Experiences, for example. Like going on holiday. Sharing memories with someone.'

'I share memories with my family and with Al and Ruth. I can go on holiday with them, too. Not that I would. I don't travel often, but when I do, it's definitely on my own,' Millie says as they turn into the hotel car park.

'You honestly think going on holiday alone is better? Why?' Ben asks.

'The last time I went on holiday with June, we had to have a debate every time we made a decision. Where to eat, what to see, what to do. Going on holiday on your own is much easier! And cheaper – it's expensive to room-share! Plus, I don't want someone using a bathroom so close to my bed, thanks.'

'Well, when you put it like that, I can sort of see why you'd think so,' Ben replies. 'But I'd choose sharing an experience over easy any day of the week.'

'Um, not to bring up painful memories, but didn't you and Sarah break up when you were on holiday? Because you disagreed about coming back?' Millie asks.

'Ah. Yup. You got me there,' Ben laughs.

'Sorry,' Millie winces. 'Did I just overstep the mark?'

'It's OK. Hope me sobbing into my hotel pillow later doesn't keep you up,' Ben replies. 'Or, you know, maybe I do.'

They open their doors at the same time, step out of the car and look up at the hotel. In typical Ben style, he had stuffed up the dates with Skye and they've spent the past hour trying to find one last minute.

'Looks nice,' Millie comments.

'It does, doesn't it, Belle?' Ben says, grabbing their bags out of the boot. 'OK, bye then,' he says, putting her bag on the ground and walking off.

'Wait, what are you doing?' Millie shouts after him.

Ben spins round and squints across the car park at her. 'What?'

She stares at him.

'Oh, I'm sorry,' he says, looking around. 'I assumed we'd go in separately. You know, because I'd hate to spoil your lone wolf entrance.'

'Very funny,' Millie replies, picking up her bag and catching him up.

'Come on, Belle,' he says, taking her bag. 'I'd be delighted to cramp your style.'

Seventeen

When they knock on the front door of the penthouse flat in Penylan on Thursday afternoon, they're greeted by a chorus of scuttles, snuffles and growls behind it. When it opens, a rapid cloud of multicoloured fur flies at their feet. Ben, ever the professional, falls to his knees and disappears in the fluff.

'Sorry!' cries a woman in a tailored teal suit, looking flustered.

'That's OK,' Ben says, getting up and dusting himself off. 'I love dogs. Are they all yours?'

'My babies.' She smiles. 'Total chaos, but what big family doesn't have its dramas? And at least they don't talk back. Most of the time. Anyway, let's start again. I'm Thandi,' she beams, stretching out her arm and delivering a firm handshake with soft hands. 'Please, come through. Would you like a drink? There's mineral water on the table already.'

'Wonderful,' Ben comments, craning his neck around the room, examining the artwork.

'You have a beautiful home,' Millie comments as they enter a large dining room.

'Thank you,' Thandi says, showing them where to sit. 'It feels like the project that never ends, but it keeps me occupied outside of work hours. The few hours I get, anyway. So, where would you like to start? This is incredibly exciting, I must say.'

'Exciting is one way of looking at it,' Ben repeats slowly, nodding his head.

'Oh, you have reservations?' Thandi asks, glancing between them.

'No, no, no reservations,' says Millie, getting in before Ben does. 'We've been interviewing all sorts of people who've reacted differently. Lots agree with you, though – it is very exciting! And we can't wait to see how it might really help people in certain situations.'

'Would you call it a situation if it's been going on for twenty years?' Thandi replies. 'I'd call it a condition. One that's made me sick for a very long time.'

'We're really sorry to hear that. Would you like to start from the beginning? Tell us how you've got here?' Millie softens her voice.

'I suppose I should start with my childhood. It might give you an insight into the kind of mind that might be susceptible to *falling in love*,' she says, taking a long sip of water and leaning back in her chair. 'I've always been ambitious. Ever since I can remember I've chased self-actualisation and I've been fixated on achievement. Being top of my class and the best at any game has always been what has fulfilled me emotionally. My mum was a hard worker, but we didn't have much, and she put most of what she had into my education. Looking back, I think my insatiable thirst for the trophies and the high marks was all part of me wanting to pay her back for everything she's done. She lent me the money to start this business, which is all I ever wanted. And that brings me to Simone.'

'Where did you meet Simone?' Millie asks.

'At uni, on our first day. She was standing in front of me in the queue to collect our room keys. She turned round and kapow! instant crush. I thought it would be fleeting, like these things always are, but then I discovered we were on the same course, and I soon realised it was something more. It was difficult to diagnose because I'd never felt like that before. I suppose very few have. I couldn't get her out of my head. Still can't. I think about her constantly, it's a nightmare. What I don't understand is how someone who is so in control of her life, like me, is so out of control when it comes to this.'

'Did anything ever happen between you at uni?' Ben asks.

'No, never.'

'Have you ever told her how you feel?' he adds.

'No. I didn't want to get hurt or lose my best friend. And I still don't, which is why we're here. Long story short, Simone and I have been best friends since that day in the queue. After uni, we went into business together. I mean, the truth is, I wasn't sure I wanted to go into this business.

All I knew is that I wanted to spend as much time with her as possible. I got lucky in that she's brilliant at the business, too, and we work well together. I thought my feelings would eventually pass, but they haven't. They've only got stronger, and it's reached a point where I'm finding it impossible to work with her. To even know her. I've been hurting for a long time now. When I think about her never feeling the same way, I double up in pain. When she talks about sliding other people, I am consumed with jealousy. When she's in the same room as me, it takes all my strength not to stare, or reach out to touch her. I feel like my life has been slowly unravelling for twenty years, and I need help. And from the sound of it, these miracle pills could save me, save our friendship and the business.'

Millie looks around the room. It's spotless, as if it could have been airbrushed.

'I'm sorry for pushing the point, Thandi,' Ben says, 'but why not just tell her? If you're best friends, I'm sure she would rather you were honest with her. I mean, let's say you did take these pills. What happens if Simone suddenly turns round and confesses her feelings for you? Wouldn't that be tragic.'

Thandi looks at him hard.

'No, that would be a disaster,' she says, unblinking.

'Exactly, why risk—' Ben continues, but she cuts him off.

'No, Ben, you misunderstand me. I don't *want* to love Simone and I don't *want* her to love me. Shared feelings between us would be a catastrophe. It would risk everything we've worked so hard for. It wouldn't just destroy our friendship, it would destroy the other friendships we have around us. It wouldn't only ruin our personal reputations, it would ruin our professional reputations, too. It would put our business at risk, and our employees to boot. I'd never do that to them. I'd never do that to my mum. It would be like throwing everything she gave me back in her face. I'd never dream of being that selfish. We've worked too hard and too long for this. Nothing feels as good as fulfilling a personal ambition. Not even Simone, despite what my hormones might suggest.'

'She got one over on you there, didn't she?' Millie grins at Ben from across the table in the hotel, her eyes resting on his for a little too long. She's just inhaled her first glass of wine.

'Uh?' His forehead twitches. 'No, she didn't. Her entire story is one-sided. How does she know that fulfilling a personal ambition is better than being in a relationship, if she's never been in one? Answer me that.' He takes a victory sip.

'I actually *don't* think it's love,' Millie replies. 'It's infatuation. She's a high achiever, who's used to getting what she wants and works for. And now she's become obsessed with attaining something unattainable.'

'Infatuation is just a big word for a crush. Crushes are

fleeting and love is long term. Big difference. You can't be infatuated with someone for twenty years, can you?' Ben asks.

'I wouldn't know,' Millie responds. 'I've never been infatuated, or in love. I don't know anyone who's been in a relationship that's lasted. Look at June's parents. Look at . . . you and Sarah.'

'Fair play.' Ben nods. 'But look at my parents. Their love has lasted for decades.'

'Well, that's amazing. But you have to admit it's a rarity.'

'It sure is,' Ben says, and smiles.

Millie nods yes to another glass, even though she shouldn't. Tomorrow's Friday. It's still a workday. And they have an early checkout. They also have to drive to their final interview in Laugharne at 9 a.m. But to end the night now seems too soon.

'Have you been infatuated with any*thing*?' he asks.

'My career, I suppose. Making sure I achieve my ambitions before I'm thirty. I made myself a vision board when I was sixteen, and I'm working my way down the list.'

'Did you have "visit Wales" on there?'

'Yes!'

'Glad I could help. Being infatuated with your career is kind of cool. And it looks like you might be on your way with this promotion, so cheers to that!' he says, raising his glass before shouting loudly across the hotel bar and making her jump. 'To Millie Jones! Chief creative officer at Slide!'

'Stop, please!' she whispers, cringing.

'You embarrass easily, don't you?' He squints.

'I'm a behind-the-scenes type,' she says, reaching across the table and bringing his hand back down.

'I think what you need is to care less about what other people think,' Ben says, putting his glass down.

'No,' she replies, her eyebrows raised. 'What I need is for you to care *more* about what other people think.'

An hour later, they amble down the hotel corridor, in a heated debate about who they'd rather be stuck on an island with, Adrian or Sasha.

'Sasha might bark, but she doesn't bite. Which means she's basically harmless. I could just sit there with my toes in the sand,' Ben argues.

'You honestly want Sasha's bark to be the only other voice you hear for three months?' Millie says, before quickly stifling a hiccup.

'I'd rather a bark than laser beam stares burning a hole into the back of my head. Does Adrian look at you like that too?' Ben asks.

'I mean, you could just climb a tree.'

'Laser beams, Belle! They'd follow you right up into the branches. And probably burn the whole tree down.'

When they reach her door, she looks at him and points a finger down the hall.

'You missed your door,' she says, and this time her hiccup

171

escapes and echoes down the hotel passage. She throws her hand up to her mouth and laughs.

He giggles too, and stares at her.

'Sorry, what did you say?' he eventually asks, with his pointy tooth showing.

'Your door, Ben.' She laughs. 'This is mine. My door. Your door!' She points down the corridor.

He looks back, then looks at her door, then looks back, then looks at her again.

'Ah-*ha*!' he shouts with the passion of a eureka moment and Millie hushes him. It's late. 'Gotcha. Well, that was fun, Willie.' He giggles. 'Do you like my new nickname for you?'

''Night, Ben.' She turns to her door as he plods back down the corridor.

Her door card doesn't work at first, which triggers a mild panic within her. Looking over at Ben, she sees him struggling, too. They catch each other's gaze and shrug. And just like that, their doors ping open at the same time.

He mouths goodnight.

Inside, Millie puts her bag by her feet and leans against the door with her eyes closed in an attempt to calm her spinning head.

All of a sudden, there's a loud bang on the door behind her and she screams, jumping away. 'Ben?' she cries as she stands on tiptoe and peers through the peephole. There's no one there.

'Ben?' she repeats through the door, before turning the

handle and inching it open. Still no one. Millie opens it wider and pokes her head right into the corridor to find Ben with his back to the wall, staring up at the ceiling.

'What are you doing?' she cries. 'You scared the life out of me!'

'Ah, but did I scare the hiccups out of you?' he replies.

'Yes! And you've probably woken the entire floor!'

'Whoops! Sorry!' he whispers, turning and creeping back towards his room.

If he asked her to follow him to his room for a drink, she would in a heartbeat. It's their last night, after all. Just a few more moments of time alone, together. She wishes she had the courage to ask him. Would he say yes? Maybe. But if he said no, she could never look at him again. She listens to her inner voice whispering no and shuts the door. She has an early start, and they have important work to do tomorrow. She heads straight for the bathroom and splashes her face with cold water. This isn't her. It's the wine.

Millie's phone vibrates. It's a message on 'Scum Chums'.

June:

> Pals, it's Friday tomorrow and I'm starting to feel thirsty. Still up for drinks?

June:

> Can't wait to catch up x

Millie:

MISS YOU! x

June:

Yeah yeah, bet you say that to all your friends

Al:

She said it to me last night

Ruth:

She texts it to me every day

Al:

Bit clingy

Millie:

Very funny, scums

Eighteen

On Friday morning, they pull up to a picturesque cottage by the sea in Laugharne. Standing on the stone step, Millie and Ben press their backs against the wooden doorway, sheltering themselves from the soft summer rain and staring out across the choppy ocean in front of them. The grey wall behind their backs is covered with tangled, windswept creepers and vines. Such a mess would normally make Millie squirm, but there's something comforting about the view.

'Beautiful, isn't it?' Ben comments. Before she has time to reply, the door behind them unlatches. They turn to see two beaming smiles greet them from the same height.

'You must be Millie and Ben. Welcome to Laugharne!' says one. 'I'm Betty, and this is my partner Marius.'

Poor Marius is radiating anxiety, delivering a vigorous handshake with clammy palms and muttering 'hello' repeatedly.

'It's lovely to meet you both,' says Ben with his broadest

smile, stepping into the hallway. 'You two are very lucky to live here, aren't you?'

'Oh, well. Maybe. I suppose we're lucky in some ways, unlucky in others. What with all the tourists on our doorstep.' Marius shrugs, laughing.

'We get enough looks already, don't we, Maz?' chirps Betty, grabbing his waist and squeezing him to her.

'Well, that's what we're here to talk about,' Millie says, feeling chilly in her puddle-soaked sandals, and wishing she'd taken Ben seriously when he told her to bring wellies. But sometimes, it's hard to take him seriously.

'Wow, check these out!' Ben says, holding up a pair of tiny boots with rainbow monsters all over them and crocodile teeth on the bottom. 'Yours, Betty?' he teases her.

'I wish!' she laughs back. 'Those are Lily's. She's at a friend's, back in a few hours. We thought it best she wasn't here.'

Millie feels instantly at home, drawn to the hotchpotch of framed photographs in the hallway. In every single one the three of them appear together, laughing at the camera.

They follow Betty into the living room, where there's a crackling fire and a tray of tea and biscuits on the coffee table. Everything is floral, and nothing matches, but somehow it all comes together. There are old paper books on every surface, ornaments in every gap and a sea of blankets on the sofas. Millie nods to the offer of tea as she sits down on the edge of the couch. It's so squishy that she fears she'll never get up if she leans back.

Betty and Marius sit on the opposite sofa. There's an awkward silence for a few seconds until Ben crunches loudly on a home-made ginger nut and their heads all turn at once.

'Sorry,' he mumbles. 'Delicious biscuits.'

The four of them giggle and the tension fades.

'Thank you,' Marius says, more relaxed.

'So, Betty and Marius. How does your story start?' Millie asks, sipping her tea.

'At high school,' Betty answers. 'We were polar opposites. Still are in many ways, I suppose. I was the class rebel, Marius was the class star. One school holiday, we were working at the same hotel. I was a waitress and Marius washed the dishes, so we spent a lot of time in each other's company. That's when we realised there was a spark between us. We got together that summer, kept it quiet for a year, then told our friends and family the minute we finished our A levels.'

'And how did they react?' Ben asks.

'Dad didn't bat an eyelid,' Betty answers. 'He was used to me doing things differently. He said he always knew I'd end up in a couple, with my personality. I hate being alone.'

'My mum was upset,' Marius sighs. 'She was worried I'd been led astray, and thought I was throwing away my future. She refused to accept that Betty was my future. I think she's finally accepted it after all these years, but sometimes I still catch her looking at me with tears in her eyes,' he says, rolling his own. 'I have to yell at her and

177

tell her to stop worrying about me. That there are lots of couples my age. I don't have to be single to be happy.'

'And we *were* happy, until a few months ago, when the government introduced all these new penalties for couples,' Betty adds. 'First there was that crazy couples' climate tax, which has pushed our monthly bills up by 5 per cent just because we have a slightly higher carbon footprint than single occupancy households.'

'Then along came the single credit incentive that rewards single people for staying single,' Marius adds. 'Simply because the government views them as more solid and stable in society. And did you know that we pay more for private health insurance than singles? Apparently, couples have a higher risk of suffering from mental stress.'

'If you add up the contributions and taxes over time, being a couple comes at a considerable expense,' Betty says. 'We were prepared to take the hit at the beginning, and we budgeted for the extra day-to-day costs of being together, like groceries, bills and such. But we're planning for the future and we're feeling the pinch. We'd love to buy this place, but it's almost impossible to get a mortgage as a couple, with the higher fees.'

'I had no idea about any of this,' Millie says, shocked. 'Why should the government be involved in your relationship status? What business is it of theirs? That would be like the government turning round and telling me that I get tax breaks because I'm single.'

'You do!' Betty and Marius cry in unison, and then laugh.

'What? Why are they promoting being single?' Millie scoffs.

'Because they're desperate to discourage couples,' Betty says, shaking her head.

'That sounds like discrimination,' Millie replies.

'It is! We've also heard rumours on the romantic relationship circuit that the government is introducing couple-parent 'drop-ins' to check on the welfare of the children,' Marius says. 'Apparently it's to make sure that they aren't growing up in households where the parental relationship has gone toxic and is having a negative impact on the child's well-being. We can understand why that's important, of course. But shouldn't single parents be subject to the same investigation?'

Millie thinks of June, and Deion, and wonders whether that might have been of benefit to them.

'So, until a few years ago, we were happy,' Betty explains. 'We still are, inside these four walls. But financially, and practically, it's getting harder and harder for couples. And for Lily, too. She has to repeatedly explain to her classmates why her parents are in a romantic relationship.'

'What does she say?' Ben asks.

'That we love each other,' Marius says, squeezing Betty's hand.

'Then they all say that's yucky and laugh at her,' Betty sighs.

'The saddest thing is, her mood is beginning to change,' Marius explains. 'She's always been so sunny, so loving, so carefree. But in the last year, we can see this shadow over her that just won't go away. She always says she's OK. But, when I picked her up from school the other day, she had food stains all over her bag. When we asked her why, she said there'd been a food fight at school. But when I looked at the other bags on the backs of her classmates, they were clean.'

'Don't forget how the other parents treat you at the school gate,' adds Betty.

'Well, they aren't hostile, but they aren't friendly,' Marius adds. 'They don't include us in their parties, and they clam up whenever I go over to say hello. I've stopped approaching them altogether.'

'We love each other,' Betty says. 'We would do anything for each other, and we aren't ashamed of who we are. But we would both take Oxytoxin in a heartbeat, knowing it would make Lily more secure – financially and emotionally. She comes first, above everything.'

Ben sits up, puts his tea down and clears his throat. 'I grew up in an official couple household,' he says. 'It was hard at times. But I learnt how to manage it. How to cope. Eventually they got used to me. We got older. The whispers stopped. With complete respect for whatever decision you make, do you really want to break up your family by doing this? Look around you. You only have to be here for three seconds to know that this is a house of joy.'

'Thank you,' Betty says.

'We aren't breaking up the family, Ben, we're fixing it,'

says Marius. 'Betty and I have been under a lot of stress because of our situation. Sometimes even taking it out on each other. I don't want us to fight.'

'Would you miss each other?' Millie asks.

'We would still be together, physically,' Betty answers. 'One of us would move to the barn at the back. We'd see each other all the time, have dinner together, share care responsibilities. We'd be platonic co-parents.'

'We're hoping that Oxytoxin will dampen the romantic spark between us, but that we'll still love each other like best friends do.' Betty gazes at Marius. 'We'll still be best friends, and that's the love that lasts, don't you think?'

'If that's the way you feel, couldn't you do that without taking a pill that permanently stamps it out? What about when Lily's older and she doesn't live here anymore? You might want to rekindle things, no?' Ben tilts his head.

'That's twelve years away. I'm not willing to take the risk,' Marius says.

An hour later, and it's time to leave. But when they open the door, they're greeted by a thick sheet of rain. The tide has swelled right up to the street and is lapping furiously at the doorstep.

Ben's staring at his phone. 'The roads to Cardiff have been closed off. Flash flooding.'

Nineteen

Betty tugs on Marius's sleeve and pulls him into the kitchen corridor out of earshot.

'This is a disaster,' Millie whispers, pacing the hallway.

'It'll be OK,' Ben says. 'We'll work something out. At least we can avoid the Friday night rush into London!'

Millie looks at him leaning against the stone wall, flicking through a magazine about the local area without a care in the world. She wonders how he can be so relaxed, and feels irritated by his indifference. It's making her feel silly about being distressed. Wouldn't most people worry in this situation? Perhaps it's easier for him because he's at home here. Or perhaps nothing distresses him.

Millie:

Roads closed. Stuck in South Wales.
No idea when I'll be back

June:

> No! Are you OK?

Millie:

> Bit stressed

June:

> Find a hotel, have a bath, order your weight in room service x

Betty and Marius reappear with some towels, a bottle of wine and a small hamper.

'We insist you stay with us tonight, in the barn at the back,' Betty says, beaming. 'It has everything you need, even a workstation.'

'There is just one thing, though,' Marius adds, glancing at Betty. 'It only has one bed.'

'That's amazing, thank you so much,' Ben says, turning to Millie for her response.

'It's so kind of you both, thank you,' Millie replies, smiling calmly.

Inside, she's having a meltdown.

As Adrian reminded them the other day, Slide has a strict no-sliding policy between employees. If anyone at Slide found out they'd shared a bed, her reputation would be toast, as would her chances of that promotion.

A few hours later, and a bottle of wine and cheeseboard down, Ben stands at the sink, washing up slowly and rhythmically as he stares out of the window. Sideways raindrops pop on the glass in front of him like hot corn kernels being swept away by the occasional whoosh of wind. Millie sinks lower into the armchair. After accepting that there is little they can do to exit the situation, she's hunkering down. The half-bottle of Cab Sav has probably helped.

He's so neat, she thinks, as she stares at his back. She likes his straight shoulders. His symmetrical head. How he isn't particularly broad or tall, he's just solid.

Suddenly, he turns around and marches towards her. Then he scoops her up from her chair like she's light as air, carries her up the ladder and throws her down onto the bed in a burst of passion. Clasping her hands above her head while his weight slowly presses down—

'Millie?' Ben says.

'Yes?' Millie replies, leaping out of her head and blushing.

'Do you mind if I have the first shower?' he asks.

'Of course not, go for it,' she replies, watching him rummage through his bag.

He glances up at her and she darts her gaze to the painting next to him, squinting her eyes in fake thought.

'What's on your mind?' he asks, smiling at her.

'What's on my mind?' she repeats slowly, buying time.

She follows up with a fake yawn.

'You,' she says. *'You, stroking my hair as you lie on top of me, looking back and forth between my eyes before*

closing yours and kissing my lips like you've been wanting to kiss them since we first met. Your soft, warm, firm hands running down my neck, over my shoulders and onto my chest. Your lips moving further down, kissing every inch of me hungrily until you reach the top button of my jeans—'

'Millie?' Ben says.

Millie sits up and pokes her head over the back of the armchair to see Ben staring at her through the crack of the bathroom door.

'Sorry, can you pass me my towel, please?' He points to the bannister.

'Sure,' Millie says, standing and pulling up the waist of her jeans.

'Thanks,' he says, narrowing his eyes at her with teasing suspicion. 'Belle, are you falling asleep at eight o'clock on a Friday night?'

'No! I'm just thinking about all the fun we're going to have when you're out of the shower,' she replies.

'Excuse me?' He laughs.

'Do you know how to play Snap?' she says, picking up the pack of cards on the coffee table.

'Doesn't everyone?' He laughs. 'Out in a sec.'

Millie throws the cards down when he closes the door and slumps into the armchair. A new panic sets in. Does Ben think she's boring? He must. Here she is, on a Friday night, with half a bottle of wine inside her and the best she can think of is Snap. Ben's probably staring at his reflection in the bathroom mirror right now, wondering how he's going to make it through the next few hours without storming outside and screaming at the sea to take him.

Adventurous Ben bends rules and breaks routine. He travels long-distance on a one-way ticket with no hotel booked. He eats insects and treks hills with impossible-to-pronounce names. He has girlfriends and sticks his fingers up at anyone who raises an eyebrow.

Millie adheres to rules and loves routine. She travels short-haul, return, with a hotel booked and a backup list just in case, and a spare outfit change in her hand luggage. She researches where she's going, reads all the reviews, and follows the itinerary which is in her backpack and on her mum's fridge. She'd never have a boyfriend because it would mean straying from her life path. She wouldn't get promoted. Her mum would die of a heart attack. June would ditch her for somebody single.

Speak of the devil.

June:

Everything OK? Call when you're safely back in civilisation x

Millie climbs up the wooden ladder to the mezzanine bedroom, where she crawls under the floral quilt of the world's cosiest double bed, wishing it was a splintered old futon with a scratchy pillow and guaranteed backache.

Before Millie can type out her reply, the bathroom door opens with a click downstairs and she hears the ladder creak. When Ben appears, she bursts out laughing. He's wearing a towel wrapped around his torso like a strapless top and has a shower cap on his head.

'What?' Ben asks.

'Nothing. You look marvellous.'

'Do you mind? Your laughter is doing nothing for my body confidence,' Ben says. 'Now, can you please close your eyes while I put on my boxers. And don't look! I know your type.'

Millie pulls the quilt over her head and feels her hair mess up. She should wash it tomorrow morning but, without her straighteners, she'll look like she's stuck a fork in the toaster, all day. Normally this would give her anxiety, but she doesn't feel as self-conscious in front of Ben. It's his sense of humour. He sees the silly side in everything. That's when his dimples are at their deepest and his eyes are at their twinkliest. A burst of eucalyptus reaches her, and she breathes it in quietly and deeply.

'I'll make the tea, you sort the cards,' Ben says, as he retreats down the ladder.

'Yes, please,' Millie mumbles through the covers.

Millie's eyes pop open at the screech of a seagull right outside the window. She turns her neck to the other side of the bed to see if Ben's awake. She's alone.

'Ben?' she says, yawning.

187

It feels like she's been asleep for hours, which confuses her. How could she sleep so deeply in a new bed, next to a co-worker, with no alarm set? She expected to sleep with one eye open, if not both, listening to her heart thudding through the pillow. This morning, she feels strangely calm. Perhaps it's the smell of the lavender on her pillow, or the sound of the sea outside. Although it is a bit unnerving that it's the only sound she can hear.

'Ben?' she says, louder.

Millie stands up, opens the curtains and stares out of the window across the wide sandy beach under blue skies, waiting for the fear of the unfamiliar to kick in. But it doesn't. At least, not immediately. Who cares that it's already 10 a.m.? Or that she hasn't exercised, eaten or pinned down her Saturday plans? Millie doesn't feel tortured by regret; she feels tortured by the realisation that this little slice of reckless bliss will soon end. And that her carefully curated routine – that she really does love most of the time – will restart in less than twenty-four hours. She feels a jab in her bladder. How long can a man spend in the loo?

'Ben?' she says, loudly. 'Are you OK?'

No answer.

'Ben?' she repeats, walking across the creaking mezzanine. She creeps down the ladder and taps on the bathroom door, softly, then louder, before pushing it open a few centimetres.

'Ben? I'm opening the door with my eyes closed,' she announces.

When there's no protest, she pushes it open fully. The bathroom is empty. Ben won't have just left her here, will he? She glances around, looking for his bag.

It's gone.

Twenty

'First pee, then panic,' Millie whispers to herself on the chilly toilet seat with her thumbs tapping at her screen in a rush.

Millie:

Where are you?

Ping!

She lifts her head abruptly. That was from right outside.

'Millie?' Ben says through the door. 'Are you toilet-texting me?'

'No!' she shrieks, turning the tap on and scrambling to finish up as quietly and quickly as she can.

'OK. I have a surprise for you,' he replies.

Millie's heart sinks. Feeling strangely calm about a spontaneous night away is one thing, but morning surprises in her pjs are another level of unfamiliar, and she isn't ready for that. Besides, shouldn't they be packing by now? It's almost lunchtime, and the car rental will be clocking up the late fees.

Surprise! The storm washed away the car.

Surprise! I've harvested fresh mussels for breakfast!

Surprise! Adrian found out and we're both fired!

Millie stares at herself in the mirror, wiping smudges from under her eyes and using her fingers as a comb. There's no time to wash it now. When she pushes the bathroom door open, she sees Ben standing with a straight back to the fireplace, holding a church leaflet to his chest.

'Are you . . . here to talk to me about Jesus?' she asks, her eyes narrowing.

He frowns and looks at the leaflet.

'Ha, no,' he says and laughs, and then switches on a serious face. 'But you have sinned. Twice! One, you fell asleep before we could play Snap. Two, you took up so much of the bed with your extreme starfish pose that I had to sleep on the floor.'

'I accept no responsibility for what I do in my sleep,' she says, her cheeks flushing with embarrassment at the idea of him seeing her sleep. She flicks the kettle on. 'So, what's the big surprise?'

Ben steps towards her, smiles and holds out the leaflet. On the front cover in big letters is TENBY – *Discover the Delights of Our Little Harbour Town. It's Shrimply the Best!*

Millie flicks through the leaflet and looks up at him.

'Let's go!' he cries. 'The storm has passed, it's a beautiful day and you can see where your mum went on holiday.'

'Hmmm,' Millie says, weighing it all up in her head.

'But that's not actually the surprise,' he says, leaning behind the armchair and dragging out a wicker basket covered in white ribbons and overflowing with an assortment of picnic foods. Millie's eyes light up as she spots peanut brittle, caramel fudge, fresh pastries and bacon butties. There's also a hot flask and a mini bottle of champagne resting on a tartan blanket inside, next to two tiny flutes.

He looks pleased to see her smiling.

'When did you have time to do this?' She laughs.

'I woke up early, as anyone would with their head resting on cold, hard wood, not that I'm bitter or anything, then I went next door and Betty mentioned a place down the road that does these summer picnic baskets, and I got there just as they were opening.'

Millie loves Morning Ben, talking at lightning speed.

'But, in a shocking twist,' he continues, 'that's not the surprise either.'

'If you pull a kitten out from under your shirt, I'll do anything you say,' Millie says, smiling.

He pulls a piece of paper out of his pocket and begins to read.

'11 a.m., depart Laugharne. 11:31 a.m., arrive Tenby. 11:45 a.m., park after five attempts and an argument about why I'm choosing to park in the space furthest from the exit. 12 p.m., tuck into our coffees and butties on Castle Beach.'

'Ben, that sounds fun, but—'

He holds his finger up in the air.

'12:30 p.m., board HMS *Tenby Two*. 1 p.m., arrive Priory Beach on Caldey Island. 1:15 p.m., suggest sea swim. 1:20 p.m., decide to paddle instead. 2 p.m., toast to the joys of spontaneous adventure with a lukewarm glass of cheap fizz.'

'What about the—' Millie begins.

He holds up another finger.

'4 p.m., depart Tenby. 4:33 p.m., arrive Laugharne. 5 p.m., depart Laugharne, destination Cardiff. If we catch the 7 p.m. train to London, we'll be back in Battersea by 10 p.m. at the latest. The surprise is, I made an actual itinerary, Belle. I'm quite proud of it and I thought you'd be very impressed. What do you say? Say yes. Yes, is what you say. She says yes, everybody!'

'What about the car rental?' She giggles.

'I've extended it.'

'OK. Bit presumptuous.'

'Meh.' Ben shrugs.

'Tenby is in the opposite direction to Cardiff.'

'Yes, this is true.'

Millie stirs her tea, thinking desperately of reasons why she shouldn't go. It isn't because she doesn't want to go. It's because it doesn't feel right. She'll have to re-wear dirty clothes. She'll have to scrape her hair into a bun, which she hates because she thinks she has weirdly shaped ears. Ben might have made an itinerary, but this wasn't on hers. Then again, neither was last night, and she's survived. She could even go as far as to say that she's enjoyed this short break from her schedule.

'Come on, what's the rush to go home? Have you got anything you have to be back for?'

There's Bruce, although she could ask Aarati to fill his bowl again. Surprisingly, her next-door neighbour adores the cantankerous cat, despite the patchwork of scratches on her arm. Then there's June. Millie missed Movie Tuesday, and she postponed last night's dinner to tonight. If she goes to Tenby with Ben, that'll be the third time she's flaked on their plans this week. She can't remember ever going a week without seeing her best friend.

'I was meant to meet up with June tonight,' Millie says. 'I haven't seen her since last Friday.'

'Ah,' Ben says, putting the picnic basket down and his hands in his pockets. 'Well Belle, I'm not the one with plans, so it's totally up to you.'

Millie sips her tea as her mind splits in two. She needs to spend time with June. She's been a bad friend this week. But they could always meet up tomorrow, couldn't they? June would understand why Millie wants to see Tenby, where Vivian and Nan went as children. But whether June, Queen of Sceptics, will believe her reasoning is another matter. And if June pushes her for the truth, Millie will undoubtedly crumble. The real reason is that Millie wants to spend time with Ben. Her heart is craving it. But her mind is telling her to play it safe and go back to London as planned.

Millie sinks her shoes into the soft warm sand and breathes in the salty air of Castle Beach, imagining Vivian and Nan doing the same. She's found the precise location of a photograph she has of her mum as a child in Tenby, taken by Nan. She puts her hand on her hip, turns to the side and smiles at Ben's camera to recreate the shot.

'The photo I have of Mum is in black and white. I didn't realise how colourful these streets would be,' Millie says, staring at the terraced houses above the beach, painted in pastel shades and looking back down. 'This sand is like caramel.'

'It might even feel like caramel if you were brave enough to take your shoes off, Belle,' Ben laughs. 'What are you scared of, sand between your toes?'

'Yes! For the rest of the day,' she cries. 'Nightmare. You'll regret it on the train back to London.'

'Now that we're here, I need to tell you the one rule I live my life by,' Ben says.

'What's that?'

'When you're on a beach, you have to dip your toes in the water. Even in the dead of winter. Even if there's an army of armed sharks on the shoreline. Even if dipping your toes in the water means—'

'OK, OK, I'll do it!' she says, laughing, standing up and slipping her shoes off with her feet, before gingerly placing her right foot then her left foot on the sand.

'Instant regret?' Ben looks up at her.

'Immediate.' She shakes her head, sinking her toes into the grains and flicking a few at him.

'Hey, I thought I said regrets are pointless? But still, that's not beach etiquette, Belle,' he says, standing up, dusting himself off and grabbing her hand, pulling her towards the sea. 'Your punishment is five seconds of full-foot submersion in the waves.'

'It's too cold!' Millie squeals, laughing, letting go of his hand when they reach the shore in case someone sees.

The mini waves feel like melted ice, and Millie's feet sting and turn bright white in the water. Still, there's something cathartic about plunging her toes into seawater this clear, cool and clean. She takes two steps further in and gasps as the water laps at her tingling calves. When she looks up, Ben is taking a photo of her. She pushes her hair back and smiles.

'Sorry, do you mind?' Ben says, appearing from behind his phone. 'You're blocking the shot.'

Millie looks behind her at the island backdrop.

'Very funny,' she says, turning back to him as he takes another photo of her deadpan face. 'So, we've done coffee, butties, sand-flicking, toe-dipping. What's next on our itinerary?'

Ben takes the paper out of his pocket and points towards a yellow boat tied to the harbour jetty. 'All aboard HMS *Tenby Two*!'

'Does this take you back?' Millie asks Ben, shivering on the breezy deck of the boat, as they pass a fisherman bobbing on his tiny boat in the water.

'It does,' he replies. 'I never caught a thing. Have you fished?'

Millie shakes her head. 'Our holidays were to gated spa resorts with kids' clubs.'

'Sounds all right,' Ben replies.

'They were beautiful. I mean, we didn't get our toes dirty, unless you count mud baths. And we never left the resort walls. Mum was extremely protective of us like that.'

'I'm sure it came from a good place,' he says.

'I guess. But I suppose it's also the reason I'm not the world's most adventurous spirit, too. You know, I see photos of people dangling off cliffs, rattling around in tuk-tuks, racing down rapids, and I wish I could be more like that. But I can never quite get there, like you seem to. Everything I do has to be safe, sensible. Planned in advance.'

'Maybe you're more adventurous than you think you are,' Ben replies. 'You're here, aren't you? How's the sand feeling between your toes?'

'Awful. Every move makes me itch,' she replies, with a wry smile.

Ben chuckles. Nothing makes Millie's insides flutter like the sound of his high-pitched giggle at something she's said or done.

'Well,' Ben replies, 'I'm not actually as intrepid as you think I am. In fact, my ex would probably complain that

I'm anything but. I also love my home comforts. Why do you think my flat is covered in pictures of the past? Why do you think I still have the same backpack and carry cup from school? It's because I like to be reminded of the past. Surrounded by the familiar.'

'I didn't know you spoke Italian,' Millie mutters.

Ben looks at her, confused. 'Ha, yes. Exactly! *Famiglia*. I love to be surrounded by that, too. I mean, why do you think I made friends with the first redhead I saw in London?' He smiles. 'You're like a little piece of back home for me, Belle!'

Feeling the chill of the ocean air, Millie closes her eyes and turns her face to the sun to warm up her cheeks.

'You're cold,' Ben says, passing her the picnic blanket from the basket. Millie drapes it over both their legs and leans back, watching the jagged cliffs of Caldey Island race by. The warmth of Ben's body next to hers and the boat's gentle bounce along the water's surface is making her feel sleepy.

'So, what made you move to London if you love your home comforts so much?' Millie asks, sitting up straight before she gives in to the temptation to rest her head on his shoulder.

'My mum encouraged me,' Ben replies. 'She said it broke her heart to see me break up with Sarah and cut my big trip short, because of her being ill. She convinced me I needed to spread my wings again and see the world. And yes, London isn't the world, but perhaps it will be a jumping-off point.'

Millie opens her eyes. Her heart sinks at the idea of him only being there temporarily.

'But that's a way off, I reckon,' he adds.

She closes her eyes again.

'I haven't told my parents what I'm working on yet,' Ben says. 'I think it would just upset them. Have you told your mum?'

'She thought it was genius,' Millie replies.

'Well, if we all had the same opinions, we'd have nothing to discuss, I guess.'

Just as he says this, the boat lurches and an enormous sheet of water appears from the bow and lands, drenching them. Stunned into silence, they stare at each other in frozen shock. Then they burst out laughing, the salty water droplets running down their faces and into their eyes, their whole bodies shaking and huddled together in the wind.

Back on dry-ish land, Millie examines herself in the public toilet mirror, scraping a brush through her rusty-coloured, wire-sponge hair and dragging her fingers under her eyes to remove the mascara stains. Yesterday, she'd have wanted to wear a mask; this afternoon, she feels the weight of caring has lifted. She's sampled spontaneous adventure, and it tastes good. Maybe even moreish. Exiting the toilets, she leans against the railings and stares out across the sea, taking in that intoxicating scent for the last time. In her head, she runs through the process of returning to her flat.

Kettle on.

Feed Bruce.

Unpack.

Laundry on.

Bath.

Pyjamas.

Single Me Out!

It's her hamster wheel routine for every day of the week, and she doesn't hate it. On most days, she longs for it. She counts down the hours until she's safe on the sofa, listening to the busy world outside as she folds her knees under squishy cushions and flicks through the channels in peace.

The smell of fish and chips wakes her out of her daydream and her stomach rumbles.

'Are you hungry?' Millie asks Ben, when he reappears.

'I could eat,' Ben says.

'How about two of those and a stroll on the beach?' Millie says, pointing at the fish and chip stand behind them.

'Woah, that isn't on our schedule, Belle! Are you sure? We'd probably have to get a later train back to London. I'm cool with that if—'

'Or we don't go back to London,' she says, staring at him. 'If it's okay with Betty and Marius, obviously.'

'Wow. OK, yeah. I'm keen, but are you sure?' Ben asks, surprised.

Millie takes her phone out.

2 missed calls from Mum
4 text messages from Mum
1 voice note from June

Tomorrow is Sunday, which means it's Sunday lunch at her mum's. Bar holidays, Millie has never missed a Sunday lunch with her mum and June. It'll prompt a million questions from both of them. But Millie will just have to deal with those consequences when she comes to them. For now, reality can wait.

'Before we do that, I got you something,' Ben says, handing her a small paper bag.

Millie throws him a confused look, takes the material out of the bag and smiles when it unfolds. It's a T-shirt with a picture of two naked people on Castle Beach on the front.

'Thanks, I hate it,' she says, laughing at him.

'The best bit is on the back,' he says, pointing.

Millie turns it over and bursts out laughing.

I WAS OFF MY TITS IN TENBY
DI MEDDWI'N GOCLS YN NIMBYCH Y PYSGOD

'I actually think Mum has the same one,' she says, deadpan.

Millie and Ben lie still next to each other, weighed down by the quilt and staring up at the beams of the barn above them. It should feel awkward, but it feels fine. Perhaps it's because they've spent so much time together over the past few days. Or maybe huddling up earlier on the boat was a gentle introduction. Whatever the reason, lying next to Ben feels totally natural. Her toes are uncurled and her fists are unclenched. Even her heart is steady. Not for long. When Ben rolls over to face her, she feels his hand touch hers on the duvet, sending her pulse throbbing. She resists every temptation to stroke his hand back, and instead rolls over the other way. Millie might feel comfortable lying next to Ben, but crossing the line into intimacy could ruin everything. There's just too much at stake.

Twenty-One

'Sorry sorry sorry sorry!' Millie shouts repeatedly, leaping past the hall drawers and tossing her bag into the bedroom on her sprint to the sofa.

She kicks her shoes off and swipes urgently at the TV, scrolling through the listings with one hand and calling June with the other.

'Ha! There,' Millie shouts when she sees June's face on the screen, which she's balanced on the coffee table. 'Now, what have I missed?'

'More like, what have *I* missed. What did you two do together all weekend?' June asks pointedly. 'You look like you've been crawling through hedges.'

'Work, basically,' Millie fibs, tying her wild curls into a tight topknot. 'We were in the middle of nowhere. But with hardly any distractions we managed to do a lot.'

'Grim. So, did you manage to get lots done by staying on Saturday night? And were the couples you met as dire as these two?' June says, nodding towards her TV screen.

Millie looks up and sees new contestant Blake kneeling at his girlfriend Jessica's feet on a tropical beach.

'Mate!' June shouts. 'Those linen chinos look pricey, get up! So much for him saying he was ready to decouple last week.'

As June's running commentary continues in the background, Millie nods along, tuned out. Instead, she's tuned in to the last forty-eight hours. She lets her hair down again and stretches it across her face, breathing in the salty scent from the beach. She rubs her toes, searching for a few grains to take her back.

'Don't you think?' June asks.

'Huh?' Millie answers.

'Earth to Millie! I was saying – don't you reckon this is all for the headlines? A week ago, he was the one telling Alpha Joe that he was ready to walk away. And now he wants to *marry* her? I don't buy it. Maybe the producers told him to do it,' June says.

'Yeah . . . probably,' Millie agrees, without a clue.

'Check Jessica out. She's looking for someone behind the cameras. That's a cry for help if I ever saw one. What's she supposed to do? I mean, she obviously has to say no, but it's kind of rough to do that on TV. He shouldn't have put her under this pressure. Yup! There we go. Now she's crying. Oh, thank god, here comes Alpha.'

Millie watches Jessica's blonde hair fall in front of her crumpled eyes.

Doctor Alpha Joe, the show therapist, is circling them as he drones on about understanding the difficulty of walking away from a complex five-year relationship. He likens them to a ball of two fragile woollen threads which have become tightly entangled. He tells them how important it is to unravel slowly to ensure their individual threads remain intact. He reminds them of the reasons they wanted out when they applied for the show, and he implores them to stay strong. How they might feel stressed now, but how being single has been scientifically proven to reduce stress long term. Blake doesn't look like he's buying it. He keeps on grabbing onto Jessica's hand and begging her not to leave because he can't live without her. It's distressing to watch, but it's difficult to turn away.

'I hate myself for watching this show,' Millie groans.

'Ugh, get off her!' June shouts at the screen. 'Doesn't he care who's watching? His friends, his family, his work? What happens when he goes back to the office? Does he just carry on as normal, after exposing himself like this? It's so awkward.'

Millie glances at June on the screen and wonders if there would be any type of romantic relationship June would support.

'Millie, thank fuck you and I have our heads screwed on,' June says.

'You're being a bit harsh,' Millie says, mustering the energy to disagree. 'Put yourself in his shoes. He's had Jessica in his life for five years. That's hard to walk away from.

Habits, routines. Maybe he's happy to be in a couple for the rest of his life. Maybe they should just carry on, set in their ways. I mean, them being in a couple has no impact on us or anyone else. Why do people care that much about couples becoming single? Why do they have to question their motives in the first place? Why do they think it's any of their business to "fix" them? I think we should all just stop having an opinion on something we know nothing about.'

'They did choose to be on telly, Mils. This show is literally made so that we can watch and judge,' June says, staring down at the screen. 'Besides, I'm not being harsh, I'm being . . . caring. I don't want to see anyone coupled up and miserable. I hate watching them waste the best years of their lives on one person who soaks up all their time and emotion. Blake and Jess shouldn't be sobbing on that beach, they should be independent, free, exploring the world, doing what they love. They have their whole lives ahead of them. They've made bad life choices that have landed them in this couple prison. I mean, look at Blake. He is literally on his knees, sobbing, *on national TV*. That's what being in a relationship has reduced him to. Begging. And they obviously weren't happy if they chose to come on this show. They're desperate for an out.'

'Maybe they want to do all of that together. For some people, it's possible to explore the world with a partner, you know.'

'It's not the same, Mils. You know that.'

'I think if Blake and Jess are happy to come as a pair,

they should be free to. How does Doctor Alpha Joe know what's best for them? What's he a doctor of, anyway? Has anyone ever asked that? And why tar them all with the same brush? The world is more beautiful when it's painted with a rainbow,' Millie says.

'What?' June asks, laughing. 'When did you become a motivational speaker?'

'I'm just saying, if we were all the same, i.e. single, then the world would be a very grey place, wouldn't it? And we wouldn't have *Single Me Out!*, would we?' Millie states firmly.

'Well, that's true,' June says. 'I just think that being single is what normal people want, Millie. And, no matter what you say, most people want to fit in.'

'Or,' Millie argues back, 'perhaps single people are threatened by couples because they're destroying the myth that single people are happier. They don't want to believe that being in a couple can make you happy.'

June stares at her in silence on the other end of the phone.

'June?' Millie says.

Suddenly June bursts out laughing.

'It wasn't that funny,' Millie says.

'Sorry, just got a slide. He's put a toupee on it.'

'Let's see!' Millie says, before squirming. 'Why is it always willies in fancy dress?'

June ends the call, leaving Millie alone with that image and the start of the next show on the Therapy Channel, *Life After Love*. Millie rolls her eyes, switches it off and stares at her flat.

Meow.

'There you are!' Millie sings, lowering her arms to the floor and tapping her hand against the sofa. Bruce weaves his way across the room, drawing the act out for as long as he can. When he reaches the sofa, he extends his neck towards her, stopping his nose a millimetre from her finger. Then he sniffs twice and struts back round the corner. Millie's phone beeps. It's a voicemail.

'Oh, hello, Millabelle, this is your Mother speaking. Perhaps you remember me from such occasions as the trauma of your vaginal birth, the indignity of wiping your bottom for three years, the expense of feeding, watering and schooling you for eighteen. June and I had a lovely lunch, thanks for checking. CALL YOUR MOTHER.'

Millie feels her old enemy panic rear its ugly head inside her. So, she wasn't totally truthful with her mum and June when she told them why she had to stay a fourth night. But she didn't tell a total lie, either. She was with a co-worker. They did talk about work. And it was completely platonic. No one needs to know that she was just a finger stroke away from changing everything between them.

Whoosh! sounds an email on her phone.

To: Millie Jones
From: Ben Evans
Re: Memories
Beaut x

Attached to his email is the photo of Millie paddling barefoot on Castle Beach, her hair dancing wildly in the wind. She stares at the photo, wondering who that person is. She doesn't recognise herself at all. She looks totally and utterly carefree.

Twenty-Two

Millie wears blue on Mondays. But not this Monday, because she got home so late last night that her washing is still damp and she was too tired to plan her weekly wardrobe. Instead, she's wearing a black minidress with heels, which are the only shoes she has that match. She's running five minutes late because she was too slow to catch the bus, which is making her panic. But, on the plus side, she looks pretty good, if she does say so herself – under her breath in her bedroom mirror, alone.

In reception, she sees an open lift and speeds up to a scurry, reaching the doors just as they start to close and feeling flustered and embarrassed by the scene she's caused and the loud echo of her heels.

'Wow,' Ben says, looking her up and down. 'Meetings? Going out tonight? Coming in from last night?'

'Laundry,' she says, smiling and straightening her hem. 'New nightclub?'

'Yes! Just round the corner from you. Watch out for the hairy bouncer called Bruce – he's a real piece of work,' she says, shaking her head and stepping back next to Ben when the lift stops on the second floor. Just two nights ago they were in this exact position, only horizontal. More people get into the lift, and they're squeezed even tighter together.

'Thank you for my photo,' she whispers behind the wall of suits in front of them. 'I'm going to frame it and put it next to the picture of Mum in the same pose.'

Millie would hate Ben to see how bare her walls really are. He'd think she was made of stone.

'Sounds like a great idea,' he says, shaking his left knee repeatedly.

Either she's being sensitive, or he's feeling uncomfortable about their weekend. But she can't imagine Ben has ever felt uncomfortable in his life, so she shakes the paranoia from her mind. There's a good chance she's imagining it. Maybe he just needs a pee. Of course, they can't act the same as they did yesterday. They're in the office. He's right to play it safe. No one should ever suspect they just spent the weekend together, even if it was as colleagues. Or friends. She isn't sure what they are. What she does know is that stepping into the office together, knowing their secret escape is safe between them, is a delicious new thrill that Millie's never felt before.

'How was your filthy trip away, you two?' Sasha shouts as they sit down.

Millie looks wide-eyed at her from across the desks.

'Research trip,' Ben mutters, visibly annoyed.

211

@milliej:
how did she know?

@bene:
skye arranged the travel, must have told her

@bene:
was it meant to be a secret?

@milliej:
no, just wondering

@milliej:
tea?

@bene:
yes please Belle

Phew, Millie thinks. Calling her Belle is a good sign that he doesn't think their weekend was a mistake. She'd hate things to be awkward between them. He's the only friend she has left here.

'Ooh, someone's made a special effort today. What's that saying? Dress for the job you want, not the job you have? Or have you got a hot slide booked in for later?' Sasha coos, approaching Millie with her yoghurt pot. Why Millie has become Sasha's audience for her incessant yoghurt consumption is beyond her. The way she wipes the spoon against her tongue, leaving a creamy trail, makes Millie want to vomit. It's almost like she's taunting her about the accusation of theft from all those years ago.

'Laundry day,' Millie replies, sounding tired. This is why she dresses plainly. Nothing makes her feel as uncomfortable as a comment on her outfit, even if it is a compliment. It makes her feel silly for making the effort, in a 'Who does she think she is?' kind of way.

'So, are you going to share your learnings from your sneaky couple deep dive?' Sasha says, sitting in Ruth's empty chair. 'Or is it top secret?'

'The latter, I'm afraid, Sasha. I'm sure you understand. Besides, you could have done a couple deep dive if you wanted to,' Millie replies without looking at her. In her overflowing inbox, she spots an email from Ruth that she doesn't remember getting.

HOUSEWARMING
Sam and Ruth invite you to celebrate their new home
Tuesday 17th August, 8 p.m.
Dress code: Your Secret Crush

'How do you know we haven't?' Sasha says, throwing her yoghurt pot in Millie's bin.

Millie grabs her phone and finds the nearest empty meeting room, leaving Sasha lingering at her desk.

'Um, excuse me? What do you mean, your new house? Are you living together? That's huge!' Millie cries down the phone at Ruth, who's laughing. 'Why am I only hearing about this in an invitation for a party tomorrow? I hope you don't expect me to actually dress up. For starters, I haven't

213

got a secret crush. And second, the summer party's coming up and that's more than enough dressing up for me.'

'It was last minute, Mils,' Ruth says. 'Sam's lease was coming up, she couldn't find anywhere that wasn't miles away and it just made sense. She moved in over the weekend. Millie, I live with someone. I actually *live* with someone. Ruth from eight years ago would have a heart attack.'

'Millie from right now is having a heart attack,' Millie says, laughing.

'Yeah, I can't quite believe it myself,' Ruth says.

'Me neither,' Millie replies quietly. She can't believe it or imagine it. 'So, what's it like so far?'

'I won't lie, I'm having to get used to less cupboard space, and some of Sam's ornaments aren't quite my style. But it feels cosy. Warm. Secure. I mean, who knows, the novelty might wear off quickly. But I'm banking on her sticking around.'

'I miss you,' Millie says. 'I mean, it's only been a couple of weeks, but it feels like years.'

'Well, let's catch up tomorrow. You can come, right?'

'Of course I'll be there,' Millie says.

'We'll grab half an hour at the party, just the two of us. There's actually something important I want to talk to you about.'

'OK, cool,' Millie says breezily, feeling anything but. What could she possibly want to talk to her in private about?

Millie:

Pre-drink at Buddies before Ruth's tomorrow?

June:

Hell yes, I'll need it

Al:

Will it be that bad?

June:

Couple Central

Al:

Does it matter?

June:

I just hope we don't stick out like sore thumbs

Millie:

Well, we have each other

June:

We can pretend to be a couple

Millie:

Ha, yes! X

215

Al:

Hey! What about me?

June:

You can be our adopted adult
daughter x

Millie:

Ah, we've always said we'd have a
kid together x

June:

Pretty sure we'd have grounded her
for drinking by now . . .

Al:

Thanks mums x

In the boardroom later that morning, Millie and Ben are
propped against the table next to each other, staring at the
three posters on the wall of Deion, Ginny, Thandi and the
Rogerses.

'No kids, right?' Ben says, after a minute of contempla-
tive silence.

'Agreed. Our position is that this is an adults-only product, given that it's irreversible. A treatment this final needs full, informed and proper consent, which kids can't give, and parents shouldn't be able to give on their behalf,' Millie states.

Ben grabs a marker, removes the lid dramatically and strikes a cross through Deion. He takes a step over to Ginny.

'Ginny's my favourite,' Millie says. 'This is where Oxytoxin could do some real good.'

'Agreed,' Ben says, keeping the poster up and scribbling a tick on it, before stepping across to Thandi.

'Now, what are our thoughts on the fact that in another world, this could be you?' he laughs.

'I'm nothing like Thandi!' Millie cries.

'Yes, you are! The good bits, of course. Smart, ambitious, career-focused. It's a compliment, promise.'

'Well, actually, I think I love her,' Millie says.

'Oh yeah, do I smell a crush?' Ben asks.

'No! Not like that,' Millie replies.

'So, who *do* you fancy?' Ben asks, taking a sip of his coffee.

'You,' Millie replies, matter-of-factly.

Ben throws the marker over his shoulder and rushes to her, taking her in his arms and leaning her back on the boardroom table as they kiss each other all over. They aren't in the office anymore, they're lying on Castle Beach, with the waves lapping around them, her skin covered in sand. Suddenly it starts to feel itchy and . . .

'Millie?' Ben smiles. An instant trigger for a smile of Millie's own.

'No one. Who do *you* have a crush on?' she asks him back, pressing her lips together to force the telltale grin off her face.

'Now that would be telling,' Ben says, raising his eyebrows. 'So, Thandi.'

'She's another strong case for it,' Millie says. 'She and Ginny are the only stories I feel completely comfortable with. They're both consenting adults who understand the consequences, and they aren't being pushed into it by anyone.'

'And, it'll have no impact on anyone else,' Ben adds.

Millie nods. 'What about the Rogerses?'

'They're only considering it for the financial benefits of being single, and to stop Lily from being bullied. I think there are other ways of dealing with that. Plus, I think my own heart would break if they split up.'

'Agreed. They are far too pure to front this campaign. It feels too tragic,' Millie adds.

Ben rips down the posters of Deion and the Rogerses, leaving them staring at Ginny and Thandi on the wall, his marker pen poised to write.

'So, what campaign lines have we landed on with Ginny and Thandi?' Millie asks, tilting her head to read Ben's scribble.

'For Ginny, it's Heal Your Heart,' Ben says slowly as he writes it out on a blank piece of paper on the opposite wall. 'And for Thandi it's . . . Find Your Focus.'

'I love them,' Millie says, and smiles. 'Sounds so positive, I might take one.'

'Don't say that!' Ben bursts out, startling Millie.

218

'Just kidding!' Millie laughs, surprised that her comment seemed to touch a nerve.

'Sorry, bit dramatic,' Ben says, flustered. 'I think I need a break. How about some lunch?' he suggests.

'It's Asian Chicken Salad Monday,' Millie replies, noticing his cheeks have turned pink.

'Do you really have the same thing for lunch every Monday?' Ben asks, taking the posters of Ginny and Thandi down and rolling them up.

'Yes,' Millie says.

'Why?' He shrugs.

'Because it's tried and tested. I know what I'm getting, and I know that I'll like it.'

'But you must have tasted it for the very first time at some point. So, how do you know that there isn't something else you'd love even more? Something you just haven't tried yet?' Ben asks.

'Would it make you happy if I tried something new for the first time today?' Millie answers.

'Only if it made *you* happy.' He smiles.

'OK, let's take it one step further. How about you choose something new *for* me?' Millie suggests.

'Hope you like prawn cocktail,' he says, putting a plate of pale pink goo in front of her and an Asian chicken salad in front of him.

Millie detests prawns.

'We'll soon see!' she chirps, stirring and poking at the rubbery blobs. She spears a prawn and brings it gingerly to her lips, swallowing down the bile that's rising at the back of her throat.

'Stop!' Ben cries from across the table. Millie pauses, her mouth open in front of the dripping fork.

'I can't let you do that,' Ben says, 'It's too cruel.'

He takes the fork from her hand and swaps their plates.

'If sticking to the same meal every Monday is what makes you happy, then that's what you should do. You shouldn't let anyone try to change you, let alone an eejit like me.'

Twenty-Three

'The worst is St Bridget's Day,' says the woman in red at Ruth's housewarming party the following night. 'Drowning in a tsunami of cards, flowers, chocolates and happy singles celebrating alone or with other single friends. Give me strength!'

'My dad still buys me a gift on Bridget's,' says the man in blue, chuckling. 'And when we moved in together, he gave me housewarming gifts for one. He even bought me a single egg cup! What does he think we do, eat breakfast one at a time?'

The rest of the group laugh and nod their heads in acknowledgement.

'It's the guilt that gets me,' says a woman in yellow on the other side of the circle. 'My mum puts on her best sad puppy eyes and tells me that she'll only be happy when I'm single.'

'I mean, don't hold back, Jean!' a man in black laughs, putting his arm around her.

'And whenever we take a photo, she gets Jack to take the picture! Maybe I'm paranoid, but I think it's because she doesn't want him in the photo!'

'Babe, you're not paranoid, she told you she was future-proofing the memories,' the man in black says.

'She said I'd thank her one day,' the woman in yellow laughs.

'So how do you know Ruth?' the man in black says, turning to Millie and June.

'Ex-work wife,' Millie says.

'And how long have you two been together?' Yellow Woman grins, her head darting between her and June.

'Two magical years,' June says before Millie can correct her. Then she takes Millie's hand and brings it up to her lips for a kiss.

Millie stares at the man and smiles.

'And how have your parents handled it?' the woman in yellow asks.

'My mum lights a hope candle for me in her spirituality group every Sunday evening. Millie's mum tells her that she doesn't want her turning into an old housewife. And last week, we went to a thirtieth ceremony and had to sit on a "couples' table"!' June closes the lie with air quotes. 'As if we're something to gawk at. Basically, our parents think we're total losers. But it's worth it to spend every morning waking up next to this beautiful face.'

June strokes Millie's flushed cheek, which is pointed straight ahead as she tries not to catch anyone's eye.

'Who'd like a top-up?' says Ruth, entering the circle holding a bottle of champagne.

Everyone puts their glass forward.

'Can we talk for five minutes?' Ruth whispers in Millie's ear, after she's finished pouring the round.

Millie is relieved to unhook her hand from June's and follow Ruth towards the balcony. She can hear June continue to tell the group that she's sick of being asked why she's in a couple.

'Ruth, the place looks amazing,' Millie says, pushing the balcony door shut behind her. 'I'm so pleased I came, even if it is a Tuesday.'

'Sorry, forgot about your school night rule! Thanks, hon. I'm really happy. I mean, it hasn't been a total bed of roses. Merging two lives means doubling up on items, deciding which ones go to the charity shop, making sure the place doesn't become a bomb site. And the landlord has hiked up the rent, as predicted.'

'Are they allowed to do that?' Millie asks.

'Two people cause twice the damage,' Ruth shrugs. 'I also had to declare that I was in a couple on my private health insurance, so that's gone up too. Still, at least Sam earns a decent salary or we'd be screwed.'

'That's the real reason you're with her, isn't it?' Millie shakes her head.

'Obviously,' Ruth replies, casually. 'Did you know what the health insurers said?'

'Being in a relationship reduces your life by ten minutes a day?'

'Very funny. No, they said that being in a couple brings added stress that being single doesn't, which can have a *long-lasting and detrimental impact on my physical and mental well-being*,' Ruth quotes. 'But, whatever. It's worth it to have her here. Just for that morning cup of tea she brings me in bed alone.' She smiles. 'I'm easily pleased, I guess.'

'Pff, I could train Bruce to do that, no problem,' Millie says.

'Knowing him, he'd throw it in your face, smash the mug against the side table and hold a shard of bone china to your throat,' Ruth replies.

'I'll probably leave it. So, what did you want to talk to me about?' Millie says.

Millie has been racking her brain since yesterday, wondering what could be on Ruth's mind. Is she going to tell her that she's upset Millie stayed at Slide? Hurt that she's gunning for her old job? Appalled that she's happy to put Oxytoxin on the market?

'I'm starting my own app,' Ruth says, beaming, her excitement palpable. 'It's a matchmaking app for people who want to be in a couple. I mean, there are already a few smaller hook-up apps on the market, and there's Buddy-Up, but this one is different – it is going to go deeper. It's going to be focused on finding someone to fall in love with and guiding them on how to adapt to a long-term, monogamous, committed relationship. Not only will you use it to find a partner, but it will offer tips on how to make the change from single to couple life, how to handle concerned parents, how to keep things exciting in the bedroom, couples' events. It'll basically be a pro-couple lifestyle hub. The anti-Slide.'

'Wow!' Millie says, trying not to sound sarcastic. Are there really that many people out there who want to be in a couple? Her work on Oxytoxin would suggest otherwise.

'I know what you're thinking,' Ruth says. 'That it doesn't sound like it would have a huge market. Maybe not. But I'd like it to start small, grow organically, see what the appetite is. I reckon there are more people out there who want to be in a couple than we realise. I think loads of people are single because that's what society expects of them. Who, in fact, would be far happier in a couple if that was the 'done thing'. If we could bring them all together and convince them that being in a couple is fine, I think we'd be surprised by the figures.'

'So what stage are you at with it?' Millie asks.

'I've been slogging away at the seed funding presentation, and now it's ready to send to potential investors. We just need enough money to build the platform and pay our salaries for the first year. But I really believe in this, Millie. I think it has legs!'

'This all sounds . . . amazing!' Millie cries positively, hiding her deep concern. It's one thing joining a start-up like Slide when it already had the funding. It's a whole new level of risk to start your own, without any guarantee that it'll get off the ground. Especially one as controversial as a couples app.

'Well, Sam has a few high-net-worth connections, which helped.' Ruth smiles. 'I've called it Twocan. Spelt t-w-o then can.'

'Why?' Millie laughs.

'Well, toucans are monogamous. And they have a courting ritual where they toss each other fruit, which I thought was cute. I figured it could play into the whole app – throw someone a blueberry. And the whole idea of it being *two* people, who *can*.'

'That is cute,' Millie replies, her head filling with creative ideas already.

'I miss working with you,' Ruth says, 'and I know you aren't in a couple yourself, never have been and never will be, but I want you to come and join me, Mils. I want you to be chief creative officer of Twocan. I can offer you a fresh start, an exciting new challenge, the chance to be a CCO, like you've always dreamed. And unlimited holiday.'

'You know I never take my holiday anyway,' Millie smiles, floored by the offer.

Millie's heart leaps at the thought of working with Ruth again. Then sinks fast when she thinks of the risk. In her head a siren sounds. At Slide, she's protected by working for a big conglomerate in Human. Monthly salary, holidays, sick leave, private healthcare, pension. At Twocan, she'll have nothing – not even an office or a guarantee the business will survive.

'I don't need an answer right away,' Ruth says, 'but it would be good to know in a week or so. I mean, there's always Sasha.'

'Hey!' Millie cries.

'Kidding,' Ruth replies. 'Oh look, he's here!'

Millie looks through the balcony window and sees Ben hovering in the hallway.

'What was the theme of this party, again?' Millie asks Ruth. She knows, but she needs to hear it.

'Your secret crush,' Ruth replies. 'June looks good as a redhead!'

Millie isn't listening. She's too busy focusing on the Tenby T-shirt that Ben's wearing.

'I'm glad I spotted you first,' Ben says as Millie approaches him. 'I was seconds away from giving June a slap on the back from behind. Could have been awkward.'

'And painful. June did judo at school,' Millie replies. 'Nice T-shirt.'

'Laundry day,' Ben smiles. 'And I figured you'd be here, so I thought I'd give it back.'

'What have you got on underneath?' Millie asks, lifting the bottom of his T-shirt. Her three champagnes are kicking in.

'Millie Jones!' June shouts from across the room. 'If you're going to cheat on me, you could at least do it behind my back!'

Millie lets go of the T-shirt and turns red when she sees June's audience giggling.

'Inside scoop – June and I are a couple here,' Millie leans over and whispers to a bemused Ben. 'We thought it would help us fit in.'

'I can't think of a more perfect pair,' he says.

'We're soulmates,' June says, striding up and leaning in between them to take a carrot from the crudités tray.

'Well, that's wonderful,' Ben says.

'So, did you enjoy being back in the motherland?' June asks him.

'Loved it, have you been?' Ben asks.

'I haven't, but Millie and I are always scouting for dream beach houses to buy together when we get old and bored of London.'

'Don't worry, your secret's safe with me.' Ben grins.

'What do you mean?'

'You don't have to pretend you're a couple.' Ben chuckles. 'But I do appreciate the method acting. Five stars.'

'Oh, it's not acting!' June smiles. 'We're going to live together like an old couple when we hit sixty-five. We're adopting Al. It's a done deal, isn't it, Mils?'

Millie nods, detecting a hint of discomfort from Ben as he sips his beer.

'So, who's *your* secret crush?' June asks, poking Ben in the chest.

'Well, if I told you, it wouldn't be a secret!' Ben smiles.

'Oh, come on,' June says. 'I presume she or he is in Tenby, not here?'

'Fair point.' He nods. 'She's just an old floozy I know from back home.' Ben chuckles, looking out at the party. 'Drinks like a fish, swears like a sailor and totally and utterly drop-dead gorgeous. But, sadly, in a relationship with someone else, as I recently found out. Isn't it always the way?'

'What is?' June asks, looking confused.

'You always want what you can't have,' Ben replies, glancing at Millie.

Twenty-Four

The office is dark outside the boardroom on Wednesday night, where Millie is sitting alone under cold white lights, tweaking the final elements of the pitch proposal ahead of the presentation tomorrow. As she taps away at the pitch on-screen, she reminisces about her late nights sitting in this exact seat opposite Ruth. Millie is meant to give Ruth an answer tonight. She's spent the week noting the pros and cons of joining her at Twocan on her phone. She opens up her notes.

Pros
Working with Ruth
Not working with Sasha

Cons
No security
No sick pay

No holiday pay
No office
No customers
No guarantee of success
No Ben

Millie stops typing for a second and looks across the room at the whiteboard covered in red and blue scribble. Underneath the scribble are layers of more scribble, going back years. Christmas campaigns, Slidetember, the Slidies. It would be crazy to leave now, just as she's on the brink of being recognised for everything she's worked so hard on.

'An app for couples? How many users does she expect to have? It sounds so niche, it's certain to fail,' said Vivian in a frenzied phone call on the way to work this morning. 'Promise me you won't take that role. It would be utter madness. Stay at Slide, get the promotion, make a name for yourself with Oxytoxin, then leave on a high and start your own agency. I mean, there's risk and then there's reckless.'

Staying at Slide is the sensible option. And, with the promotion, she has a huge opportunity within reach.

The light in the kitchen comes on.

Then there's him, she thinks. Ben, who is currently making every day here a good day. Ben, who she thinks about constantly. Ben, who gives her comfort just by sitting across the desk from her. Ben, who has spilled beer all over the counter and is frantically mopping it up with a coaster.

Millie is fully aware of how inappropriate her Ben crush is. But she is also fully aware that the flirtation between them is harmless fun. And of course, it doesn't mean anything. If there's one thing this pitch has taught her, it's that love might feel real to the people who experience it, but it's just hormones. Nothing more. She could put a stop to it if she really wanted to. Besides, he won't be here forever.

Millie returns to her screen for one final check of their pitch deck, as Ben approaches the boardroom with a bottle of beer in each hand.

'Shall we take this outside?' he asks, opening the door with his back. 'To be clear, I want to have a beer on the roof garden. I don't want a fight.'

'That's a shame,' she says, shutting her laptop. 'I reckon I'd crush you in a thumb war.'

'Ah, fighting talk. I like it.'

'I do actually need some fresh air. I feel like I'm beginning to fester,' she says, standing up and grabbing both of their jackets before following him up the stairs to the twentieth floor. The roof garden is Millie's favourite office spot, and at night it's extra special. A soft green lawn with a long glass wall overlooking the river, tidy beds of roses and lavender planted so symmetrically it gives Millie great satisfaction just staring at them. Above the lawn are criss-crossing strings of tiny twinkling lanterns that cast a warm orange glow. When she's up here, Millie likes to lean back in a deckchair and squint at the lanterns, imagining that the stars have dropped down. After checking that no one is watching her first, of course.

Millie takes a rug from the communal box and lays it across two deckchairs in the centre of the lawn, as Ben places the bottles on the table between them. All she can hear is the soft hum of traffic from below and the occasional siren in the distance.

Ben opens a bottle of beer and hands it to her.

'Drinking before a pitch?' Millie fake-gasps, taking the bottle, stretching her legs out and leaning back. Normally she wouldn't drink on a weekday night before a big meeting, but she's feeling confident about the pitch and figures one won't hurt. Ben sits down, stretches his legs alongside hers and looks up at the lights. He closes his eyes for a few seconds to bask in the glow, and looks so beautiful in the moment that Millie takes a mental snapshot of him in this light.

'So, think we're finished?' he asks, lifting his head and turning to her. She abruptly turns her head back in case he sees her staring.

'What?' she replies quickly, startled by the suggestion.

'The presentation? Are we finished?' he repeats.

'Oh, yeah, I think so,' she says, calmer. 'I can't believe how much we got done today! Go us.

'A toast to the dream team,' he says, lifting his bottle in the air and stretching it towards her. Millie reaches across to meet it, still staring straight ahead.

'Belle, what are you doing?' he cries softly.

'What?' she says, turning to him.

'We have to look into each other's eyes when we say cheers! It's ten years of bad luck if you don't.'

'Ten years? That's a pretty long time,' she replies.

As they stare at each other and re-clink, it feels like the world pauses. For just a few seconds, everything is still. Everything but Millie's racing heart. Suddenly uncomfortable, she breaks off their stare and takes her gaze up to the lanterns. Ben, after a while, does the same. She needs to say something. Anything.

'So, I have a question for you,' Millie says. 'How long do you think you'll be here?'

'If we're done, I'd say half an hour or so?' he replies breezily.

'No, I mean at Slide,' she says. 'You mentioned you wanted to go travelling again.'

'Ah,' he says. 'Yes, I do want to. Plus, you know, I don't think it's fair to deprive people of Boy Eats World for too much longer. My three fans need me, Belle.'

Millie's mood nosedives at the thought of him being far away.

'But,' he continues, 'I doubt it'll be for a while yet. I'm enjoying it here too much.'

And all is OK with the world again.

'How about you? You've been here for eight years, haven't you? You aren't bored of it yet? Would you ever pack it all in to travel the world?' he asks.

No. Millie wishes she could say yes, but she'd be lying.

Travelling isn't part of the life plan. It was never on her vision board. You couldn't pay her a million pounds to pack it all in, not when she's worked this hard to get where she is. She'd spend the entire trip wondering what could go wrong and worrying about falling behind. People like her don't go travelling on a whim. People like Al do. People like Ben do. Planless, carefree, caution-to-the-wind types. Millie stares down at his legs stretched out next to hers and imagines them both on the sand of a tropical beach instead of the roof of the office. No matter how hard she tries, the vision makes her feel anxious, not excited.

'Honestly?' she replies. 'I don't think I could. It's just not me,' she responds.

'What if the trip had a very precise and well-planned itinerary?'

'Even if I planned it down to the minute, it could still go wrong. Besides, it's not just about the itinerary, it's about the whole life plan.'

'Ah, the career,' he nods, looking disappointed. She wonders why.

'It's not just the career, it's the home comforts. I love my life the way it is. And anyway, I have responsibilities here that I can't ignore.'

'Such as?'

'For starters, I've got a cat.'

'And who are you to say that your cat doesn't want to see the world, sampling the finest local cuisine?' Ben asks.

'Do you think the mice in Vietnam taste different to the ones here?' Millie replies.

'Oh, undoubtedly. I've heard the mouse pho in Vietnam is to die for.'

'What about the *cat*-su curry?'

'Ha, very good,' Ben says, laughing.

When their conversation goes quiet, Millie's thoughts grow loud. She wonders what Ben really thinks about her obsession with routine, her aversion to risk and her fear of change. They're so different, they shouldn't work. So why does it feel like they do?

Millie hates disappointing people. Earlier she felt like she'd disappointed Ben by saying she'd never go travelling. And now she has to disappoint someone else she cares about. It's a moment she's been dreading for the last hour, but her mind is made up. She clicks on Ruth's number and waits, practising her speech in her head.

Twenty-Five

'Very impressive!' Adrian booms after the presentation on Thursday morning, leaning back in his chair as Ben sits down. 'I can see how much work went into this. Lots of research. Strong insights. A solid creative idea. You two have given us plenty to think about.'

Ben nudges Millie's knee under the boardroom table.

'I just have one question,' Adrian asks, looking at his notes. 'Your strategy is to target one specific audience. Single adults who've had their hearts broken. That's a limited market. How would we get scale? Go wider? Attract different audiences?'

Millie and Ben have anticipated this question, and they have a simple answer.

Millie clears her throat. 'We wouldn't.'

Adrian raises his eyebrows. 'What about parents, teens, couples? This campaign is just about a cure for the broken-hearted. What about Oxytoxin as a preventative?

Wouldn't we want to help adults avoid being lovesick altogether?'

'If we target parents and teens, we risk a backlash,' Millie explains. 'As it is, Human doesn't have the best reputation. To come out with a product that shows adults making teens take a pill feels too controlling, too Big Brother, too inhumane. If teens want to take Oxytoxin when they're older, they can. And in terms of couples, you only have to glance at social media after an episode of *Single Me Out!* to see how divided we are in our feelings towards romantic relationships. Everyone seems to think that couples are a bit weird, but people tell the truth on the Internet. Our social listening research shows that, to our surprise, lots of people, with the courage of anonymity, are in support of couples in a "back the underdog" kind of way. So, bringing out Oxytoxin to break couples up might come across as a bit couple-bashy.'

'Whereas if we focus this campaign on helping to mend broken hearts,' Ben continues, 'it paints Oxytoxin in a much better light. We'll come across as kind, not cruel.'

'Heal Your Heart,' Adrian repeats. 'It's a snappy tagline, that's for sure. Good work, you two.'

While Adrian isn't looking, Millie tries a cheeky sneak peek at his earlier notes on Sasha and Margot's presentation, but he snaps his notepad shut before she can see what it says.

'Yes! Chicken satay!' Millie says, smiling. 'What did you get?'

'Vegetable tagine,' June says, poking at it, testing it and nodding in approval. 'S'good!'

'You seem super chirpy this evening, Mils,' June says, curling her legs up onto Millie's sofa with her Surprise Meal for One from Pantry. 'And I can't believe you ordered a Surprise Meal. Something's changed. What's up?'

'Oh, nothing major. Just that I think Ben and I might have nailed the Oxytoxin pitch!' Millie sings. 'And I'm feeling stoked that it's finally over.'

'Amen!' June says. 'I feel like we've been strangers this past fortnight.'

'Do you know, Adrian has never once described my work as "good" to me, ever. I mean, even if I don't get the job, that's a win in itself.'

'Of course you're going to get the job,' June says. 'You're the best one.'

'Oh, I don't know.' Millie shakes her head. 'Sasha might have nailed it, too. But at least I can say it wasn't a total train wreck.'

'I was surprised when you texted me to hang out,' June says.

'I was surprised you weren't stuck at the office,' Millie replies.

'I assumed you'd be with Ben, having a cosy celebration for two somewhere.'

Was that a dig? It feels like one, but June isn't subtle. If she wanted to come out and say something, she would. She'd probably use a megaphone.

'A cosy celebration?' Millie laughs, feeling uncomfortable. 'What's that supposed to mean?'

'You know what I mean, Mils,' June puts her fork down and stares at her. Millie detects a mood shift.

'I really don't!'

'It's so bloody obvious that you two fancy each other. I've never seen you look at anyone that way. Ever. You look at Ben like he's a human-sized peanut butter, honey and banana cheesecake. And he looks at you the way I look at my bank account on payday. Honestly, when you two are together, it's like there's no one else in the room. I've never seen you like that with anyone. It's a bit nauseating, to be honest.'

'That's so untrue!' Millie cries.

'No, it isn't,' June replies. 'You luuurve him.'

'Oh, as if,' Millie dismisses June's taunts. 'I do not.'

'He luuurves you,' June teases again.

'Can you stop?'

'No, *you* stop,' June replies, childishly.

'I do *not* love him,' Millie states.

'Riiight. OK then,' June says, unconvincingly.

'I don't,' Millie repeats softly.

'If you don't at least fancy him, why does your nervous rash make it look like you're wearing camo when you're with him? And, actually . . . right now. What are you nervous about, Mils? Huh?' June asks.

Millie throws her hand to her chest and feels the hot skin underneath.

'Because you're making me uncomfortable!'

'OK, fine!' June replies, louder. 'Let's change the subject. How did Ruth take the rejection?'

'She was fine,' Millie says quietly.

June's taunting has unsettled her. Sure, Millie fancies Ben. He's beautiful. Sure, she likes being with him. He's fun. Sure, when she's not with him, she misses him. But the same could be said of any friend. She likes being with June. She misses June when she hasn't seen her for a while. But it doesn't mean she loves June, in *that* way. Millie wonders what June has seen between them. What makes her think that Ben loves her? She can't deny that the possibility that he fancies her makes her heart flutter.

'Maybe it's time you got back on Slide, Cobweb Pants,' June suggests, putting the kettle on. 'Talking of which, have you decided what you're going as tomorrow night?'

'No idea,' Millie moans. 'And I've run out of time, so it has to be something I can find in this flat.'

'Hmmm . . . a sexual fetish in this flat.' June looks around. 'You could strap Bruce to your head and go as Ben? Cheap, warm and true?'

'June!' Millie cries. 'Enough. You're going to make it weird between us.'

Bruce narrows his eyes at them both from across the room.

Ping!

241

Millie frowns when she sees who the message is from and squints when she sees the photo.

Sasha:

Busted!

Millie's heart stops.

—

'Millie, I did you a favour by taking that photo!' Sasha says on Friday morning, faux casually, opening her yoghurt pot. 'I wanted to shock you into being a little more cautious next time. I mean, if you're going to have a dirty weekend away with someone from the office, maybe don't leave the photo evidence in full view on your work computer?'

'It wasn't a dirty weekend away, it was a work trip,' Millie states firmly.

'Conducting interviews on the beach with champagne, were you? Interviewing a boat captain, were you?' Sasha asks.

'What the hell were you doing on my computer on Monday morning anyway?' Millie asks angrily, her pulse rising from the confrontation.

'I wasn't on your computer, I happened to walk past and see it. I was actually trying to lock it for you before anyone else saw it. Bit defensive, aren't we?' Sasha replies, her eyebrows high.

Millie slaps the yoghurt pot out of Sasha's hands, sending it flying across the canteen and into the window, where it slowly glides down the glass, leaving a pale pink streak. Then she grabs Sasha's phone, scrolls to the photos and deletes the picture of her and Ben on the beach and, as a final jab, plops it into Sasha's coffee.

'Did you hear what I said?' Sasha interrupts, scraping up the last dregs of yoghurt.

'Sorry?' Millie asks.

'I said, you're lucky it was me who saw it, and no one else. I'm just worried about you. I mean, you know Adrian's rules. It was a risky move, with the promotion announcement tonight. It's hardly professional, is it? Especially when Ben might be under you soon. If he isn't already.' She winks, sticking her tongue deep into the pot.

'Please. We were on a work trip and decided to see some sights while we had the chance. You're making something out of nothing.'

'If you say so,' Sasha coos. 'But if you ask me, you two seem *very* close. You might want to be careful about the vibe you're throwing out. Weekend trips, little private messages, tea for two. People will start to talk.'

They'll start to talk because you're gossiping to them, Millie thinks mutinously. First June, now Sasha! Though maybe she does need to be careful. Is it that obvious?

'So, the summer party,' Millie says, ignoring her. 'Anything I can do to help?'

'It's all under control, hon. But thanks for the last-minute

243

offer. It's been such a struggle to organise it with the pitch. I guess I'm lucky that I'm a multitasker and don't panic easily.'

'Outfit ready?' Millie asks. 'Got all your bondage gear here?'

'Oh, I'm not going in bondage anymore. I'm going as Adrian!' She laughs. 'What can I say? I'm kinky for bald guys.'

'He's going to love it,' Millie replies, sickened by Sasha's game playing.

Twenty-Six

Ben pauses and frowns as he approaches Millie at the roof terrace bar in his clown suit that night.

'I can't tell if your sexual fetish is a ghost or an Ancient Greek,' he says, leaning against the bar next to her. Millie has wrapped herself in a white sheet from her laundry basket.

'Funny guy!' she replies, reaching over and squeezing his nose, sending fake blood spurting across the floor. 'Ew!'

'I warned you,' Ben says.

'No, you didn't!' Millie replies, laughing and wiping her hands on a paper napkin.

'My bad. So, explain yourself, Belle.'

'Egyptian cotton bed sheets,' she answers. 'It was all I had.'

'Ah,' he mouths. 'Drink?' he asks.

Millie has been nursing a near-empty champagne glass for the last half hour, taking it slow in case she needs to

say a few words on stage later. But she nods to his offer.
One more won't hurt. Her stomach has been in knots since
she arrived, and it might help her loosen up a bit. She hasn't
told Ben about the photo, and she can't decide if she should.
One side of her is questioning the point of bringing it up
again, the other side is demanding he has a right to know.
If she tells him, she might have to explain why Sasha felt
the need to confront her – and why it rattled Millie.

Ben hands her a glass of champagne and turns round to
rest his back on the bar, bringing a neat whisky up to his
lips. *He must be the only person in the world who can
make a clown suit look sexy.* He catches her staring at his
lips, and she glances away.

'A whisky is a bit heavy for 6 p.m., isn't it?' Millie jokes.

Ben takes a sip, draws his breath in sharply through his
teeth and splutters.

'Yeah, I thought it would make me look sexy and mysteri-
ous,' he says, lowering the glass and wiping his mouth.
'But who am I kidding? Barman! A cold bottle of your
most neon-coloured alcopop, please! I can't live this lie any
longer,' he says, and laughs, putting the whisky on the bar
behind him before squeezing Millie's arm and leaning into
her ear.

'So, how are you feeling, Millie Jones, Chief Creative
Officer?' he whispers loudly.

'No! Don't jinx it!' she cries, smiling.

'Well, it'd better not be Sasha,' Ben mutters. 'I did *not*
sign up for that. Ruth told me that Slide has a "no twats"

hiring policy, but what about a "massive twats" firing policy?'

'Talking about twats,' Millie says, nodding towards Adrian, who's on the dance floor attempting to do The Belt with some of the creative interns. The Belt is a new dance craze that isn't safe for anyone over twenty and isn't cool for anyone over ten. When the interns move away, he limps off.

Millie and Ben turn their heads at the same time when they hear screeching laughter from the other side of the garden. It's Sasha, who's doing an impression of Adrian doing The Belt, in front of the board. Cue the selfies, kisses and hysterical laughter.

'To be honest, her outfit is uncanny,' Ben replies. 'Dressing up as a penis for a sexual fetish party is pretty meta. Although let's be honest, she didn't have to dress up as one at all.'

'Because she's a huge knob already?' Millie says.

They catch each other's eyes.

'She showed me the photo,' Ben says. 'I'm guessing she did you, too?'

'Ah,' Millie answers. 'Yep, that was the topic of Yoghurt Yap this morning.'

'I hope you're choosing to ignore it, like I am?'

'I totally am,' Millie nods.

A brief but uncomfortable silence falls between them.

247

'Good evening, Sliders!' Adrian shouts into the mic he's holding, handcuffed as he paces up and down in front of the crowd in his prisoner fantasy outfit. 'I hope you're all having a good time tonight. Before we get started, let's give it up for Sasha! I think we can all agree that she's done a brilliant job at dressing as the best-looking Slider here!' The crowd applauds as Sasha puts her hand up, looks around and blows kisses across the terrace.

'I'd like to take a few moments now,' Adrian continues, 'to talk about what a remarkable year it's been for Slide. We're financially fit, we're getting more global recognition, and we can be truly proud of what we have achieved in the last twelve months. I don't have to remind you of the success of The Slidies, the first awards programme of its kind in the world that rewards our highest-rated users. Thank you, Millie!'

The audience turns and cheers, while Ben grabs hold of her right hand and lifts her arm in the air like a boxing champion. Millie covers her face with her left hand and looks into his eyes through a gap between her fingers. Suddenly, everyone else is out of focus, and he is all that she sees.

'Our platform is changing people's lives for the better,' Adrian booms, bringing them back. 'Our community is liberated, in control, and can celebrate being proud sexual beings!'

Ben gently lowers her arm and squeezes her hand before he lets go. Remembering her earlier conversation with Sasha,

Millie darts her eyes around the crowd to see who's watching. To her relief, everyone's eyes are on Adrian.

'And every single one of you here in this room has had a part to play in our phenomenal success,' Adrian continues. 'So, you can all give yourselves a pat on the back. But, like every year, there are some people who have gone above and beyond. Some people who deserve recognition for their dedication, for putting in the hours and having flashes of pure genius.' Adrian pauses and pans the room.

Millie looks down at her feet.

'As you're all aware by now,' Adrian says, his face switching to serious mode, 'Ruth Clarke has left Slide to pursue personal interests. We were sorry to see her go, but we wish her all the best. She was an inspiration and a visionary to many of us here, and her important role as chief creative officer will be a tricky position to fill. But, as it turns out, not impossible. Because we've found someone right under our noses. A creative force with the kind of commercial smarts that can send us global. She's been here for a while. She's a team player. She's a fighter. She's a winner. And she's won the vote of the board as of 4 p.m. this afternoon. Please welcome to the stage our new chief creative officer!' Adrian pauses for effect.

Millie takes a deep breath and looks up, smiling, her stomach on fire with nerves.

'Sasha Hunter!'

Millie smiles widely and claps robotically along with the others. Her eyes glaze over as she watches Sasha throw her hands to her mouth in a nauseating performance of mock surprise.

Ben turns to her, stone-faced and shouts over the applause, 'Are you OK?'

Millie glances at him and nods furiously, before excusing herself to go to the loo, where she calmly walks into a stall, closes the door behind her and sits on the toilet seat. Waving at her cheeks, she swallows repeatedly in an attempt to dissolve the rock in her throat. She mustn't let anyone see her crushing disappointment. She pictures Vivian advising her on what to do next.

Chin up, back straight, pull yourself together.

Millie hears the door to the loos open and steps approach her cubicle.

'Millie?'

'I'm fine,' Millie shouts, tugging at the loo roll to hide the sound of her shaking voice.

She pats her face, takes a few deep breaths, smiles and opens the door.

'Thought you might need this,' Ben says, holding a glass of champagne towards her. 'And this,' he continues, handing her the oversized daisy from his clown suit pocket.

'Thanks.' She smiles. She chugs the champagne and twirls the daisy in her fingers. 'What are you doing in here? If anyone catches you, they'll think —' Millie starts.

'I don't care what they think,' Ben says, leans against the sink and takes a swig of his alcopop. 'And you shouldn't either. Everyone knows you should have got the job. It's not a reflection on you, it's a reflection on them. It's this shit company. The type of company that markets something like Oxytoxin is the type of company to promote someone like Sasha. They've made a terrible choice. And I'd like to say they'll see that soon enough, but I don't think they will. Do you even want to work at a place like this? If this decision makes you question that, maybe it's a good thing.'

'Well, why you do work here then, if you hate it so much?' Millie asks, feeling indignant that he'd be so dismissive of the eight years she's dedicated to the company. She turns from the mirror to face him.

'I think you know why I'm still here,' he says.

Perhaps it's the sound of June chanting *he luuurves you* on repeat in her head. Maybe it's because Millie's career-first care factor has just come crashing down after the announcement. Or it could be the fact that she's just downed her fourth champagne and it's gone straight to her head. Mostly it's the way Ben is staring at her. So deeply, it's like he's staring *into* her.

Millie doesn't take chances.

But right now, she feels confident that this is one chance she can take.

He's still here because of her.

Millie puts her champagne glass on the counter.

'It's because of—' Ben starts, but Millie doesn't let him finish.

Instead, she steps forward, takes his face in her hands

and brings his lips to hers. She hears the clink of his bottle next to him, and feels his warm arms wrap all the way around her, bringing her so close into him she can barely breathe. They kiss harder, not caring to come up for breath. His hands move up her back and onto her neck, sending shockwaves of shivers down her skin. His fingers run through her hair as they carry on, even harder. They rotate to lean against the wall. The women's loos. *They're in the work loos. The women's loos. Do the women's work loos have cameras?* Suddenly Millie starts to feel hot and flustered in his grip. What the fuck is she *doing*?

Millie quickly pulls away from him.

'As I was saying,' Ben says, looking shell-shocked and running his fingers through his hair, 'it's because of the corporate benefits and early Fridays.'

Millie smiles half-heartedly.

Suddenly the door bursts open and Skye marches in, looking green and swerving. She does a double take at Ben before shoving open the first stall door, burying her head in the toilet and vomiting loudly.

'What the hell am I doing?' Millie whispers, before putting her head in her hands. 'Could this night get any worse?'

'Ouch,' Ben says softly, throwing his bottle in the bin.

'I don't mean that,' Millie mouths. 'Ben, this could mess—'

A huge retch sounds from Skye's stall, so loud it's impossible to hear themselves.

'Are you OK?' Ben and Millie shout at the same time.

252

'Fine! Sorry!' Skye gasps in between gags.

'Let's not talk about it here, eh?' Ben whispers, putting his hand on her shoulder and squeezing it gently. 'I'll see you outside.'

Millie watches him walk out, a hint of despondency in his gait. A sad clown.

Skye's stall door swings open and out she steps, wiping her mouth.

'Oh my god, Millie, I'm so sorry,' Skye says. 'Adrian was making us do a shot competition and I can't handle tequila. Did I interrupt something?'

'No, don't be daft!' Millie chirps. 'Ben has a ridiculous habit of walking into the wrong toilets.'

'I love Ben,' Skye coos. 'He's the nicest person here. Apart from you, of course. I wish you two were in charge. You'd make such a great team.'

Millie and Ben are sitting quietly on the rose garden chairs with a bottle of wine, watching the party unfold on the dance floor in front of them. Neither of them has spoken a word in at least ten minutes. All Millie can think of is that kiss. How his lips felt on hers. How much shit she would be in if anyone found out.

'Do you think we should talk about what just happened?' Millie finally musters the courage to ask him, not daring to look at him.

'I think we should,' Ben takes a sip of his wine. 'But I don't think here's the right place, or now's the right time. I think it's a conversation for clear heads.'

They fall silent again. After a few minutes, Ben nudges her with his shoulders.

'Stop worrying,' he mouths, and smiles at her.

As the drinks get smaller, the moves get bigger. Outfits are ripped off; outfits are tried on. Sasha's bald cap is doing the rounds, along with some pretty brutal impersonations.

Millie glances over towards Adrian's table to see what he makes of it. To her horror, he's staring directly at her. He wiggles a finger at her and pats the seat next to him.

'I'm being summoned,' she shouts at Ben over the music, and stands up.

'G'luck,' Ben says, with a tipsy salute.

Millie sits down slowly next to Adrian, feeling sick about what he'll say, and about how she'll respond after a bottle of wine and three shots.

'I just wanted to check in with you,' Adrian says. 'Make sure you're OK. You must be disappointed.'

Millie shakes her head. 'I'm fine, Adrian, Sasha is brilliant for the role. The team will be in excellent hands.' She smiles, her stomach rolling when she thinks of Sasha sitting next to her in Ruth's chair on Monday morning, angling the picture of Lupo the greyhound on her desk.

'Well, glad to hear you're taking it well. It was a close call.'

'Can I ask what gave her the edge?' Millie says.

'Ambition, scale, blue-sky thinking. Sasha didn't limit her ideas to one product, one sector, one campaign. She's come up with four products, four sectors and four campaigns. An incredible amount of work in just a couple of weeks.'

Perhaps Sasha did deserve this after all.

'So, what are the four products?' Millie asks.

'One's called Oxytoxin Teens, and targets co-parents with kids acting up at school, and that's all about securing their future.'

Strange. That's the exact same angle Millie and Ben had been considering.

'One's called Oxytoxin Twos, and targets couples with financial challenges, and that's all about avoiding the stress.'

So is that.

'The third is called Oxytoxin Fix, and targets single people who've been dumped and are struggling to get over it. A bit like yours, I guess.'

Exactly the same as ours.

'Then her fourth idea is identical to yours, in fact. So it must be good!'

'Let me guess,' Millie says. '"Stay focused"?'

'Right, it's called Oxytoxin Pros,' Adrian says. 'If you both came up with the angle, it seems like a must-do, right?'

Millie doesn't answer him. She looks over at Ben. When he catches her eye, he offers her a thumbs up and a thumbs down. Millie suddenly feels a surge of warmth towards him. Ben might be the newest member of the team, but he feels like her best friend. Maybe more, now that they've crossed the line. She looks out on to the dance floor at the rest of the team and realises just how much of an outsider she feels here. Sasha's at the centre, swinging her bald cap around at an army of admirers.

Millie is seething. It is one thing to lose; it is another to lose to your own ideas that someone stole. *That's* what Sasha was doing on her computer on Monday, hacking into her emails. And she had the gall to act like she was doing Millie a favour.

'Well, thanks for checking in,' Millie mumbles to Adrian, standing up. Her head spins; she knows she's drunk. She's at a work event. She hates scenes. And yet, she marches across the dance floor and up to Sasha.

Twenty-Seven

Millie takes Sasha by the wrist, half dragging, half leading her over to the chair where Ben is waiting, his eyes filled with confusion.

'Hello, lovebirds,' Sasha says, panting and taking a seat in between them, oblivious to Millie's mood. 'Millie, I don't know what to say. You played the game well, and someone has to win. Guess I'm just the more ruthless of the two of us.'

'You're right, you are *ruthless*,' Millie replies, surprised and impressed by how level her voice sounds. 'Mostly because you hacked into my emails and blatantly stole our work.'

Ben sits up suddenly and turns to them both.

'Let me break it down for you quickly, Ben,' Millie says, sobering up. 'I've just heard that Sasha's idea for Oxytoxin isn't one idea. It's four. Oxytoxin Teens, to help parents *secure their future*. Oxytoxin Twos, to help couples *avoid the stress*. Oxytoxin Fix, to *heal your heartbreak*. And Oxytoxin Pros to *stay focused*. Sound familiar? What *were* you doing at my computer on Monday, Sasha?' Millie asks, feeling her voice start to shake with anger.

'What are you trying to say, Millie? I've already told you, I was trying to lock your computer. If anyone's hiding things around here, it's you. And you,' she adds, turning to Ben. 'Perhaps I should show your "work trip" photos around the party and get a verdict? Maybe put it up on the big screen and ask for a show of hands?'

'Oh, fuck off, Sasha,' Ben says. 'You won the pitch, now give it a rest.'

'I'm not going to sit here and let her accuse me of stealing when she has no proof!' Sasha cries. A few people near them turn round and Millie shushes both of them quickly.

'Let's not do this here,' Millie says, quickly regaining her composure. Now is not the time for her to react with her heart instead of her head.

'No, let's not,' Ben says, standing up and offering her his hand.

'What are you doing?' Millie whispers to him, looking at the crowd near them, red-faced by his offer.

'I think we should go,' Ben says quietly.

'I don't,' Millie says, staying seated with her hands firmly on her lap. 'And can you please stop offering me your hand, people are staring.'

'I didn't think you'd be such a sore loser, Millie,' Sasha says. 'Thanks a lot for ruining my big night.' She stands up, pings on her bald cap and disappears into the dance floor crowd.

Ben rubs his face before sitting back down. 'Why the hell

do you want to stay here? Let's just leave! It's not like we want to hang around with anyone else, is it?'

'No, Ben!' Millie hisses back. 'What do you think that'll look like to everyone else? That's how rumours start. It was bad enough Skye catching us in the loos, and now this.'

'Who gives a shit, Belle! Let them think what they like!' Ben cries.

'I give a shit what they think, Ben! And please don't call me *Belle* in front of people,' she says, lowering her voice. 'Look, I can handle this myself. I don't want *anyone* thinking I need some kind of saviour.'

'I'm not trying to be your saviour, I'm trying to save us both from spending any more time in the company of these utter twats. And any embarrassment by having a big argument.'

'Well, it's a bit late for that now, and you're just making it worse!' Millie cries.

'Look, whatever. Handle this situation however you like. But *you* kissed *me*, Millie – don't act like I'm the one ruining your bloody reputation. I'm leaving.'

Ben slams his glass on the table and walks off without looking back.

◖◗

Millie's eyelids feel like sandpaper and her tongue tastes like something she'd wipe off the bottom of her shoe after a night out.

Ping!

It's a voice message from her mum.

'Millabelle Jones, chief creative officer of Slide. Have you got used to it yet? I'm so proud of you, sweetheart. Congratulations. See you tomorrow at lunch. I'll put the champagne in the fridge.'

Al:

> I'm guessing congrats are in order, *grand fromage*?

Ruth:

> Tell me everything! X

June:

> How's the new CCO this morning?
> Call me when you're conscious.

Millie sighs as she types a separate message to June.

Millie:

> I did something really stupid last night. Can I call?

Millie's phone starts ringing immediately.

'What happened? Are you OK?' June asks, sounding worried.

'No, it's fine. I'm fine. Well, not fine, actually. I didn't get the job,' Millie responds flatly.

'Oh Millie,' June replies. 'I can't believe it. I'm so sorry. But that's not stupid, that's them being idiots.'

'That's not the stupid thing. The stupid thing is . . . I . . .' Millie stops before she confesses about the bathroom kiss. It'll be the first time she's kept something from June in their lives, but today is not the day for the third degree. She changes direction. 'I had a fight with Sasha. A loud one. Sasha won the pitch. She got the promotion. Then I found out that she stole our ideas. Although I don't have any proof, so I can't do anything about it. And then I took it out on Ben, so he might not be talking to me.'

'What the fuck, that's crazy, Millie!' June says.

'*I'm* crazy,' Millie says.

'No you're not, you're normal. If you *didn't* confront her about it, *that* would be crazy.'

'Yeah, but you know I don't do confrontation. I was a completely different person last night,' Millie says, thinking of the kiss in the office loos. 'I was out of control.'

'Oh, stop beating yourself up. I bet you there were people silently applauding. The only thing you did was have a fight. I fight with my colleagues all the time, 'cause they can be utter twats.'

It isn't the only stupid thing Millie did. But Millie isn't ready to talk about the other thing. She's not sure she ever will be.

Twenty-Eight

'How long have you been here?' June whispers, approaching Vivian's front door. Millie is leaning against the wall outside.

Millie turns her head lazily. 'I just needed five minutes,' she says, and sighs.

'How's the head?' June murmurs.

'It's a two-day hangover,' Millie moans.

'Ready to break the bad news?' June smiles, rubbing Millie's shoulder.

Millie has been avoiding her mum's calls for the past twenty-four hours. Their weekly Sunday lunches are usually where good news is celebrated. Not today.

They hear Vivian marching down the hall. Millie sighs as she drags herself off the wall and puts on a half-hearted smile.

'Hello, darling. Your skin looks dry,' her mum says, as soon as she opens the door. She holds Millie's chin and turns it towards the light.

'I'm just tired,' Millie says.

Her mum taps Millie's cheek three times. 'Hard at work, as always. That's my girl. Still. You need to protect that precious skin,' she calls as she marches back down the hall and into the kitchen, the two of them following behind. Vivian reaches into the fridge and brings out a bottle of champagne.

Millie wanders over to a familiar paper recipe book on the counter. It's the only keepsake that Vivian has from her mother, Veronica. They didn't speak for years after Millie was born. Veronica was appalled at Vivian for having a child so young, when at twenty-five she should have been focusing on her career. But Vivian was rebellious and determined. Despite this stormy relationship, sunny memories were made with Veronica's cookbook. Millie recalls sitting at the kitchen counter after school and flicking through the pictures while Vivian made her recant the peaks and troughs of her day. She strokes the grease stains, wondering what meal they were cooking when these marks were made. Millie only met Veronica once, when she was six years old. The memory is vivid. Pale blue eyes staring at her in what seemed like disbelief.

'My goodness, Vivian, she doesn't look anything like you,' Veronica remarked. 'Isn't that funny? You insist on having a baby at your age, when you should have been focusing on yourself, and you end up with one who could be somebody else's. Don't expect me to babysit. This is all on you.'

It was the first and last time Millie had seen her mother cry. Tears running over soft cheeks that burned Millie's own as she stormed out of Veronica's living room hugging her close on her hip. Outside the house, Vivian placed Millie gently on the floor and crouched down to her level. She looked into her eyes without blinking, gripping her shoulders tightly with both hands.

'Millabelle Jones, you are my baby. And you are perfect. Don't you *ever* let anyone suggest otherwise. It's you and me, Millie. Forever,' she said with a shaky voice that belied the firmness of her grasp.

From that moment, Millie had made a silent pledge to please her mum. To help Vivian prove that Millie was perfect in every possible way. Top student at school. First-class honours at university. *Chief creative officer.* When Millie was little, being placed on a pedestal of high expectations made her feel special. Today, it's giving her vertigo. June was pushed too, but never to the same extent.

'So,' says her mum, smiling as she hands Millie a glass of champagne. 'Shall we toast you, then? Come on, I'm dying to know. Was everyone thrilled at their choice? When do you start? Do you get a new office? Pay rise? Press release?'

'Actually, Mum, I get nothing,' Millie states casually.

'What do you mean?' Vivian's flute pauses midway to her mouth. 'Did you negotiate? I mean, I know you don't like confrontation, Millie, but you can't be a doormat. Sometimes you have to upset the apple cart in order to get the apples.'

'I didn't get anything, because I didn't get the job, Mum.' Millie says it quickly, brutally – it is the only way she can get the words out. 'Sasha, the other senior creative, got it.' Millie shrugs. 'It's fine, she's good for the role. Let's just say she's a lot more *Slide* than I am.'

'It is *not* fine!' Vivian exclaims, putting her glass on the counter with a loud clunk. 'She can't be better than you! And you've been at Slide for eight years, how can anyone possibly be more Slide than you?'

'Well, apparently, they are. Please can I have a top up?' Millie replies, wondering if hair of the dog will help.

'Who is this Sasha?' Vivian asks, her eyes growing wider and her lips getting tighter.

'She's a snake. She stole Millie's pitch ideas and presented them as her own,' June says, taking a sip.

'More like . . . an ostrich. Long legs. Sticks her beak into other people's business,' Millie replies nonchalantly, ignoring the tuts and gasps that are on a loop from her mother's side of the kitchen.

'What do you mean, she stole your ideas? Are you going to report it? You're not going to give in, just like that? Millie, where's your fighting spirit?' Vivian cries.

'It's already been announced, Mum. Besides, I'll look like a sore loser if I suggest it. Even if she didn't steal my ideas, Adrian said he wanted someone ruthless, and that's what he gets with her. It's over. It's done.' Millie stretches her arm out across the counter and grabs the champagne bottle herself.

'Not your fault, Mils, you worked so hard on that pitch. You can't win them all,' June says, putting her arm around Millie and wincing in anticipation of Vivian's inevitable outrage at the phrase.

'Oh, I hate that expression, it's utter nonsense! Why can't you win them all? Millie has been winning them all her whole life. Those idiots at Slide don't understand how lucky they are to have you there.'

'Mum, please don't. I'm not really in the right frame of mind to think about it,' Millie sighs, taking a large glug.

'You are perfect for that role, Millie! I can't think straight, I'm so furious.'

'I'm *not* fucking perfect!' Millie explodes, silencing her mother. 'Sorry,' she puts her glass down. 'I didn't mean to shout.'

'Well that outburst is long overdue,' June mutters.

'They've upset you, of course they have,' Vivian says, ignoring June's snide comment. 'Right, that's it. I'm putting feelers out tomorrow for other roles.'

'I don't want to leave Slide right now, Mum. *Please*, just drop it. And please do *not* put feelers out. Look, it's my fault. I am who I am. I play it safe, and that's not what they wanted.'

'Playing it safe isn't always the best option, Millie. Sometimes you need to take risks, be ruthless, be a snake. I blame myself. Maybe I mollycoddled you.'

'I wouldn't say that,' June sniggers. 'I'd say milliecoddled.'

'June, please! This is important!' Vivian shouts, walking

through to the dining room and taking a seat, before dramatically leaning back on the chair.

'Mum, I'm the one who's supposed to be upset about this, not you!' Millie shouts from the kitchen. 'Can you please say something helpful?' Millie mutters, nudging June.

'Vivian?' June picks up the champagne bottle and wanders through to the dining room. 'If you ask me, this is the best thing that could have happened to Millie. A CCO is too busy to work on the details of a campaign, so essentially Millie will still be running Oxytoxin. Won't you, Millie? Her name will still be all over the credits. It's one of the most exciting projects the company has ever undertaken. Then, with that experience, perhaps she can leave Slide on a high.'

Vivian sits up and holds her glass out for a top-up.

'Well, that's true.'

'If you think about it,' June continues, 'perhaps the reason they didn't give Millie the promotion is because she's the only one who can be trusted on this Oxytoxin project. They know Millie is the *perfect* person for the task.'

'I suppose you're right,' Vivian folds her arms.

'I'm also starving,' June replies, returning to the kitchen. 'When does the food arrive?'

'Thank you,' mouths Millie.

June clinks their glasses and kisses the air. She turns the kiss into a snog by sticking her tongue out and rolling her head around.

'Stop, please,' Millie begs.

'Changing the subject, I have some news,' June says.

Millie and Vivian turn to her in anticipation.

'I found out on Friday I'm being put forward for partner!' June beams.

Millie steps forward and wraps her arms around her and gives her a shake. June lets out a fake groan.

'Junie! That's amazing!'

'Congratulations, sweetheart, that's fantastic.' Vivian places a hand on her shoulder.

'Why did you wait so long to tell us?' Millie cries.

'Well, it was a bit awkward with your whole situation, to be honest. I figured I should probably let that settle first,' June replies, uncharacteristically coy.

'Oh, rubbish, don't even think of that! This is the best news ever!' Millie smiles.

She means it. It's the type of happy news she needs after forty-eight hours of wallowing in a pool of self-pity.

'Shall I open another bottle?' Vivian asks.

'Absolutely!' Millie replies, rubbing June's arm again. 'June Moon, Partner, Stumble & Guest.'

'Sounds rather good, doesn't it?' June scrunches up her face.

'Sounds great!'

'Message.' June nods to Millie's screen on the counter. Millie picks it up.

Ben:

I'm sorry about how I left last night

268

Relief floods over Millie. She was dreading seeing him in the office tomorrow, with what was said – and left unsaid – at the party. Millie isn't sure what she feels more nauseous about, the kiss or the fight. Although the flashback pains her, she remembers the kiss feeling good. The aftermath, not so great.

'Something amusing you?' June says. Millie looks up to see her raising an eyebrow in suspicion.

Ben:

I'd had a few and lost my cool

'What?' June says. 'Millie, hello? I'm trying to talk to you. You're being rude.'

'Sorry! What was the question?'

'I asked you what was amusing you.'

'Nothing,' Millie responds quietly.

Again June lifts one eyebrow.

'OK, fine – Ben. He's just messaged. Think we're all good.'

Millie puts her phone down and gives June her full attention.

'Well, at least we're talking again after Friday,' Millie says. 'Otherwise it would have been really awkward at work.'

'He's too in love with you to make it awkward,' June says.

'He isn't in love with me!' Millie says, waving her away.

'Also, shhh.' She nods towards her mother, who's returning from the front door with the food delivery. 'We're mates, nothing more.'

'Well, we're *best* mates, and you text each other way more than we do,' June scoffs.

'That's because I see you all the time,' Millie replies, shrugging. 'I don't need to text you when you're standing right next to me.'

'You see him all day, every day!' June hisses.

'Who do you see all day, every day?' Vivian asks.

'Bruce,' June replies.

'Ah.' Vivian nods.

While Vivian and June lay the food out on the table, Millie replies to Ben.

Millie:

> Don't worry, you didn't have any cool to lose in the first place, nerd

Ben:

> Zing

Ben:

> Also, false

Ben:

> I am cool, look, I can prove it

Millie giggles, zooming in on a picture of Ben's feet in dog paw slippers resting on a coffee table in front of the TV, with a crossword on his lap.

Millie:
I'm sorry, I stand corrected

Millie:
Also, quilt, four down

Ben:
I knew that

Ben:
Look, I found another one

The picture is a close-up of the crossword, with mad scribble all over it that spells out . . .

'S m a r t A r s e,' she quietly reads to herself.

Twenty-Nine

A fluffy slap in the face wakes Millie up abruptly. Bruce's bottom is horribly close to her lips, and his tail is flicking her cheeks repeatedly, as if he's attempting to revive her from a faint. She hoists her body up onto the pillow, while he turns his head and eyeballs her.

Millie, still watching him suspiciously, reaches for her phone on the side table. It isn't there. Squinting her eyes to her dressing table, she can't see it there either. A sudden loud vibration in the bed sends Bruce upwards and outwards, all four limbs stretched at angles from his sides. Millie reaches under the duvet and retrieves her phone, tutting at herself when she sees the battery is at 10 per cent. She must have fallen asleep on it after her long phone call with Ben. She checks the last call and tuts at herself again. Going to sleep at 1 a.m. on a Sunday night isn't a strong start to the week. She smiles, though, remembering snippets of their hours-long conversation, mainly about the changes Sasha might

272

make to the team. Millie's betting on a dedicated yoghurt fridge by the end of the week. Ben's betting on a taser on her desk to keep them in line. Then there was the argument about what dessert is best on a hangover, after the obligatory salt intake of fry-up, cheese toasties and ramen noodles throughout the day. He argued for cheese. She argued that a) cheese isn't a pudding, and b) cheesecake is life.

'Shit!' Millie says when she sees it's almost 8 a.m., swinging her legs to the side of the bed and putting her feet down. 'Shit!' she says again when she stands on something. Lying on the floor is the daisy from Ben's clown suit that he gave her in the office loos at the summer party. Millie picks it up, hobbles over to her dressing table and hangs it on the mirror.

It'll be quicker to run to work and shower there, she decides, opening her wardrobe to search for clean workout gear.

'Shit!' she repeats, louder. She forgot to put a wash on. Frustrated, she opens the laundry basket to find last Wednesday's running outfit, her mind feeling foggy as she pulls the Lycra over her head and catches a glimpse of herself in the mirror. She wishes she hadn't. Her face is so pale it looks transparent, and her eye bags are the colour of the pavement outside. Who is she this morning? Millie isn't the type to miss her alarm, forget about laundry day and . . . crap. She turns to see Bruce staring at her from the hall. There's no cat food left. She was supposed to order it yesterday.

Hopping into her joggers, Millie hurries through to the fridge to see what she can whip up in the zero minutes she has. Do cats eat scrambled eggs? No, there's no time to cook. She pulls out a Fuel for One box and glances at the label. Lamb fillet and sweet potato. It's Bruce's lucky day.

Despite it being summer, the park air feels cool this morning. Millie breathes it in through her nose and out through her mouth in a steady rhythm, attempting to distract herself from the stabbing stitch in her side and hoping the fresh air will clear her head. It's currently clouded with conversation replays from last night, which are making her sides ache even harder. She starts laughing when she remembers the competition for their best thumb impression, lying back on the pillows with their phones at their chests, their chins splayed. Perhaps, one day, they could be just friends. The prospect seems impossible right now. Her crush on Ben is undeniable, but she's hopeful it will pass. Millie closes her eyes briefly and flashes back to the kiss at the summer party. Her insides curl up as she does, remembering the feeling of his lips on hers. That eucalyptus smell filling her nose. His surprisingly strong hands running their way up her back towards her neck and pulling her closer.

'Woah!' cries an alarmed voice.

Startled, Millie opens her eyes, just in time to see a dog walker right in front of her. She gasps and veers to the left of him, staggering across the grass and stumbling into a tree. She stands up and waves an apology with muddy, scraped hands. She imagines what her mum might say.

Pull yourself together, Millie!

OUT OF ORDER

'Nooo!' Millie moans when she sees the sign on the shower at work, followed by a long groan when she spots herself in the mirror. An Alice band of sweat and . . . she sniffs her skin . . . her dirty running outfit has left a foot smell all over her. She splashes herself with water and sink soap that smells of toilet spray.

At least her work clothes are fresh, she thinks, unfolding the black cigarette pants and black lace blouse and . . . oh, for fuck's sake. What is wrong with her today?

'Is it Casual Monday?' Sasha comments, glancing at Millie's running shoes.

'I forgot to pack my pumps this morning,' Millie replies.

Neither of them will forget Friday night that easily.

As Sasha adjusts the height of Ruth's seat to make it taller than anyone else's, she stares at Millie's hairline.

Millie dumps her bags down on her desk and starts searching for her water bottle.

'Didn't you get my email?' Sasha says, swivelling her chair round to face Millie and crossing her legs.

Millie stares at her blankly.

'I want a senior to sit in with the creative interns. To keep them in check and offer a little guidance and feedback. So I've moved your desk there, just on a trial basis. As you were running late this morning, I thought I'd give you a hand, so I sent Skye to move your stuff.'

'But this has always been my desk,' Millie replies, feeling her breath getting shorter and her hands start to tremble as she begins to realise just how many things Sasha might start to unravel now that she has the reins – and a reason for being vindictive.

'Well, it's time for a shake-up!' Sasha cries. 'Sometimes I wonder what those creative interns actually do every day. Judging by the quality of their ideas, I'm guessing they sit there picking their noses until the clock strikes six. Well, now you can watch them.'

@bene:

you're online but I can't see you

@bene:

invisible cloak? are you giving the finger to Sasha right now

@milliej:

desk move :(

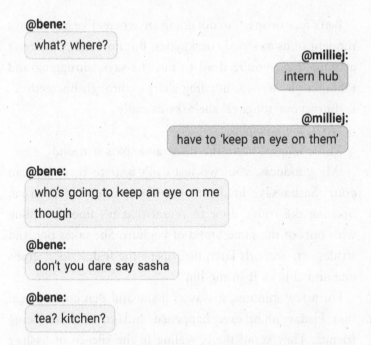

@bene:

what? where?

@milliej:

intern hub

@milliej:

have to 'keep an eye on them'

@bene:

who's going to keep an eye on me
though

@bene:

don't you dare say sasha

@bene:

tea? kitchen?

Millie is stirring the teabags in the kitchen when Ben appears carrying the cactus from his desk. He's drawn a smiley face with a pointy tooth on a sticky note and attached it to one of the spines at the top. He holds it up to his face and grins. Seeing his cheery face in the flesh always brings her such comfort. She's going to miss having the real one on tap across the creative hub.

'Just a little something to remember me by,' he says. 'His name is Ken. He enjoys long walks by the river and conversations about the weather. He's to help you remember me.'

'Why, are you going somewhere?' she asks, smiling. 'And can you take me with you?'

Ben's face drops. 'I'm not going anywhere. I've just always thought of us as strictly deskmates. But now that you aren't at your desk, you're dead to me,' he says, shrugging and taking a victory sip, inhaling sharply through his teeth.

'Burn your tongue?' she asks casually.

'Yeth,' he whispers.

Millie laughs, takes the plant and spins it round.

'My goodness, you two just can't *bear* to be apart, can you?' Sasha says loudly as she comes round the corner, opening the fridge door to reveal that it's floor-to-ceiling with pots of the same brand of yoghurt. She takes one and strides off. Seconds later, Ben opens the fridge door, grabs one and chucks it in the bin.

For a few minutes, it was as if she and Ben could forget that Friday night ever happened and go back to being friends. They stand there, reeling in the silence of Sasha's comment, until Millie makes her excuses and heads back to her desk with Ken Plant.

Ben is like a sugar rush. A temporary pick-me-up. He gives Millie such a high when he's there and sends her crashing down when he's not. At home that evening, following an afternoon of silence on work messenger, she slumps back onto the sofa and holds up the vision board she made with Vivian when she was sixteen years old, that mapped her life intentions. It's almost fourteen years old now, and the pictures are starting to curl up at the edges. She lowers it to watch Bruce slowly lick his paws. A wave of irrational envy washes over her. She wishes she were a cat. Bruce doesn't have to worry about work, relationships – romantic or otherwise – or turning thirty. He doesn't lie in bed awake at night, wondering why it feels like he can't move forward with his life.

Millie is the only one whose life is going backwards. Ruth is smashing it with her start-up. June is kicking ass at work and in the bedroom, probably literally. Al . . . well, she isn't sure what Al is doing. But for some reason Al doesn't seem to care. Maybe Millie should try to be more like her. Care less. What *has* Millie done in the last year to be proud of? She's in the same old flat. Same old job. And now she's even further away from being made chief creative officer than ever before. It feels like she's gone right back to the start. Perhaps she should get a fringe. Maybe that'll shake things up a bit.

Millie:

Should I get a fringe?

June:

No.

Millie:

Why? I think it'll suit me.

June:
It won't.

Millie:
I'll love it

June:
You'll hate it.

An unexpected knock on the door sends a panic through her. She tiptoes to the keyhole and frowns at the visitor.

'Dairy Devils?' says the delivery woman when Millie opens the door gingerly.

'No?' Millie says.

'For "Belle Jones, the one and only true chief creative officer"?' The woman looks at her note, confused.

'OK, yes, thanks,' Millie says, taking the parcel and opening the lid. Inside is a family-sized peanut butter, honey and banana cheesecake with writing in cursive on top.

I'm fondue you.

Millie smiles as she shuts the front door with her foot and carries the precious cargo to the coffee table. As she stares at it pensively, her smile slowly fades. She picks up her phone and makes a call.

Thirty

Millie and June sit beside each other on the sofa, staring at the cheesecake on the coffee table in front of them.

'OK, so what am I looking at?' June asks.

'It's a cheesecake, from Ben.'

'And why am I not eating it?'

'It's a cheesecake. From Ben,' Millie says.

'OK. Granted, it's random, but what's the big—'

'I kissed Ben,' Millie blurts out.

June's eyes widen.

'I kissed him at the party in the loos, but it was a stupid drunken mistake that I made because I was upset about the promotion. I didn't tell you because I was confused.'

'Bloody hell, Millie!' June says. 'That's not like you!'

'Yes, thank you! I know that!' Millie cries. 'But it didn't mean anything.'

'Maybe it didn't mean anything to *you*,' June says after a few seconds of shocked silence, glancing at the cheesecake.

'What do you think it means?' Millie says.

'I think it's pretty clear. It means that kiss was more than just a kiss,' June replies. 'For him, anyway. I mean, the writing is literally on the wall, or, in this case, on the cake. *I'm fondue you.* Ben loves you, Millie. This is an *I love you* cheesecake.'

'It could be an *I'm sorry* cheesecake,' Millie suggests.

'If it was an *I'm sorry* cheesecake, it would say . . .' June pauses momentarily to think. '*I'm so so-brie.*'

Millie giggles.

'Can we *brie* friends again,' June grins, pleased with herself.

Millie sighs, scraping the side of the cake with her spoon before slipping it into her mouth and leaving it there while she rests her chin on her hand.

'How was it between you two in the office this morning?' June asks.

'It was fine until Sasha made a snide remark in front of us. Then it got super awkward and we didn't speak for the rest of the day. I mean, what does *fond* even mean? You're *fond* of friends. Perhaps this is a *let's be friends* cheesecake.'

'We're best friends and I wouldn't send you this cheese-cake,' June replies. 'I'm telling you, it's an *I love you* cheesecake. Sorry to freak you out.'

Millie is freaking out. But it isn't the *I love you* cheese-cake that's doing it. It's how the *I love you* cheesecake has made her feel. Inside, she's dancing a celebration dance. But the celebration dance quickly turns into a flailing arms panic. She glances at June, who's preoccupied with a piece of biscuit base. Should Millie tell her what's really going on in her head, or will that freak June out, too? Any talk about couples makes June very uncomfortable – not that that's what this would be, but this crush does go deeper than any she's had before, so Millie feels like she needs help navigating whatever these emotions are. She knows June won't judge her, if she's just honest.

'You know,' Millie starts. 'Ben used to have a girlfriend. So, I guess he's the relationship type. If that's a thing.'

'He's totally the type!' June cries. 'It took me two seconds to spot that when I first met him. I have an excellent relationship-type radar. And because he's the type, you need to tread carefully. Maybe distance yourself from him. I don't think you can be friends with someone you have feelings for, if you're the relationship type, so this can only end badly if you carry on.'

Although June's right, and it's probably what they need, Millie winces at the idea of even more distance between them. Today was bad enough, being on the other side of the office and opposite Sniffy Steve. She really missed him. Ben, that is, not Steve. It turns out that without Ben, Slide is quite shit.

'I guess it'll be easier now we don't sit opposite each other,' Millie sighs.

'It will be,' June replies. 'And if I were you, I'd just act like none of this ever happened. Don't mention it at all. He'll get the message soon enough.'

'What, completely ignore this?' Millie asks, pointing at the cake. 'Not even a thank you?'

'You don't want to start a dialogue. Just pretend you never got it,' June replies, smudging the message until it's illegible and then licking the back of her spoon. 'Say that Aarati nicked it, or something.'

'Seems a bit harsh,' Millie says.

June throws her spoon into the box and leans back on the sofa. 'This is a cruel-to-be-kind situation, Millie. You're doing him a favour in the long run. You aren't the relationship type, and the sooner he knows it the better. You know what is harsh? Leading him on.'

June stares at the box and sits back up again. 'OK, just one more bite.'

'Well, you've just done one sit-up, so you've earned it,' Millie says, putting her own spoon down and staring at June as she continues. She watches June chew and wonders how she'd take it if she told her the whole truth. About Tenby. About her feelings. About how this cheesecake really makes her feel. After a few seconds of chewing, June turns to her.

'Why are you staring at me? Are you eat-shaming me?' she asks.

'So, I haven't told you *everything*,' Millie says.

'Oh boy,' June says, swallowing. 'There's more? What is it?'

'I did something a bit stupid. And I should have told you at the time, but I was embarrassed. Actually worse, I was worried you'd try to stop me.'

'You got your vagina pierced?'

'No! Be serious.'

'I'm deadly serious. I've been thinking about getting Vivian a voucher for her birthday.'

'That working weekend away wasn't exactly a working weekend. And by that I mean we didn't do any work at all. We sort of had a minibreak together. There really was a storm, and we were stuck overnight. But then . . . he had the idea of staying for the day. Then, well, I suggested we stayed for another night . . .' Millie grimaces.

'So what? Friends go away for the weekend together. You didn't have to fib about it, you could have told me,' June replies.

'I guess I didn't tell you because the truth is, it didn't feel like a friends weekend. It felt like a more-than-friends weekend. I mean, we even shared a bed. By accident, but still.'

'How do you share a bed by accident? Did you fall into it, blackout drunk?'

'No. It's a long story.'

'But you didn't slide?'

'No,' Millie says.

'Okaaay,' June replies, slowly. 'Sorry, what's the issue? Apart from the fact that poor Ben probably thought he was *well* in there.'

'I wouldn't have spent the weekend with anyone else from work. Not even Ruth. Normally I'd want to get home, do laundry, have lunch with you and Mum. But I *wanted* to stay.'

'*Really*? You *liked* Tenby that much?' June asks, purposely missing the point.

'No!' Millie laughs. 'I wanted to be with *him*. I want to be with him. All the time, June. I think that maybe I'm . . . *fondue* him too.'

June swallows the cheesecake that's been sitting in her mouth and takes a long sip of water.

'Please don't vomit,' Millie pleads. 'Look, I don't know, I'm confused. I've never had a crush like this before. I thought I just fancied him, but it feels stronger than that. It's like my brain is infected. All I can think about is Ben Ben Ben, like a big clanging clock in my head. It's making me do stupid things, like lie to you and Mum. And it's distracting me from my work, which might be why I didn't get the promotion. I literally ran into a tree this morning because I was in such a daze. Ever since I met him, it's like I can think of nothing and no one else.'

June chucks her spoon into the box again. 'Jesus, when I teased you about *luuurving* him, I was only joking!'

'I don't love him!' Millie cries. 'I think. I don't know. I just like him. But more than like him. Is there anything in between like and love?'

'Loke?'

'I loke him. Ugh, what's wrong with me? How can I, of all people, be having this conversation?'

'Millie, don't be so hard on yourself. So what? So, you told us a little fib or two. I've told you fibs before! That top I was wearing the other weekend? It *is* your top. And to be clear, the only reason you didn't get the job was because Sasha stole your flippin' ideas. So what? It's not the right job for you. Perhaps it's a sign that you need to think about moving on. And these feelings you have for Ben? The Millie I know would put it down to hormones. You're not the relationship type. These feelings will pass. You'll be fine.'

'Maybe,' Millie says, unsure.

'I think you've got three options. First, give Ben a go and see what being in a couple is like. I mean, Ruth raves on about it, so perhaps it isn't all bad. Although this option does come with a strongly worded caveat.'

'Which is?'

'I will disown you if you ever tell me that you've got to "check with Ben".'

'OK.'

'Or start calling yourselves Billie.'

'Yeah, right,' Millie says, and laughs. 'Anyway, that is *not* an option. Can you honestly imagine me in a couple? Can you imagine me losing control of my own life, all that change and all those sacrifices? Having to explain my life choices to people who want to know why I'm in a couple? Having to deliver another crushing blow to my mother?'

'Oh, thank fuck for that!' June blurts out. 'You actually had me worried for a second. No, of course I can't imagine you in a couple, the idea makes my head hurt.'

'Second option?' Millie asks.

'Second, you slide his brains out and hope it's enough to scratch the Ben itch. The B-itch, ha! Anyway, hopefully when you wake up next to him he'll have bad breath or that white crusty dribble that looks like dried-up mozzarella juice. Maybe you could be a terrible slide on purpose. Adopt a weird fetish, like humming the national anthem or screaming your own name in his face.'

'Third option?'

'Wait it out and see if your feelings pass. Like I said, I'm sure they will. Eventually he'll quit trying, and then one day you'll wake up and realise you haven't thought about him for a while. He'll just be someone that you used to know.'

'All that does is make me feel sad,' Millie mutters.

'I could keep you distracted by texting, calling and visiting you constantly,' June suggests.

'You do that now.' Millie squints at June.

'I could send you some revolting visuals to speed things up. Ben picking underneath his big toe and wiping it on your sofa, perhaps?'

'June!'

'Ben picking his belly button, rolling the fluff in his fingers and leaving it on your keyboard?'

'Why does he have to pick anything?'

'If none of the above works, there's always a fourth option. One that's been staring us in the face.'

'Which is?'

'You could take a course of Oxytoxin.'

'Very funny,' Millie says. 'I don't think it's quite come to that yet.'

In truth, it's not the first time that taking Oxytoxin has crossed Millie's mind.

Thirty-One

When Millie and Ben walk into the boardroom on Monday, they're greeted by a pharmacy of different Oxytoxin pill packages, posters and leaflets. Sasha is standing proudly at the top of the table in a white lab coat while two of the creative interns scurry around her to put everything in place. Tomorrow she's presenting their campaign ideas for Oxytoxin to three big cheeses who are flying in specially from Human in San Francisco. Millie is secretly pleased it won't be her. Judging by the crappy start to her week, she'd stuff it up by randomly choking on her own spit, getting the hiccups mid flow or forgetting what the pills are called.

'Welcome to the Oxytoxin pop-up shop!' Sasha crows, spreading her arms out wide. 'A temporary store that offers everything you need to protect yourself from the trappings of romantic love. Interested, you two?'

Millie blanks her.

'Wow,' Ben says, running his finger over the table as he examines the products. 'Talk us through them.'

'Well, here you've got Oxytoxin Pros, the love suppressant for professionals who want to focus on fulfilling their goals.' Sasha holds up a matt black pill packet with a glossy pink embossed logo of a heart with a line through it. 'We wanted to give it a sexy, discreet, premium feel.'

Millie and Ben nod as they step towards the next product.

'Next, you have Oxytoxin Twos, the love suppressant for couples who are struggling to handle the financial, practical, social and logistical complexities that their relationship brings,' Sasha says, holding up a plain white packet with grey font on it. 'We kept this functional. It even comes with a fridge magnet on the back, so busy parents can keep it in sight and in mind. We all know how distracting kids can be!' She chuckles. 'Who'd have them?'

Ben moves on before she finishes, and stares at the poster in front of him.

'Who's this?' he asks, frowning.

'That's our school campaign. I want these posters in every school across the UK on launch day,' Sasha says with a smug grin.

Millie marches across the room to the whiteboard and grabs the eraser. She spins round, runs at Sasha and wipes the eraser across her face until the smug grin has gone and all that's left is a mess of multicoloured smudges and a look of horror.

Millie steps forward and looks at the poster of two teenagers staring defiantly into the lens.

'That's Taylor and Avery, our manufactured pop duo Tave. Not only are they going to be the faces of Oxytoxin Teens, they're bringing out an album that discourages teens from falling in love called *Love is for Losers*. Cool, huh?' She smiles with her mouth open and her chewing gum visible.

'Not that cool if it leads to bullying,' Ben mutters, 'which it inevitably will.'

'Very cool if it leads to fewer kids getting distracted and dropping out,' Sasha responds.

'Because it's obviously impossible to be in love and achieve your life goals?' Ben asks.

'It makes it much harder. With Oxytoxin Teens, teens around the country will get a helping hand at eliminating all the stress that comes with being in love, and can focus instead on securing their future. We considered targeting parents with this one, but we decided that might be frowned upon. You know, teens are almost consenting adults. We certainly wouldn't want a backlash. But if we can make teenagers want it, we're winning.'

Millie can't help but admire the approach. She thinks back to Deion and wonders how he'd feel about Tave. His feelings seemed too strong to be turned by a fake teen group. Her heart sinks when she imagines him losing the support of his peers, being branded a loser and sinking further into the pit of unhappiness he seemed to be stuck in with his dad. She suspects it's his unhappiness that'll screw up his future, not his relationship.

'What the actual fuck is this?' Ben says loudly.

Millie turns to see him holding up a plastic ostrich.

'Ah, that's Oxy the Ostrich!' Sasha laughs. 'The design isn't finalised yet. He needs a bigger mouth and loads more feathers.'

And a bold red lip, Millie thinks, amused that Sasha can't see the resemblance.

'But what is it for?'

'For dispensing the pills, silly!' Sasha responds. 'We're calling it Oxytots, and it'll be aimed at the preschool market.'

'That's pretty fucked up.' Ben stares at her.

'Parents have a duty to do the best for their kids, and make the decisions for them until they have the mental capacity to choose for themselves.'

'The problem here isn't that kids could end up falling in love. It's the cowards who fear it. I don't know what trauma you suffered in childhood to make you promote this monster in the first place, but you need help. Talk to someone. Your dream is a nightmare. Preventing kids from being themselves? Forcing teens to take pills because of peer pressure? Suggesting couples are financially irresponsible? Can't you see how dangerous and reckless that is, Sasha?'

'No, I can't,' Sasha says defiantly, crossing her arms. 'Oxytoxin gives people a choice and offers parents peace of mind. Would you really deny them that?'

'How is this giving kids a choice? You're telling people there's something wrong with them if they fall in love by creating a "cure". That they need treatment. Falling in love won't be a choice if you create a cultural belief that says love stops you from succeeding at school, in your career, in your social life. It's not a choice when you're made to feel defective if your decision is different to everyone else's.'

'Well, I'm sorry you feel that way, Ben,' Sasha says. 'But in the next twenty-four hours you're going to have to put your personal beliefs to one side because you're presenting the strategy across all four of these products.'

'Fuck that. Find someone else. I'm having nothing to do with this,' he says angrily, throwing the ostrich down on the table and storming out of the room.

'Ben?' Sasha shouts after him.

He turns round at the boardroom door with a face like thunder.

'Aren't you forgetting something?' Sasha smirks.

Ben shakes his head, takes the couples deep-dive research from under his arm and tosses it onto the boardroom table.

'Like you haven't got this already,' he says, before turning and marching out the door.

Millie looks at Sasha.

'Well,' Sasha says. 'Looks like you'll be presenting after all.'

@milliej:
you OK?

@milliej:
tea?

@milliej:
hello???

Later that afternoon, Millie returns to the boardroom to start familiarising herself with the surroundings for the pitch. Millie wonders if he thought she would follow him. Yet another sign of their differences. Millie would always see a project through. She'd never abandon a team. She might . . . *loke* Ben, but today he showed a volatile side that she's not sure she likes at all. Millie doesn't do drama. All she wants is for her life to return to normal. Perhaps it's time for Millie to kick Ben off her hamster wheel. He's making it dangerously close to spinning out of control.

Millie wanders behind the Oxytoxin Pros station and runs her fingers over the black packets. Looking towards the glass wall, she slowly lifts one up, slips it into her pocket and leaves.

Thirty-Two

Are you in a couple?

Do you feel as if your life is out of control?

Are you craving the sweet taste of the single life?

It's time to start your life over.

We're searching for applicants for Season Two of Single Me Out!

Apply anonymously on singlemeout.com

And now, back to the moment we've all been waiting for!

Millie pauses mid-scrub of the kitchen sink to watch *Single Me Out!* winner Jessica accept her Starting Over Single prize money and reunite with her family and friends on the show's finale. She looks radiant as she accepts bouquet after bouquet, beaming into the blizzard of camera flashes that erupts from the crowd. You wouldn't think it was the same person from a month ago, who first appeared on the cameras

296

looking stale and grey. Being single suits her. She's got the glow of someone who doesn't have to deal with someone else's issues anymore.

Millie blows her hair out of her eyes and returns to scrubbing the stains off her kitchen sink, the last on her list of to dos in this three-hour-long deep clean. Removing every trace of grime that's gathered in the past month is her way of grabbing the wheel and getting her life back on track. Of pressing the reset button to life before Ben. It was a better time, she convinces herself, when her professional reputation was intact and she was on her way to achieving her dream job. She knows she agreed to her and Ben's strategy of targeting consenting adults only, but had she been working alone, perhaps she wouldn't have shied away from expanding the range and scale of Oxytoxin. Perhaps she'd be sitting in Ruth's seat, instead of with the interns, who earlier today spent an hour debating whether black velvet chokers were in or out. Millie followed along, uncharacteristically doe-eyed and giggly. Still, she has no one but herself to blame.

When Millie's phone starts ringing, she doesn't answer it. Only two people ever call her, and she's not willing to speak to one of them right now. Vivian's been pushing her to apply for an executive creative director position at Big, her agency, with daily calls to remind Millie that her career clock is ticking. That time is running out. That she needs to hurry up, because once she hits thirty, she'll be left on the office shelf. Because people over thirty don't have their finger on the pulse where the young are concerned. But Millie would rather stick pins in her eyes than work for her mum. She gets enough pressure from her at home. When the kitchen sink is sparkling clean, Millie pings her gloves off and picks up her phone.

June:

Big news! Call me! Excited!

Millie calls immediately and switches the kettle on in preparation for a long conversation. When June answers, Millie can hardly hear her for the thumping music in the background.

'June?' Millie says loudly, as if she's there herself.

'Millie!' June shouts down the phone.

'Where are you?' Millie yells.

'We're at a bar! On a Monday! Where *aaare* you?' June shouts back, dragging out her words.

'Who's we?' Millie asks.

'The team, we're celebrating! Millie, I did it! I've been made partner! I have my own office with a big glass window!'

'June!' Millie shrieks. 'That's amazing, I'm so proud of you! I'm taking you out to celebrate this weekend, so don't you dare go and give yourself a four-day hangover.'

'OK, I'll just have a five-day party instead,' she says. 'Are you OK?'

'I'm good! I'm blitzing the flat,' Millie says.

'And I'm blotto!' June replies, laughing.

'You deserve it!' Millie shouts, hearing June's assistant Jonathan call her in the background.

'Now get off the phone and go and have fun,' Millie says.

Millie smiles as she puts her phone down. Of course, she's thrilled for June, who's been desperate to make partner for the past two years. So why does she feel so deflated? Probably because June's promotion only serves to remind Millie that she didn't get one. That, for the first time ever, her life isn't moving forward. She feels like a failure. She shakes the dark thought from her head, replacing it with a promise to pick herself up. Whining won't get her anywhere.

Millie and June weren't allowed to whine when they were little. Vivian taught them that finding a solution to a problem should be the first response, not complaining about it. And God help you if you cried. She wouldn't shout. She'd just stare at you with her cool blue eyes until you exhausted yourself, calmed down and eventually stopped. Her mum has always been fearless, self-reliant and confident of her own worth. A force to be reckoned with. At eighteen, she started in the post room of London's biggest advertising agency. At nineteen, she convinced a creative director to accept her as an intern in the creative department. At twenty-two, she took his job. And at twenty-eight, she opened the doors to her own agency.

The doorbell rings, making Millie jump. She rinses and

dries her hands and makes her way to the hall, brushing her hair back with her fingers before opening the door.

'Hi,' he says.

'Hi,' she replies.

'Can I come in?' Ben asks. 'I won't be long. I just want to chat.'

'Yeah, of course,' she responds, wondering why he's carrying a duffle bag, and feeling pleased that her flat is spotless.

'Wow,' Ben comments, looking around at her blank walls and bare shelves. 'I had my suspicions that you were a hoarder, but this is mind-boggling. How do you keep your focus with all this clutter?' He points at a blank wall.

'Well, it makes it easier to clean,' she replies.

'My strategy is to hide the filth by displaying everything I own.' He shrugs.

Suddenly Ben's eyes bulge open, his mouth expands and he lets go of his duffle bag. Millie looks down to see Bruce's claws lodged in the top of one of his trainers from beneath the hall drawers.

'Bruce!' she shouts, crouching down to detach the paw. 'I'm sorry, he does it to everyone.'

'I guess that makes me feel better,' Ben says, wincing as he limps over to the sofa and slumps down, rubbing the top of his foot. 'If anyone back home asks why I'm limping, I'll just say I was fighting crime. Very dangerous crime.'

'Well, Bruce is the neighbourhood thug, so it wouldn't be too far from the truth,' she says, then realises what he's said. 'Home? Hence the bag?'

'Yep,' he says, sitting back up.

'Tea?' she asks, breaking his stare to step into the kitchen and switch the kettle on.

'Please,' he says. 'And then let's talk about how I handed in my notice earlier.'

Millie slams the mugs down on the counter and spins round just as the kettle reaches boiling point. 'You quit? When?'

'That was a dramatic reaction!' He laughs. 'You'd make a good soap star.'

'Well, that was a dramatic announcement!' she cries, turning her back to him to fill the mugs in silence, the teaspoon clinking against the china.

Millie's head is spinning. Is this a good thing? It should be a good thing. Perhaps Ben leaving is the fix she's been looking for. Out of sight, out of mind. She should be relieved. She *should* be. No more tea in the kitchen. No more lunch roulette. No more impossible hangman puzzles on the office messaging system. No more fun. No more reason to be there herself. Then again, no more crazy thoughts running through her head.

'After the meeting,' Ben says, moving to the kitchen stool closest to her. She puts the tea down and leans next to him on the island. Millie from five minutes ago would be sounding the alarm bells. After all, she's just spent the last three hours pledging to distance herself from him. Now she's drawing closer. The truth is that when Ben is in the same room, all she wants to be is right by his side. Well, even when he isn't in the same room.

301

'How long are you going home for?' Millie asks, trying to be nonchalant.

Ben stares at her with soft eyes and a smile that says sorry.

'I'm on a one-way ticket, Belle,' he replies. 'I don't think I'm coming back.'

'Oh!' Millie says. 'But when did you . . . ?' She doesn't complete the sentence.

'I've been thinking of leaving Human for a while now, even before I got Ruth's call for an interview at Slide. I really liked the sound of her, so I thought I'd give it one last shot with a move to London. But, as you can probably tell, it's not the kind of company I want to work for. This Oxytoxin project was the nail in the coffin. I should have walked after our first meeting. I think you know that the only reason I stayed for as long as I did was because of you. So, thank you for making my month here bearable,' he smiles. 'Very bearable, in fact. I've had more fun in the last month than I have in a long time.'

Millie feels her chest compress with the weight of what he's saying. Ben isn't coming back. Whatever this was, or perhaps still is, it's finally over. It's precisely what she wanted. To rewind to life before Ben, when she was happily on her hamster wheel with her regular routine. So why is there a lump forming in her throat at the thought of him being so far away? Millie looks into her mug and blows on the steam with a shaky breath. She can't look up now or he'll see that her eyes are starting to glisten.

'Millie?' he says, leaning closer towards her. 'Are you OK?'

'Fine!' She smiles, blinking away the wet. 'I think I'm just tired. I think everything is catching up with me.'

'There's something you should know, Belle,' Ben says.

'What is it?'

'Do you remember when we first met? When I took your coffee?'

She nods.

'That wasn't an accident. I stole it.'

'You stole my coffee?' she replies.

'I saw you, and I knew I had to meet you. With my caffeine addiction, I would never have stomached your mock-milk swill otherwise.' He winces. 'That, Belle, is precisely why I need to get out of here. I need some distance. I'd love to say we could be friends. And perhaps we can in the future. But right now it's becoming harder for me to be near you. Because every time you're close to me, all I can think of is kissing you. Well, even when you're not close. It's quite torturous, to be honest.'

Millie stares at his face, now blushing, as he starts to get off the stool.

'Wait,' she says. 'Just sit there.'

He lowers himself back down again and watches her stepping forward, between his thighs. Millimetres away, without the blur of champagne vision, she can count every speck of blue, green and gold in his eyes. She places her hands on his flushed cheeks and brings his lips to hers, feeling his knees tighten around her hips and his hands on the small of her back, pulling her into him. They kiss. Softly at first, and then harder. When she comes up for breath, he tilts her head to one side and puts his lips on her neck, his tongue touching her ear with gentle kisses that send lightning bolts from her head to her toes, every inch of her covered in goosebumps.

Millie steps away, takes his hand and leads him to the bedroom, where she pulls him on top of her. Her legs squeeze his waist towards her and his weight makes her ache for more.

'Stop a second,' Ben says, lifting himself up and searching her face. 'Are you sure we should do this? This could mess things up even—'

Millie interrupts him, putting her lips on his and continuing their kiss. He pushes her arms up above her head and strips her shirt off in one move, before she starts scrambling to unbutton his. In seconds, every barrier between them is gone. All Millie feels is hot skin as she nuzzles into the soft-scented hair on his firm chest. Ben rubs his whole body up and down hers with every hungry kiss on her lips, neck, chest and stomach, as Millie closes her eyes and silences her internal sirens with moans of pleasure. A montage runs through her mind. The moment he spun round with her stolen coffee, his electric eyes meeting hers. The secret smiles he would send her across the desk after each message, as if it were just them in the room. The golden sun highlighting his face on Castle Beach.

Ben lifts himself off her again and looks into her eyes as if he can't believe they're finally here. He smiles with that pointy tooth smile that makes her insides turn to mush and lowers himself back down onto her. Millie sighs as she finally lets herself go.

Early the next morning, Millie lies in Ben's shoulder crevice as he softly runs his fingertips up and down her back under the sheets. In a few hours, he will be gone. Perhaps forever. Perhaps this was the right way to say goodbye.

'Is that the flower from my clown suit?' Ben asks, pointing towards her dressing table.

'Oh,' Millie says, embarrassed. 'Yes. Did you want it back?'

He chuckles. 'Of course not, I gave it to you.'

Ben turns to her and lifts the bed sheets over them.

'Come with me,' he says.

'What?' Millie scoffs.

'Come with me,' he repeats, leaning up. 'Take the leap. Leave Slide. You know you aren't happy there. We could take a month. Shit, we could take three months. Longer, if you haven't killed me by then. We could go anywhere we want – South America, Asia, India. Wouldn't you like to stick your fingers up at Sasha? You could look for a new role when you're back. A better role, at a company where you don't have to sell your soul to get ahead.'

'Ben,' she says, frowning. 'I've told you before, I'm not that kind of person. I don't cope well with change. Please don't put that on me.'

'Put what on you?' he asks.

'Make me out to be boring, just because I don't want to quit the only job I've ever had and take off without a plan. I have a life here, Ben, and it might be dull to you, but I like it. I have my mum, June, Al, Ruth, Sunday lunches, Fridays at Buddies. I don't want to walk away from that.'

'I'm not making you out to be anything! Boring is the last word I'd use to describe you. I just want you to come with me, that's all,' he says. 'And I don't mean it in a purely selfish way. I just think a change of scene would do you some good. I bet your June would agree with me.'

'Um, you barely know June,' Millie scoffs. 'That's the last thing she'd say. What will do me some good is space and time to get my life back in order. That's what I want.'

'I don't believe you!' Ben cries, making Millie's heart race. 'I've seen you at the office, I've seen you in Tenby. I know which Millie was happier, and I think you do too.'

'We aren't all like you, Ben!' she cries, sitting up and looking for her shirt. 'You like spur-of-the-moment, you like doing the opposite of what everyone else is doing, you don't care what people think. You break rules, you hate plans and you're risky. And you're bringing me down with you. It's 5.30 a.m. and I have a pitch today. This is hardly a good start, is it?'

'I might be risky,' he says, sitting up. 'But at least I'm honest. At least I'd never let myself be Sasha's puppet.'

'What are you saying?' Millie says abruptly, frowning and feeling stung.

'I'm saying, you're too scared of everything, Millie. You're scared of change. You're scared of confrontation. You're scared of what people think. One day you'll look back and wonder what life could have been, if only you'd been brave enough to actually do what you wanted to do.'

Ben rubs his face with his hands and stands up.

'Ben, you can't throw a tantrum because I don't want to quit my life and run away with you. It's not who I am. You should know that by now!' Millie shouts. 'And if I'm so scared of confrontation, what do you think this is?'

'Fair enough,' he sighs. 'Perhaps I need to remember that not everyone thinks like me. Everyone's entitled to their opinion. You've always said that your career comes first. I hope Oxytoxin brings you all the success you're looking for.'

Ben raises his eyebrows and buttons his shirt.

A relationship with Ben? It would never have worked. When he disappears through that door in a few minutes, she can return to the Millie she knows. But if that's what she wants to do, why do tears stream down her face the second he slams the front door? Why does every gulp of air hurt as she staggers into her bedroom, grabs the daisy from the dressing table and tosses it in the bin? Why are her fingers shaking uncontrollably when she takes the packet from her drawer, removes the pill from the foil, puts it on her tongue and swallows?

Thirty-Three

On Saturdays, Millie's alarm rings at 7.30 a.m. At 7.45 she eats breakfast with Bruce. At 7.55 she's in her running gear, scraping her hair back into a high ponytail in front of her dressing table mirror. At 8.00 she shuts the front door.

Today, her Saturday-morning routine has been disrupted by the disappearance of Bruce. She shakes the pellets around in his bowl three times and there's still no sight or sound of his beefy paws thudding across the wooden floors. She puts her smooth-peanut-butter toast down, wanders across to the hallway and opens the front door.

'Bruce? Breakfast!' She shouts down the old and empty stairwell outside her flat.

Leaving the door open, in case he's being stubborn and ignoring her calls on purpose, Millie crouches to peek under the hall table, his usual hideout. He's not there, but something is. Millie puts the last piece of toast in her mouth and stretches underneath to retrieve it. When she pulls it into the light, her face scrunches. It's Ben's daisy that she threw away earlier this week. Bruce must have fetched it from the bin. Sometimes she wonders if her cat is part dog.

She twirls it with her fingertips as she stands up. The party – Ben – is the last thing she needs to be reminded of.

Millie never replied to Ben's messages this week. Not out of anger; it was more of a defence mechanism. Watching him walk away on Tuesday morning sent a wrecking ball into her chest. Hopefully the final pill she's taking tonight will heal her bruises.

'Millie?'

Millie gasps and spins round, dropping the flower on the floor.

'How long have you been standing there?' Millie says, hiding the flower with a shaky foot.

'Sorry,' Ben says, rubbing his unshaven face. The overgrown stubble brings out his eyes even more, if that's possible. 'The front door was open. I didn't mean to give you a fright. I found him in the street and I didn't want to leave him. I tried picking him up, but after five seconds I decided that having hands is actually quite useful.'

Bruce appears from behind Ben's legs and darts straight to Millie's feet, where he starts scratching at her slippers. She kicks him away with her other foot.

'I promise I'm not being a weirdo who hangs outside your house, I was just here to put this in your letterbox,' he says, holding up a white envelope. 'I feel like a bit of a dick now. I was hoping I could just leave it there and then leg it before bumping into you.'

Millie flicks the flower behind her under the drawers with her foot, sending Bruce scrambling after it, while Ben plays with the letter in his hand. The sound of Bruce gnawing through the plastic breaks the silence.

'So, should I take that, then?' Millie says, pointing at the letter.

Ben rubs his forehead and laughs uncomfortably. 'Actually, now that I'm here, have you got five minutes? Look, I know I'm the last person you want to talk to, and maybe you never want to talk to me again after what happened, but I'm catching a plane tonight and I need to explain a few things before I go. Get them off my chest, you know. I promise I won't ask you to come.'

'Where are you going?' she asks.

'Back to Sydney,' he replies.

'Woah, that's far,' Millie comments quietly, feeling panicked by the distance that will soon be between them and wondering whether he'll meet up with his ex-girlfriend. Maybe they'll get back together. Maybe that's the plan.

'For how long?' Millie asks.

'It's an open ticket,' Ben replies.

Calm down. Space is what you wanted.

Ben hasn't done anything wrong. Millie can't punish him for calling her out on her fears; his points were all true. Perhaps a chat will bring the closure she wants to this mad chapter of her life and help her start afresh. Besides, she's a few hours away from taking the second pill. What's the worst that can happen? The first Oxytoxin must be having an effect on her by now, even if her rushing pulse suggests otherwise.

'Let's walk instead,' Millie says, nodding towards the front door.

'Really?' Ben looks at her quizzically.

'Yes. I don't mind,' Millie replies.

'No, I mean . . . really?' He smiles, looking her up and down.

'Oh, right,' she giggles, realising she's still in her pyjamas.

Distracted much, Millie?

'Come on, Belle, I know your style is *comfortable* but you could occasionally make some effort,' Ben teases her. She's going to miss those dimples. Wow, he really does listen. She's going to miss that.

She shuts her bedroom door and clutches at her cramping stomach as his nickname for her rings in her head, and the way he says it with the 'l' on the tip of his tongue. It's only been five days, but she's missed him, despite how they left things. She's missed this. Being with him feels so right in one way, but wrong in so many others. Too many others. She's *this* close to having things back the way she wants. She mustn't let him derail her. As painful as it might be to watch him walk away, the pain won't last long. Not after tonight's final dose.

311

'I'm sorry I didn't reply,' Millie says, softly tapping the surface of the water with the tip of her trainers.

'I'm sorry about what I said,' Ben replies, doing the same. 'It was harsh, to say the least.'

'Don't be. It wasn't because of anything you said,' Millie continues. 'What you said was true – I am afraid of lots of things.'

'Well, so what? Maybe I'm not scared of enough things,' Ben replies. 'You once told me I should care more about what people think. I think about that comment a lot. I know I should. But I guess we are who we are.'

'Ben, I didn't reply to your messages because I felt like we both needed space. And just to move forward with our lives. I thought it was pointless to try and be friends. It would feel a bit false. A bit forced. I'm black and white, I don't cope well with blurred lines. So I thought it would be easier if we became . . . fond memories. I guess I could have just told you that, but I didn't know what to say. It didn't seem right to put it in a text.'

'Well, there's nothing to be sorry about,' Ben replies. 'You love your life just how it is. You're happy on your . . . hamster wheel. And knowing that you're happy on it alone, makes me happy.'

She's never mentioned her hamster wheel to him. Strange. Maybe they're more similar than she thinks.

'And I think what'll make *me* happy is having what my parents have,' Ben continues. 'A relationship. I guess I'm just the relationship type.'

Millie plays with a stone under her shoe, keeping her eyes on it. What's she supposed to say to that?

'And that's just fine for you,' Millie replies. 'Obviously.'

'It is fine,' he nods. 'And I would be fine, if I could just get you out of my head.'

Millie moves her scarf up when she feels her cheeks start to burn.

'I even considered taking Oxytoxin,' Ben says, and laughs.

'You must have been feeling desperate,' she says, thinking of the pill in her dressing table drawer.

'I was. But then I came to my senses,' he adds.

Tell him about the pill. You have to tell him about the pill.

'Ben, I need to tell you something—' she starts.

'I'm in love with you, Millie Jones. I am. I suspected it the moment I spotted you in the canteen queue, and I knew it the moment I watched you in the wind on Castle Beach. Don't worry, I don't expect you to be in love with me back. It's my problem, not yours. It's been on the tip of my tongue since Tenby, and I just had to get it off my chest. I couldn't leave without telling you. I know we don't want the same things, and that's fine. I'll come to terms with it eventually. I just thought that if I don't tell you now, I never will. And I'd spend the rest of my life wondering what you might have said.'

After a few moments of silence, Millie speaks.

'Ben, I don't know what love feels like, but I know there's *something* between us. I know that, for the past week, I've thought about you a lot. About *us* a lot. What it would be like to be in a couple. I've imagined coming with you and leaving this life behind. Quitting Slide, packing my case, meeting you at the airport to fly somewhere far away. But I can't.'

'I thought as much,' he says, his hands jangling the contents of his pockets.

'It's not because I don't have feelings for you. I do have feelings for you. Maybe it's love. But I've worked my guts out to create this single life for myself, and I don't want to give it up. We're talking dreams I've had since I was sixteen. Promises I made to myself. I feel like if I quit this life of mine, this life that I love, I'd be letting my sixteen-year-old self down.'

'I get it,' Ben says.

'I can promise you one thing, though,' she says.

'Oh yeah?' Ben says, as he stares across the water.

'If I was going to be in a couple with anyone, it would be you.'

He smiles and turns towards her, wrapping her in his arms and resting his chin on her head. She inhales that eucalyptus scent deeply for the last time.

'Well, thank you for saying that,' Ben murmurs.

'Ben, there's something else I need to tell you,' she says, unravelling herself from his grip. He keeps hold of her shoulders, his face lingering just a few inches from hers. She cranes her neck up, looks into his eyes and says, 'The night you walked out, I—'

314

Before she can finish, Ben lowers his head and kisses her deeply, squeezing her into his chest. Leaning in, she kisses him back. The world stops. It feels like they're alone again. But they aren't.

When they come up for air, Millie's eyes shift left to the person standing behind him, staring at her.

'June!' Millie mutters, gently pushing a startled Ben away from her.

'Um, hi?' June says, her head bouncing between them both, holding a coffee in one hand and a cheese toastie in the other.

'What are you doing here?' Millie asks, brushing her hair out of her face.

'What do you mean, what am *I* doing here? What are you two *doing* here?' June scoffs. 'I *thought* you'd be on your run.' June is talking quickly, her eyes searching for anything to land on but the two of them. 'So I decided that, as you've had a tough time of it lately, I'd get you a surprise breakfast!' She laughs bitterly and lifts up the coffee and toastie. 'Didn't realise you'd end up surprising *me*!'

She nods towards the water. 'Those ducklings are cute, aren't they? What a scene. How romantic! Anyway, I'm waddling, I'll leave you guys to it. I mean, *waffling*. Looks like you've got a few things to catch up on. Ben, hope you're well. Are you growing a beard? Did you know that beards are dirtier than toilet seats? Something to think about. Anyway, maybe I'll see you later, Mils.'

June spins round and walks back down the path.

'I should go,' Millie says, panicking.

'Why do I feel like June has a problem with me?' Ben asks.

'She doesn't have a problem with you, she's just worried,' Millie explains, stepping away from him.

'Well, she is your soulmate. It's her job.'

Millie detects a hint of bitterness.

'What time's your flight?' she asks.

'Ten o'clock tonight.'

'I'm sorry.'

'You've already said that,' Ben replies. 'All that's left to say is goodbye, I suppose.'

'Have a good trip, Ben,' Millie says, turning away from him and hurrying after June.

'Wait, Millie!'

She pauses and turns around again.

'What was it you wanted to tell me?' he shouts.

Millie stares at him from across the pond.

'It doesn't matter anymore,' she shouts back.

And it doesn't. She can finally put Ben to bed. Not like that, of course.

Thirty-Four

June is waiting alone on a chair by the entrance gates when Millie catches up with her.

'I was beginning to think you wouldn't follow me,' June says, looking up.

'As if I'd do that,' Millie responds, out of breath.

'I really didn't mean to interrupt you two,' she says, handing Millie her breakfast. 'By the time I reached the pond it was too late, and you would have seen me anyway. I thought I'd look like a perv if I watched you in silence. And a creep if I just tiptoed away. Sorry,' June says, straight-faced.

'There seem to be a lot of sorrys being said in the park this morning,' Millie comments. 'And you didn't interrupt anything.'

'It sure looked like something from where I was standing,' June says, stealing a corner of Millie's toastie.

'OK, fine, it was something. But you happened to arrive in the three-second window of a random, spur-of-the-moment

317

goodbye kiss. Before that, we were just talking. Clearing the air, getting some closure,' Millie replies.

'I know I don't have any experience in romantic relationships, but isn't kissing usually a catalyst, not closure?' June asks, raising her eyebrows.

'I suppose,' Millie replies.

'What does it mean?' June asks.

'What does what mean?' Millie says.

'The kiss. What does it mean?' June repeats.

'He told me he loves me,' Millie replies.

'Jesus,' June says. 'What did I tell you? He's the relationship type. God, I'm good.'

'Well, it doesn't matter anymore, anyway,' Millie replies, feeling a rising irritation at June turning the conversation back to herself and treating the situation so flippantly. 'He's on a flight to Sydney tonight, and doesn't know when, or if, he's coming back.'

'Thank fuck,' June says, ripping off another piece of toastie. 'Just imagine, you could have been on that flight. Sipping champagne, holding hands, whispering sweet nothings to each other under the blanket, ha! Eurgh, no thanks, dude. Save that for some other sad loser!'

Millie yanks the toastie away from her.

'Hey!' June says.

Millie and June have only ever had two proper arguments in their entire lives. The first was when June kept on wearing Millie's tops without asking. The second was when June started sneaking out in sixth form to go clubbing, and

Millie refused to join her and threatened to tell Vivian. Millie senses a third is on its way. Millie leans back on the chair and starts picking at the rest of her cheese toastie.

'You're being a dick,' Millie says, surprised at her outburst. 'If you met him properly and gave him a chance, for once, you might realise he's actually lovely. Really lovely. The loveliest. And you might be a little more *understanding* about why I'm so confused about it all.'

'Well, I'm sorry that we aren't all as charmed by him as you, Millie,' June says. 'But if we're going to be honest, something which you haven't really been up until now, you've been a dick recently, too. Ignoring my messages. Standing me up at the cinema. Lying to me about your work trip. Skipping Sunday lunch. Kissing him at the office party and not telling me about it. Who *is* that? That's not the Millie I know. You change when you're with him. And what's most annoying is that whenever Ben is in the same room, no one else exists. He's like a weird Millie magnet that pulls you in and no one else has a chance of even having a conversation with you. He might well be the loveliest, but as far as I can see, he isn't good for you.'

'First, am I not allowed to have other friends? Must it always be just you, Mum, Ruth and Al? I'm allowed to see other people, June! Second, did I not just come chasing after you? You, June. You don't see me still standing there with him, so he can't be that much of a magnet. And I resent the suggestion that I'm weak. I just cut short an important – possibly life-changing – conversation with

319

someone I'm totally in love with, to come and check that my best friend is OK. Magnet, my arse. You're being really bloody unfair.'

June frowns at her. 'In *love* with?'

Millie stares at her in shock.

'I didn't say that,' she eventually replies.

'Um, yeah, you did.'

'It was a slip of the tongue,' Millie replies defensively.

'Like the one by the pond a few minutes ago?' June asks.

'Very funny,' Millie says sulkily.

'I thought you took the Oxytoxin?'

'I did,' Millie replies.

'So why would you even have love on the brain? Shouldn't it be out of your brain by now?' June prods.

'I don't know!' Millie cries. 'I need to take the second dose tonight.'

'Do you think that's wise?'

'Of course it is, why wouldn't it be? I obviously need to.'

'I thought you were going to take it to prevent falling in love with him. I didn't realise you already were in love with him. I mean, as reluctant as I am to suggest this, because the idea of you being in love with him makes me freak out, but maybe you should think about that a bit more? There's no going back after the final pill, right?'

Millie takes a long sip of her coffee, still in shock from her own confession and wondering if she's made a huge mistake by letting Ben go.

'What's the point? He's leaving in a few hours. It'll be over soon,' she says.

'It's only Australia. It's not like he's disappearing off the face of the planet,' June replies. 'You could chase after him, stop him at the airport. You know, if it came to that. Find out what it's like to be in a, you know, *couple*. Ugh, that sounds really weird.'

'Can you picture me doing that?'

'No, but then I could never have pictured you saying you're *totally in love* with someone either, and here we are.'

'I know myself, June. I'm not the couple type. Besides, I've looked at the stats, and relationships don't last forever. Do you honestly think I should turn my entire life around for this one person, just for it to end eventually? Do we know anyone whose relationship has lasted longer than a few months, apart from Ruth?'

They pause.

'Ours?' June says.

'True. God, why can't it be as easy as us?'

'I think it's obvious what we need to do,' June says, standing up. 'We're calling Al and Ruth for backup. We're going back to yours. And we're going to write a good old-fashioned pros and cons list, like we used to.'

Millie and Ruth are in the kitchen making tea, just like the good old days.

'Can I ask you something, Mils?' Ruth says, stirring. 'How do you know it won't make you happy if you haven't tried it?'

'It's just feels like way too much change,' Millie replies. 'My life is already divided into neat quarters: my career, my friends, my family, myself. That's all I have time and emotional space for.'

'But I split my time with Sam. She supports my career. She's one of my best friends. She's now part of my family. Of course, myself is just for me. That's not for sharing. People who aren't in relationships think that couples are surgically attached, but even couples need their space.'

'How did you know you loved Sam?' Millie asks.

'I think it's different for everyone,' Ruth replies. 'For me, it went something a little like this. At first, it felt like a massive crush. I couldn't stop thinking of her, and just seeing her name light up on my screen made my insides flip. I knew it was more than a crush when I started to see her everywhere and in everything. I'd notice little things on my way to work that I'd want to tell her about. And when we spoke at night, I wanted to hear about every detail of her day, however mundane. I knew it was love when I realised I was prepared to make certain single-life sacrifices for this woman. Not that she expected me to, of course.'

'See, that's what I'm not sure of. I don't know if I want to sacrifice what I have for him.'

The list is long. It's also inconclusive. There are the same number of pros and cons when it comes to being in a relationship with Ben. Whether or not Millie should be in a relationship with Ben cannot be strategically deduced. The four of them lean back on June's sofa to contemplate their work.

'We could assign each point a different weight of importance?' Millie suggests. 'Surely losing your freedom is, on the grand scale of things, more important than sharing your food?'

'I'd like to repeat that I still object to that point. I haven't lost my freedom with Sam,' Ruth says, huffing.

'But this is me, Ruth,' Millie says. 'I feel like I would.'

'On the sharing food point, what if it's cheesecake?' June replies. 'I mean, it was hard enough for the two of us to share a cheesecake the other day.'

'Hey, where was my invite?' Al whines.

'Ben and I did actually share a cheesecake once,' Millie says, remembering the night in the hotel room. 'It was lovely.'

'What's with the cheesecake obsession? And why am I suddenly craving one?' Al says.

'OK, what about this point?' Millie says. 'Splitting my time between Ben and my friends would be level ten. Sharing my wardrobe space would be—'

'Level eleven. The idea of sharing wardrobe space with someone actually makes me break out in a cold sweat.' June shudders. 'Please tell me you don't do that, Ruth.'

'No! We have very separate wardrobes. Although, I do occasionally go in and nick her good pyjamas when she's away on a work trip. And her boots. Sometimes a shirt, too. It's pretty handy that we're the same size.'

'I'm a bit jealous now,' Al says. 'Maybe I should be in a couple.'

'Hold on, who says he'd ever leave things at mine? He has his own place,' Millie says.

'Yeah, for now he does!' June says, loudly. 'But being in a couple means moving in together. Isn't that what most couples do, if they don't break up? Um, case in point right here,' June says, pointing at Ruth.

'She's right,' Ruth nods. 'Ben might slowly start creeping his belongings into your flat. First it'll be a toothbrush. Then it'll be a pair of pants in your side table. Next, you're accidentally putting on a shirt of his. That was me, a few months ago.'

'*Accidentally*?' Al lifts an eyebrow.

'Having someone to cook for you is a plus,' Ruth says, pointing at the pros list.

'Ah, but you'd also have to cook for him, or worse, what if he cooks you something you hate?' June comments, standing up, walking over to the flip chart and pointing at *Having to agree on what to eat* under the cons list. 'And then you have to force it down your throat and tell him you really love it.'

'Are we still talking about food?' Al asks.

They giggle.

'What if he cooks it for me every week, and for the rest of my life I have to eat something that makes me gag and then smile afterwards, like he's done me a favour?' Millie asks.

'Seriously though, are we still talking about food?' Al asks, smirking.

'Well, that's a whole other issue,' June says, pointing at *Only ever sliding one person* under the cons list.

'But on the other hand,' Millie says, pointing at the *Having a slide on tap* under the pros list.

'Face it, Millie,' June says, 'you're eating stew and sliding in missionary every Tuesday.'

'Then comparing notes with Ruth in the morning,' Al mutters.

'Hey!' Ruth cries. 'We aren't like that. We're at least twice a week.'

'God, I hate stew,' Millie says.

'I know you do,' June replies.

'You'd never cook me stew.'

'Never.'

'But you can get over that,' Al says. 'You can be honest and say, "I don't like stew". And you can take charge in the bedroom. I mean, isn't the point of a couple, rather than a slide, that you can be completely honest? Ruth?'

'I faked it at the beginning with Sam.'

'In the bedroom?' Al interjects.

'No! Well, sometimes. What I meant was that I put out the best version of myself. I pretended I had a CrossFit membership, then had to scramble to get one when she suggested a date there. Cost me an absolute fortune. Went once. But the more time we spent together, the more honest I could be. And, shocker, she accepted me, warts and all. That's what's great about a relationship. You can be authentic.'

'But Sam isn't asking as much of you as Ben is asking of me. He isn't just asking me to be in a couple. He's asking me to quit my job, go travelling, leave this – and all of you – behind. Sam never asked you to do all of that. Him cooking me stew isn't a big deal to me,' Millie says.

'Do you know what *is* a big deal?' June says, highlighting a statistic on the board.

89% of couples are unhappy.

'Where did you get that stat from?' Ruth says. 'I bet you I could find one that says the opposite.'

'And what about that?' Millie takes the pen and highlights another headline.

Couples live longer than single people, says new study.

'So, you live longer, but you're miserable at the same time? I can see the appeal,' Al says sarcastically.

'Again, objection!' Ruth cries.

Millie sighs and strolls back to the sofa, where she plonks herself down on a cushion and stares at the list. As she sits there, it dawns on her that the answer is right there. And that the answer has been there all along, even before they made this stupid list. It has nothing to do with the length of each column, the weight of what's more important or what the latest research says that completely contradicts the research that came before it. It has to do with the fact that Millie had to make a list in the first place. If she truly loved Ben, would this list even exist? A romantic relationship shouldn't be built on facts and statistics. A romantic relationship should be built on emotions and feelings. It isn't something you control or deduce, it's something you fall into with open arms, unafraid of the pain you might endure when you land.

Millie can't deny the part of her that wants to jump. The part of her that craves to see him every day. The part of her that would gladly accept most of the cons on this list, because to love someone is to sacrifice putting yourself first. But nor can Millie deny the part of her that wants to step back. To stick to the single life she knows and loves. When life was simple, when her future was clear, when her vision board was coming to fruition. To include Ben would mean giving up so much. Time spent with the people most important to her. What would happen to the beach house that she and June have dreamed of? Being with Ben wouldn't just change the life that Millie has so carefully curated, it would erase the future she's so carefully planned. June's future, too. After all, isn't June the true love of her life? How can she have both?

She hurries to her room and opens her dressing table drawer, pulling out the packet.

'What are you doing?' Ruth asks, looking shocked as Millie returns.

'Making this decision once and for all,' Millie says, removing the pill from the foil and rolling it around in her fingers.

'Millie, are you sure you want to do that? There's no going back,' June says, stepping forward.

'Millie, don't!' Ruth cries, jumping up.

But it's too late. Millie puts the final dose in her mouth and takes a hard swallow. There's a painful lump in her throat. It isn't the pill.

Thirty-Five

Millie prises open her heavy eyelids and stares up at the ceiling of her safe space. She wasn't in the mood for a Saturday night out with the others after the list exercise. She'd made the list. She'd taken the pill. But her mind was still buckling under the weight of the what ifs and why nots. What if taking Oxytoxin was a huge mistake? Why not give Ben a chance? As soon as the others left, she dragged herself over to Vivian's, where she slunk into her childhood bed to lay her racing mind to rest.

She taps her phone on the side table. It's 3 a.m. She's already been asleep for eight hours. Sinking further under the duvet, she pulls it over her face, feeling sorry for herself. Millie has read the small print on the packet at least twenty times. Nothing in the side effects suggests she'd feel like this. Like she hasn't slept in months. Like she hasn't eaten in days, but also like she never wants to eat again. Like she's empty.

She wonders where Ben's plane is right now, and then

silently tuts at herself. Aside from her fatigue, it's as if nothing has changed. All she can think of is him. Their last conversation. That one night. That kiss. Is Oxytoxin a total sham? She pats her face under the covers. It feels puffy. An allergic reaction, perhaps.

Millie always goes to her mum's when she's ill. There's something comforting about the smell of her old bed when she's under the weather. Looking shaky on arriving, Vivian quickly ushered her into her bedroom, switched off the lights and spent the evening bringing her peppermint tea and plain toast. Her mum might not be overly sentimental, but she's certainly practical in a situation like this. That's how she cares. Whatever *this* is.

Millie said she had stomach flu. She couldn't tell her the truth, obviously. The truth would lead to a loud meltdown that Millie doesn't have the energy for. Storm Vivian is the last thing she feels like facing.

Against her better judgement, Millie opens the flight tracker app she downloaded before she fell asleep and searches for his plane. He's over Turkey. She watches as the plane edges along the screen and she imagines him in the seat, moving further and further away. Her stomach lurches for the hundredth time. She clicks her phone off and crams it under her pillow, out of sight. Is this what lovesick feels like? Maybe it's a case of it gets worse before it gets better. A minute later, she snatches the phone back and opens her messages. She just wants to reread the last one he sent. It was the morning before their chat at the pond.

Ben:

> I'm sorry for everything. Take care, Millie x

Why didn't she just reply? If she'd replied to him, he wouldn't have brought that letter to her flat. He wouldn't have found Bruce, they wouldn't have gone to the park, they wouldn't have had that conversation or that kiss. *That kiss.* Millie shuts her eyes again and imagines his face on hers. The feel of his soft stubble, his lips. She continues to scroll back through all the messages they ever sent each other, right to the beginning, reliving those moments in her mind. The hangman puzzle.

Ben:

She never did work it out. And, as she stares at it, she starts to feel desperate for the answer.

Millie reaches into her handbag on the floor by the bed and takes out the letter. It's still unopened. She can't bring herself to read what it says and get served another painful reminder of what could have been.

Ping!

Millie flinches, like she's been caught in the act.

June:

> You still up? How are you feeling?

331

Millie:

AWFUL

June:

😩 Side effects?

Millie:

Mind racing

June:

Thinking of . . .

Millie:

Him. Haven't stopped

Millie flinches again when her phone starts to ring loudly. She answers quickly before Vivian wakes up.

'What do you mean, you haven't stopped thinking about him?' June says, with a telltale drunken hiccup. 'I thought that was the whole point of Oxytoxin?'

'It's not working, June! My stomach hurts, I'm nauseous, I'm so tired I can barely lift my head, yet I can't get to sleep! And I want to know what this bloody hangman puzzle means that Ben sent me!'

'What hangman puzzle?' June says.

'The first text he ever sent me was a hangman puzzle, and I don't know what the answer is. I never worked it out and now it's too late to ask him.'

'Could you call him when he lands? Or text him?' June says. 'You know that he'll want to hear from you. If that's what it will take to make you feel better.'

'I can't start up a conversation again! That'll make

me look like a total weirdo,' Millie whispers. 'I'm not supposed to be thinking about him, remember? Yesterday was goodbye.'

'Look, maybe Oxytoxin takes a few days to kick in. Or maybe it doesn't work for everyone. Shall I come over? I can be there in five. You can spoon me and pretend I'm Ben. I'll put that red wig on my chin to make it more realistic.'

'Sounds like you guys had a good night,' Millie replies.

'Tequila!' June sings. 'It makes me happy!'

'Not sure you'll be singing that tomorrow. I think I can smell it from here,' Millie laughs through sniffs.

'Seriously, though, are you OK?' June asks.

'I'll be fine,' Millie says, gathering herself. 'It's probably just the last few weeks catching up with me. Just need to get over myself, really. Get a grip. I'll be better in a few hours, I'm sure.'

'I won't be,' June moans.

'Drink some water, get some sleep,' Millie replies.

'I hate seeing you like this, Mils,' June says, softly.

'And I hate being like this,' Millie replies.

'How do you feel about him right now?' June asks.

'It feels like I still love him.'

'What! Who do you love?' a shrill voice sounds from behind the door, before it flies open.

Millie has déjà vu. When Millie and June were fifteen, they snuck out of the flat at midnight to meet friends in Soho. When they crept back in at 4 a.m. the next morning, Vivian was standing in the dimly lit hallway in her long black dressing gown, tapping her foot. June burst out laughing. Millie knew better and instantly shut up. Vivian spent the next hour reprimanding them for being stupid and irresponsible. This morning, not much has changed.

'I'm not angry,' Vivian says, with flared nostrils, leaning against the kitchen counter.

'Are you sure? Because from here, it looks like you've got steam streaming out of your nose,' Millie replies, sipping her tea.

'Do you think this is funny, Millabelle?' Vivian scoffs.

'I really don't,' Millie responds. 'I feel sick about the whole thing.'

'Like I said, I'm not angry, I'm just worried about you,' Vivian repeats, trying her best soft tone. 'You're suddenly in love with a colleague? You kissed him at an office party? You lied to us about where you've been and why you've been there?'

'It *was* a work trip originally, I didn't lie about that,' Millie defends.

'You've put your entire career and professional reputation at risk,' Vivian snaps.

'Mum, I'm thirty, not thirteen. You can't scold me anymore. It's my life!'

'You're certainly behaving like you're thirteen, sulking in your childhood bedroom. And you wonder why you didn't get that promotion! I can spot an office slide from a mile away, Millie! The looks across the desks. The little sniggers. The lunches. Colleagues who've slid think they're *so* clever at hiding it, when everybody knows! And everybody is talking about it.'

'Oh my god, Mum, I haven't slid anyone,' Millie fibs. 'And please stop saying that. No one at work suspects anything.' She won't mention Sasha. 'And besides, we don't have to worry about it anymore. Ben's gone. And I've taken Oxytoxin.'

'It obviously isn't working!' Vivian cries.

'I only took it yesterday. Let's just wait and see.'

'Well, at least he's gone. Good riddance to bad influences.'

Millie's blood pressure surges. But before they get into a full-blown row, she takes a deep breath in to stop herself from exploding. There's no point having an argument. Ben is gone. And with any luck, her feelings will, too.

'What's that smell?' Millie suddenly asks, her eyes popping open.

'Eucalyptus,' Vivian replies. 'From a new diffuser I bought yesterday.'

Millie sinks her face into her hands.

'You know I only ever wanted the best for you, Millie,' Vivian says, switching the kettle back on. 'I've seen a few talented people get stuck in relationships, and I won't let that happen to you. Relationships suck the life out of you. I know you're an adult now, but you'll always be my girl.'

'I know, Mum,' Millie sighs.

'More tea?' Vivian asks.

Millie nods, and watches her mum turn before opening the app again.

Ben's over Iran.

Ping!

AI:

> You OK? Worried.

Millie:

> Why aren't you in bed?

AI:

> I am! Not mine hehe

Millie:

> Boom

AI:

> Can you swing by Buddies tomorrow?
> I have things to say

Millie:

> Sure x

Dearest Belle,

By the time you read this letter, I might be 10,553 miles away from you in Sydney. I've booked a one-way flight and I won't be back any time soon. I need space, and Australia has lots of it. It has lots of sand, too, so

perhaps it's a good thing you aren't coming. Although I
hope our trip to Tenby changed your mind a bit. I hoped
that it would change your mind about us, too, but I've
accepted now that it did not. Don't worry, this letter isn't
a guilt trip. And nor is my actual trip meant to be. I've
had itchy feet for a while, and I think some Bondi sand in
between my toes could fix that. This letter is just a little
note to say thank you for the last few weeks. Without
you, I would have left London some time ago, and I'm
so glad I gave it a shot. It was . . . an experience. But
an experience that I needed to help me make important
changes in my life. To leave Human for good, and think
about what I want to do with myself. So, thank you
for keeping me here for as long as you did. Thank you
for the laughs. Thank you for the tea. Thank you for
the hangman puzzles. And finally, thank you for being
my mate here. I hope you know that, despite what has
happened between us, I'll consider you a friend, always.

With love (don't freak out, not that kind of love) from

Ben

Ben has landed. He is 10,553 miles away from her. If that's
not distance, what is?

'Chin up, phone down,' Al says, handing Millie a beer
over the bar.

Millie throws her phone in her bag, imagining how she could drink ten of these bottles quite easily, even though it's Monday tomorrow.

'How can you drink after last night?' Millie laughs. 'I heard tequila was involved.'

'Hair of the dog always works for me,' Al says, swilling the bottle around in her hand.

'I've never understood that,' Millie replies.

'So, how are you feeling?' Al asks.

'Pretty shit, to be honest,' Millie says, taking a swig. 'But I don't know if it's the pill or the situation.'

'Any side effects?'

'No effects whatsoever, it seems.'

'Millie, I want to know what we were *really* doing yesterday,' Al says, changing the subject abruptly. 'At yours. With the pros and cons list.'

'What do you mean?'

'What was the point? I mean, you're so clearly into him, why not just go for it? Stop fucking whining about it and do something! You know, follow your heart! Sorry for being blunt, but you're making a right meal of it when it doesn't have to be. He loves you. You love him. Love each other. If you still can, after that weird-arse pill you took.'

'What, in a couple?' Millie grimaces.

'Uh, yeeeah, in a couple.' Al grimaces back, mimicking her. 'What's the big deal? I mean, I know it's not everyone's cup of tea, but how do you know it's not yours if you don't try it?'

'Well, you were there,' Millie says indignantly. 'The whole point of making the list was to decide whether being in a couple is something I want to do. And, it turns out, I don't. Or at least, I shouldn't. There are too many downsides.'

'What like, sharing food?' Al scoffs. 'June eats half your food straight off your plate and I don't see you complaining about that.'

'That's different,' Millie says.

'How? Maybe your problem is that you've been in a couple with *June* for too long.'

'I have not!' Millie laughs.

Al shrugs.

'Al, I'm hardly in a couple with June,' Millie says, straight-faced this time.

'OK, perhaps you aren't *in a couple*. But you do care about what she thinks. Maybe too much. June hates the idea of couples. And, being that you're two peas, that makes it very hard for you to even think about being in one.'

'*Hate* is a strong word, Al. Couples just make June uncomfortable,' Millie says. 'More so than most. You know what happened with her parents.'

'Yeah, it was fucked up,' Al says. 'But what happened to her parents is not for you to worry about. Just because they had a shitty relationship, doesn't mean that you will. Anyway, whatever,' Al says. 'It might be too late anyway. I just think that being in a couple with Ben should have been your decision, and I feel like it wasn't. Sure, we went through the practical downsides, but I feel like the main reason you aren't going for it is because you're embarrassed. You feel like it's freakish, or something. But Millie, stuff what other people think. Go with your gut. And your head. If they're telling you that you want to be with him, then that's what you should do.'

'My gut is screaming right now,' Millie says. 'It's like I've swallowed shards of glass.'

'Well, maybe that's a sign.'

'Don't you care what people think of you?' Millie asks, contemplating Al's comments about June. She can't deny the shame she felt when she saw June in the park. Or the guilt she felt when she imagined being with Ben for the long haul, like his parents, and breaking the news to June that the beach house wouldn't work, or having kids, like they discussed a few years ago.

'Do I care what people think? Hell, no!' Al laughs. 'I mean, take a look around us, Millie. I've been working in this fleapit for six years. Six years! You think I'd work here all this time, after getting a first-class degree in journalism, if I cared what people thought of me? I know everyone thinks I'm a loser, but I'm happy here. I'm close to home, I work with mates, the tips are good and I get to hang out with you guys every Friday night. And, when I feel like it, I'll do some writing on the side. I can sell my eggs on eBabe again if I ever need a salary top-up. I've done it before. And let's not forget, free beer! Sure, it's not a high-flying career. But I'm flying high on happiness.'

340

'That was beautiful.' Millie laughs. 'Also, no one thinks you're a loser.'

'Right,' Al laughs. 'Tell that to my dad. But it's OK. I think *you're* a loser for letting Ben get away, when I think he could have made you happier than maybe you could ever imagine.'

'Ouch,' Millie mutters.

'Yes, ouch,' Al says.

'Too late now, right?' Millie says, downing the rest of her drink.

'I don't believe in too late. One for the road?'

'How about five?'

Thirty-Six

@sashah:

Happy Monday! Can we have a
quick chat? Boardroom.

@milliej:

I'm in the middle of something
important. Half an hour?

@sashah:

see you in five minutes, Millie.

Sasha glances up from her phone, but continues to type, as Millie enters the boardroom.

'Have a seat,' she says, suggesting that Millie needs her permission, when in fact Millie is already halfway to sitting.

Sasha slams her phone on the table and leans forward on her elbows, wrapping her red talons around each other.

342

'So, I had a very interesting call from San Francisco this morning,' Sasha says, smiling. 'They were thrilled with our pitch. They loved how we scaled it up to include different audiences and markets. And in particular, they are thrilled with the idea of rebranding for Oxytoxin Teens. They are so thrilled, in fact,' Sasha continues, 'that they've given us the rest of the Oxytoxin business, without a pitch. This is huge. It's even bigger than Pros, Teens, Twos and Fix, Millie. So big that they've asked us to transfer a creative team to San Francisco for a month to work at Human HQ. And I've already chosen the creative team for the task.'

'Who?' Millie asks, knowing the answer by the look on Sasha's face.

'You and me!' Sasha cries. 'The work needs our most senior team, which is us. We can rent together short term near the campus, get lifts in together and grab drinks in the valley after work. Have you seen the campus? It's like a luxury holiday park. Plus, I know a couple of people at Slide San Fran who could show us where to hang out at weekends. Are you excited?'

All Millie can picture is trying to find a space for her milk among a thousand yoghurt pots.

'That sounds . . . amazing,' Millie eventually responds. 'So, what does the rest of the work involve? Are they bringing out more products?'

'A vaccine,' Sasha grins.

'A vaccine?' Millie asks, her eyebrows creasing.

'For toddlers, Millie!' Sasha cries. 'Parents are now

going to be able to prevent their toddlers from falling in love using an Oxytoxin vaccine! Giving them even more choice and peace of mind. Plus, it saves them the hassle of trying to convince their spawn to take a tablet. It's genius, really.'

Millie's heart is pounding through a tight chest and she's counting down from ten to reach some level of calm before she can respond.

'So, what do you say, flatmate?' Sasha asks, grinning at her. 'You and me?'

'What the *slide*, Sasha?' Millie cries. 'Babies?'

'What? Millie, we'll be *saving little children* from heart-break! Isn't that a good thing?' Sasha responds, before her eyes lower to Millie's neckline. 'Are you OK? You look like you have some sort of rash. Do you wear a lot of polyester?'

'I'm not going to San Francisco with you,' Millie says, staring at her.

'What do you mean?' Sasha asks, frowning. 'To be quite frank, it wasn't a question, it was a statement. I *am* your senior, your superior. We *are* the Oxytoxin creative team. We *have* to go to San Francisco at the end of the month to work on the vaccine campaign. I've already said we would. Skye's sent me a load of flats to look at, which I was going to forward to you later.'

'I'm not going to San Francisco with you because I'm leaving,' Millie states.

'What are you on about?' Sasha says, staring at her.

'I'm resigning,' Millie replies, smiling. A few moments

ago she might have been more dramatic about it. But Millie doesn't do confrontation.

'Sorry, *what*?' Sasha says, louder. 'Millie! Since when? You can't just quit! We're launching our biggest campaign ever next month. Are you going to walk out on that? You're crazy! We could end up in San Francisco permanently, working at Human, not Slide. I mean, isn't that the fucking dream?'

'It used to be,' Millie replies, calmly. 'But to be honest, it's more of a nightmare now.'

Millie reaches for her phone and scrolls through her contacts.

'Millie, wait!' Sasha calls to Millie from the boardroom door, as Millie storms into the office kitchen. She puts her phone in her pocket and turns round.

'What now, Sasha?' Millie sighs, as Sasha approaches her.

'Can we . . .' Sasha says, looking uncharacteristically uncomfortable and pausing for a painfully long time.

'Can we what?' Millie says impatiently.

'Look, can I buy you a drink?'

Millie is taken aback, but intrigued enough to say yes.

'I've spent years trying to be your friend here,' Sasha starts, after their first sip of wine. 'It was impossible when Ruth was around, the two of you in your tiny two-woman clique, letting no one else get close. Those fucking Friday lunches that no one else was invited to.'

'We didn't exclude anyone on purpose,' Millie replies. 'It's just that we worked together for a long time. We'd been doing Friday lunches since the start. It's hard to break a habit. Believe me, I know. Look, I'm sorry. I didn't realise how much it bothered you. To be honest, I thought you hated me. You don't act like a fan. And accusing someone of stealing your yoghurt isn't a great way to make friends, is it?'

'I thought you were bullying the new girl!' Sasha cries. 'Like some kind of strange initiation. Weirdly marking your territory, or something.'

'Do you still think I stole your fucking yoghurt?' Millie asks, one eyebrow raised.

Sasha looks at her, then drops her gaze. 'No,' she mutters.

'Come again?' Millie asks.

'No! OK? Fine. I didn't want to look stupid in my first week here, so I couldn't take it back. I thought it was better to just pretend I still thought it was you. I . . . find it hard to apologise. But, as we're clearing the air, I'm . . . sorry.'

'Thank you for that,' Millie states. 'And, what else are you sorry about?'

Sasha tightens her lips.

'Go on,' Millie encourages her.

'I didn't *steal* your research notes, Millie,' Sasha replies.

346

'I merely saw them. And I didn't hack into your computer for them, I found photocopies of them in the print room. There was a huge pile of them, scattered all over the place. I read them while I was waiting for something to print, and . . . what can I say? I was inspired. And in the interests of making the best possible campaign, I used them. Can you honestly say you wouldn't have glanced at my work, if you'd seen it lying there?'

Bloody Ben.

'OK, I believe you,' Millie says, stifling a giggle. 'But I'm still waiting.'

'Fine. I'm sorry,' Sasha replies. 'Even so, Millie, you and Ruth made me feel excluded from my first day. I felt like a third wheel for years. I feel like you owe me an apology too.'

'I'm sorry,' Millie replies genuinely.

'When Ruth left, I thought we'd get closer. I thought we could start doing Friday lunches. Be a proper team.' Sasha looks at Millie and shrugs.

'If you were so desperate for us to be a team, why did you toss me over to the interns?' Millie asks.

'One word. Ben. I could see what was happening between you two! It was Ruth all over again. The private messages, the inside jokes. The adorable tea-making. Those fucking lunches!'

'Ben and I just clicked. I'm sorry,' Millie replies. 'In hindsight, I guess we were cliquey. We should have included you more. But you and I, we're just . . . different.'

'Are we? I reckon we're more alike than you think. We're

both ambitious. We're both still here, working on Oxytoxin, unlike Ben and Ruth. You don't see me dumping you to swan off with a girlfriend, or because I have a moral problem with the pill.'

'When you got the promotion, I was devastated. I felt like everything I'd worked so hard for was for nothing. But the board picked the right person for the role. Go to San Francisco on your own, you don't need me.'

Sasha's lips turn up at the corners. 'Thank you.'

'Now,' Millie continues. 'As long as we're being honest, there's something else I need to tell you.'

'Sounds like we might need more of this.' Sasha sighs, topping up their wine glasses.

'I took Oxytoxin. Two weeks ago.'

Sasha pauses mid-pour and her eyes widen. 'Why the hell would you do that?'

'I . . . have my reasons. They aren't important. What is important, though, is that I don't think it worked. I feel no differently about my situation.'

'Really?' Sasha frowns, tilting her head. 'It seemed to work for our test cases. Thandi emailed this morning confirming that she's definitely felt a change.'

'And the others?' Millie asks. 'Deion, Ginny, the Rogers?'

'Deion and his dad have come to some sort of agreement about his schoolwork. Ginny has chosen to wait a bit before taking the pills, and the Rogers have decided against taking it at all. In fact, they've swung the other way and have started some kind of *pro-couple* petition which has about fifty thousand signatures. I suppose it's a hundred thousand if each signature counts for two.' She titters. 'But I can't work out why it wouldn't work on you. Where did you get it from?'

'I took a packet from the pitch,' Millie says. 'From your pop-up shop.'

Sasha throws her hand over her mouth and her shoulders start shaking.

'Are you OK?' Millie asks, leaning across the table. 'I'm sorry, Sasha, I didn't . . .'

'Millie!' She drops her hand, laughing. 'Those packets were prototypes from the design studio. They weren't real, they were filled with flour!'

Millie sits bolt upright in her chair as the news hits her. A wave of relief suddenly washes over her, and, when she realises that what she feels is relief, rather than disappointment, it all becomes clear. She knows what she has to do. And she knows who she has to call.

Millie:

I need to talk to you x

Millie rushes through the park towards home, holding tightly onto Ken Plant. She feels as light as a feather with the relief of being Oxytoxin-free, and she's bubbling with excitement at the phone call she's about to make.

She puts Ken carefully on her kitchen island and takes a seat on the stool, her hands shaking as she presses call on her phone.

'I've changed my mind,' she states decisively, grinning like a loon as she strokes Ken Plant's sticky note face, but her smile fades as the silence stretches and she waits for an answer.

Thirty-Seven

One month later

The front door of the old warehouse is half rust, half steel. With Ken Plant in one hand, Millie pauses before knocking, checking her freshly manicured fingernails haven't been chipped afterwards.

This is it. Deep breaths.

She quickly glances at her reflection in the window next to the door, and leans in. There's nothing on her face. She's lipstick-smudge-free. Her hair is behaving and . . .

She grins.

. . . there's nothing lodged in her teeth.

She inhales, reaches up and knocks three times. The echoes reverberate inside. When she's greeted by silence, she takes her phone out and dials Ruth.

'Where are you?' Ruth says.

'Outside!' Millie replies.

'Oh, sorry! I'll come down now. It's a bit of a trek. Great for the butt, though.'

A few minutes later and faint, squeaky footsteps from inside start to grow louder until they're on the other side of the door. The door opens with an ear-piercing screech, making Millie's spine tingle. It's a far cry from the smooth, faint whooshes of the automatic doors at Human.

'Welcome to Twocan!' Ruth beams, wearing a pair of paint-splashed dungarees. 'It still needs a spit, a lick and a polish, but it's come on since last week, hasn't it?'

'It really has!' Millie says as she steps inside and looks up at the skylights, which are covered in moss. The exposed brick walls of their new HQ are faded, and their eclectic mix of charity shop desks are stained, but it's a start. Millie smooths her hair down one side, smiles and continues looking around.

'He's not here yet,' Ruth says.

Millie releases her lungs.

'You all right there?' Ruth laughs.

'I'm fine. Why do I feel so nervous?' Millie says, breathily, placing Ken on the reception desk, which is currently a single chair with a Twocan sign swinging above it.

'Because he doesn't know you're here and it's going to be a rather huge surprise,' Ruth replies.

'Thank you,' Millie says. 'For this. For bringing me on. And for bringing him on.'

'I hardly needed much persuading, Mils,' Ruth said. 'You two are the dream team. Hey, who's this little guy?' Ruth asks.

'Ken Plant. Temporary receptionist,' Millie smiles, dusting his face. 'Calm, but prickly.'

A loud bang on the door makes them jump.

'Oh my god, it's him,' Millie says, swatting at her hair again, sitting on the reception chair and then standing up again, pulling her blouse down and leaning on the counter.

'Can you calm down, please? It'll be fine,' Ruth says as she shoves on the front door handle and yanks it open. The light streams in and the silhouette in the doorway steps forward.

'What are you doing here?' Millie says, relaxing her pose.

'Well, it's nice to see you too, Millabelle. What a welcome,' Vivian says, removing her massive sunglasses. 'Who were you expecting?'

'Our new chief strategy officer,' Millie replies.

'Vivian!' Ruth cries. 'Come in. It's far from done, so you'll have to use a little imagination. Maybe a lot of imagination, looking at it. We're probably two weeks away from completion.'

'I think it's fabulous!' Vivian smiles. 'It reminds me of when I set up on my own. Big ceilings, open pipes, exposed brick. Very urban chic. Anyway, I'm sorry to arrive unannounced, but Millie didn't invite me or answer my calls, so I had no choice. I just wanted to pop round to congratulate you on your first official day, Chief Creative Officer.'

'You could have *waited* for an invite, or for me to answer your calls,' Millie says under her breath, next to Ruth.

353

Millie and Ruth exchange glances and stifle their smiles with pursed lips.

'Oh dear, what's happened here? What's this sorry little excuse for greenery?' Vivian says, poking Ken with the arm of her sunglasses. 'I'll put you in touch with my urban landscape architect. If I invest in a company, I want to make sure it creates a decent impression.'

Millie steps forward and rolls the chair away from her mother's reach. 'That's Ken Plant, and I like him just the way he is,' Millie says, frowning.

'Small, wrinkly and limp?' Vivian replies.

'Hey, who's been reading my old Slide reviews?' chirps a familiar voice at the front door.

Millie's heartbeat goes into overdrive as she turns round and sees him for the first time since the park. Since she ran away. Since that kiss.

'Millie!' Ben cries with a strange expression – half smile, half frown, putting his cartoon coffee cup down slowly on a cardboard box next to him. He wipes his hands on his trousers, then through his hair before extending an arm towards Vivian for a handshake, which is reciprocated half-heartedly. 'Hello, I'm Ben! Are you our new Chief *Welcome* Officer?' He smiles, glancing at Millie and frowning again.

Vivian stares at him with her icy eyes while Millie shakes her head vigorously in the background.

Ben soon realises that the safest thing to do is stop talking, and instead darts his wide eyes between them both in confusion.

'Ben, this is my mum, Vivian. Mum, this is Ben, our chief strategy officer. Also, hi,' Millie says, stepping forward.

Millie and Ben do an awkward arms-outstretched dance before hugging.

'It's good to see you,' Millie says softly in his ear.

'You too, Belle,' Ben replies, even more softly. 'I had no idea you'd be here. Are you joining Twocan?'

Millie nods her head excitedly and opens her mouth to explain, when her mum interrupts.

'Lovely to meet you, Ben, I'm Vivian. And one of your investors,' Vivian says, interrupting the moment and forcing a smile before giving Millie a withering look.

'Oh, right, sorry.' Ben squeezes his eyes shut. 'Just give me a moment to remove this giant foot from my mouth!'

'You look very tanned, have you been on holiday?' Vivian asks.

'I've been in Australia for a few weeks. Sorry, can I just make it very clear that I'm not really on Slide?' Ben says with a serious face.

Millie mouths sorry from behind her mum's back.

'Mum, let's go to the balcony. We have an amazing view from up there that I'd love you to see.'

⬤▬

'Have you gone completely mad?' Vivian says, folding her arms and leaning sideways on against the balcony railing. 'I mean, I thought the whole idea of Twocan was off the wall, but then you go and hire a man you have history with? Do you know how complicated and messy that could get? And what if you start falling for him again, surrounded by all this talk of couples?'

'I don't have a history with him, Mum,' Millie says. 'And, technically, Ruth hired him.'

'Oh, stop trying to deny it, Millie, you've already confessed to everything,' Vivian replies.

'No, I mean—' Millie tries to continue, but Vivian interrupts her.

'Wait a moment,' Vivian says, as if a light bulb has suddenly been switched on. 'You took Oxytoxin, didn't you? So, maybe this will be OK? Unless he's the type to hold a grudge. Is he? What if he's a stalker? Maybe you should slip some Oxytoxin into his coffee when he's not looking. From what I can tell, he isn't exactly the sharpest tool in the box.'

'Well,' Millie starts. 'Funny thing, actually. As it turns out, the Oxytoxin pills weren't Oxytoxin after all. So I haven't taken it.'

'What were they?'

'They were fake pills. Filled with flour. For the pitch.'

'So when are you going to get some real ones?' Vivian says, starting to fluster.

'I'm not.'

'I think it would be sensible, Millie.'

'Mum, I'm still in love with Ben.'

Vivian blanches.

'I haven't told him yet, but I'm planning to, this weekend. I'm just hoping he still feels the same way about me.'

'Millie, no!' Vivian throws her head in her hands. 'No, no, *no*! You've been brainwashed, haven't you? I knew this would happen, working here, with Ruth. You want to be in *a couple*, Millie? And you *work* together? What's got into you? Is this some kind of delayed teenage rebellion? What happens when you break up and you're stuck working with him? You're honestly going to take that risk?'

Her mother's stream of consciousness eventually fades, making room for Millie to speak.

'It might seem like a risk to you, but it isn't for me,' Millie responds calmly. 'Look. You've always told me to stand up for myself and go after what I really want. That's what I'm doing. I'm standing up for myself. I'm standing up to you. I'm standing up to everyone who thinks there's something wrong with being in a couple. And I know I used to be one of them.'

'You know full well that I meant stand up for yourself at work!' Vivian cries. 'Can't you see how being in a couple could hold you back? You're going to be distracted, you're going to lose focus, you're going to lose time, money. You're going to be trapped, Millie.'

'It might be hard for you to believe,' Millie says. 'But I think I feel more trapped being single and set in my ways. I used to think that being in a relationship would make me lose out. But Ben feels like a . . . a bonus. Besides, I'm only twenty-nine, Mum. I've got thirty years of work ahead of me. I have time for both Ben and my career.'

'Next you'll be calling him your *other half*,' Vivian tuts.

'I promise you, I'll never call him that,' Millie winces. 'We're both our own, independent people who just happen to enjoy spending time together. Hopefully.'

'But you enjoy spending time with June. I used to think you enjoyed spending time with me. You've got Al and Ruth. Aren't we enough? I mean, how much time can you possibly have to spare on him? You're too good to be in a relationship, Millie. Why would you want to share all this with someone? Why would you want to make that sacrifice? This is Mandy all over again. You're going to lose your spark, just like she did.'

'Mum, I know it's hard for you to believe, but you don't need to be worried about me sharing my life or making sacrifices. I'm very happy. Being in a couple will be my choice. I'm not ill. I don't need to be rescued. I don't need to be pitied. You know me, I only make sensible decisions, and I'm sure this is one of them.'

'I used to know you,' Vivian said. 'Now I'm not so sure.'

Vivian puts her sunglasses back on firmly.

'I'm sorry I'm not the perfect daughter you thought I was. Although if you think about it, being in a couple makes me more like you than ever. I've inherited your rebellious streak. You rebelled against Veronica when you chose to have me in your twenties, and now I'm rebelling against you. You wanted to prove Veronica wrong with me, and I'm sorry, but I want to prove you wrong with Ben. I want to show you that I *can* be happy and successful *and* in a couple, despite your concerns. I do appreciate you want what's best for me. And I'm convinced this is it.'

After a few minutes of silence, Vivian speaks.

'You said you haven't told him yet,' Vivian says.

'Not yet. This is the first time I've seen him since . . . that night I told you about.'

'So there's still a chance he'll say no,' Vivian mutters.

'Mum!'

'Well, sorry, Millie, but he might not give you the answer you want. Maybe he'll give you the answer *I* want,' Vivian smiles wryly.

'I suppose. But I hope not. And if you care about my feelings, you'll hope not too,' Millie replies.

'Fine.' Vivian sighs. 'I do only want what's best for you. And it's hard for me to stand here and tell you that being in a couple for the rest of your life is just that. I hope you understand what you're getting yourself into. If this relationship doesn't last, you'll be left heartbroken and unemployed. I pictured a future for you of financial independence, freedom to travel the world at your will, the ability to do what you want without sacrificing your space, time, wants and needs. Freedom from taking on someone else's problem.'

'That's just it, Mum,' Millie replies. 'Before meeting Ben, I didn't want to travel at all. He helped me find the confidence to try new things.'

'OK, Millie. If you can honestly say that being in a couple with Ben will give you that, then who am I to tell you otherwise? It wouldn't be my choice, but it's not my choice to make. I just hope we don't lose you. I hope you don't lose *yourself*.'

'I promise I won't lose anyone, least of all me.'

'Will I like him?' Vivian asks.

'I think so,' Millie says.

'Well, at least he's Welsh,' Vivian ponders. 'You are wrong about one thing. You're still perfect to me. You always will be, and if you attempt to tell me otherwise one more time, I'm going to display all your teenage photos on the wall. I'll dig out every sighting of the bucket hat for when you bring Ben to meet me properly this Sunday, for lunch.'

'Really?' Millie smiles. 'Of course, there is a chance that Ben might say no.'

'He'd be mad to,' Vivian replies, turning towards the balcony door before pausing.

'Don't you dare get matching tattoos.'

'Too late, sorry,' Millie says, grinning at her.

'Don't joke about that, Millie,' Vivian says. 'Next thing you'll be holding hands whenever you're next to each other.'

'Never. You know I'm far too practical for that. Holding hands is very inconvenient.'

Vivian smiles at her and places a hand on Millie's arm.

'Perhaps you haven't change that much, after all.'

Millie approaches her mother, takes her hand and kisses her on the cheek.

'Thanks, Mum.'

Suddenly the balcony door bursts open.

'Have you seen the news?' Ruth says, panting.

BREAKING NEWS: COUPLES STAGE PROTESTS AGAINST NEW ANTI-LOVE DRUG FROM HUMAN

'So that petition the Rogers started, calling for couple equality? It's reached 250,000 signatures now,' Ruth says, as the four of them stare at the computer screen.

'Are those couples? There are thousands of them!' Vivian cries. 'Where have they all been hiding?'

'We all know what this means, don't we?' Ben grins.

'It's time for Twocan to fly!' Millie cries.

Ben grabs hold of her left hand and lifts her arm in the air like a boxing champion. Millie looks up at him, and for a few seconds it's the summer party moment all over again.

Thirty-Eight

'So, what are we celebrating?' Al asks, raising her glass.

'Twocan getting funded!' Millie shouts.

'Millie being a chief creative officer before her thirtieth birthday,' June says.

'June becoming a fat cat,' Ruth adds.

'Like I need another one of those in my life,' Millie replies.

'I take it tonight's on you, June?' Al takes the menu. 'Because the wagyu sounds delicious.'

'Yeah, you'll be lucky if I shout you a ragu,' June responds.

'We're also celebrating you, Al,' Ruth says.

'Well, it's hardly a kick-ass start-up, a fancy new job or a big promotion,' Al mutters, sipping her ginger ale. 'But I'm glad my workmates have dropped the nickname.'

All three look at her blankly.

'Al . . . cohol.'

'To Al . . . cohol Free!' June cheers.

'So, when do you officially start at Twocan, Mils?' Al asks.

'In approximately one day, twelve hours and thirty-six minutes,' Ruth replies, looking at her watch and beaming.

'Watch out, your co-worker's a bit of a keeno,' Al says. 'Next thing, she'll want you to go for a team lunch!'

'I can't actually believe it took me so long to finally say yes,' Millie adds.

'I can, you cautious little hamster,' June replies. 'It's a good thing, most of the time. Speaking of which, I assume you know exactly what you're ordering?'

'Well,' Millie replies, her hand hovering over the menu. 'Seeing as I'm in the mood for change, I thought I could leave it to chance tonight.'

Al gasps dramatically.

'Hold on a minute . . . who are you, and what have you done with Millie?' June asks, her eyes squinting, looking around the bar.

Millie looks up at the ceiling and traces her fingertip up and down the menu until they shout at her to stop. Her face falls when she leans over the menu.

'Prawn curry.' She sighs. 'Do I get a second go?'

'Nope. Against the rules,' June states.

'We're forgetting some other news that deserves a celebration,' Al says, looking at Millie.

Millie frowns, confused.

'You haven't taken Oxytoxin!' Al cries.

'Well, I'm happy I still have options,' Millie explains.

'Says the woman who used to hate options,' June says, and laughs.

'Oooh, I have another one!' Millie says, raising her glass. 'June has reached a 4.5-star Slide rating, which makes her an official All-Star Slide.'

'Thank you, thank you,' June says, looking around her. 'I'd like to thank Jesus, my agent . . .'

'. . . and my best friend, Millie Jones,' Millie interrupts, 'chief creative officer at Twocan, without whom none of this would have been possible, who also happens to be funny, smart and extremely stylish.'

'God, I love how we finish each other's sentences,' June says.

'You complete me,' Millie adds.

'Get a room, you two.' Ruth laughs.

'So, what's happening with Ben?' Al asks. 'On, off, over him, under him?'

'I'll tell you tomorrow,' Millie replies with a shy smile, glancing at June.

'Oooh,' they all murmur in unison as the waiter appears beside them, saving Millie from any further interrogation.

'I'll have the lamb and pomegranate salad, please, with a side of polenta chips,' Millie says, and smiles.

'You did read the menu, didn't you?' June stares at her with a deadpan face.

'Yep.'

'What were we all so worried about? You'll never change,' June says, laughing.

Thirty-Nine

Millie has been pacing the pond for ten minutes, wringing her hands with nervous energy, her stomach in knots. She checks her watch for the third time. It's five minutes to 8 p.m., which is when she asked him to be here at their spot by the goose. The last time they were here, Ben confessed he still had feelings for her, she unexpectedly kissed him and then ran off after June, leaving him in the literal and metaphorical dark. She's surprised he's coming at all. Could his feelings have disappeared in a few weeks? Her stomach sinks at the thought. She's turned him down so many times, she wouldn't blame him.

She pauses to catch her breath and give the setting one final check. With June's help, Millie has spent the last hour turning their spot into a luxurious little Scandi retreat at sundown with faux fur, knitted blankets and fairy lights framing the chairs. A bit strange for October, Millie worries, but it looks pretty, nonetheless. Above them, a string of lanterns is tied between two lamp posts, their orange orbs reflected in the inky water below. On the table between the chairs is a picnic, which she has carefully curated to reflect little moments in their relationship. If you can call it that. Fish and chips from Battered Sea. A cheeseboard to show she remembered his favourite dessert-that-isn't-a-dessert. Two flasks of hot tea and a packet of lemon cream biscuits. And of course, a bottle of wine in a cooler bag for a bit of Dutch courage.

She sees him approaching down the path, his hands in his pockets and his headphones on. He looks just like he did on the day they first met. Millie feels the sudden urge to spin round and be sick into the pond. She takes a deep breath in and a big swallow down and smiles at him instead. Ben takes his hands out of his pockets and brushes his headphones back, resting them on his neck, which is craned up at the lanterns above.

'Did you do all this?' He smiles broadly, running his fingers across his new beard, which makes Millie fancy him more than ever, if that's even possible.

'I wanted to do something a little special after last time,' Millie says sheepishly. 'You know, when I was a dickhead for giving you mixed messages and then running away in the middle of an important conversation.'

'Rings a bell,' Ben replies, squinting. 'But you weren't a dickhead. You were just looking out for *your friend*. Still, I'm glad you felt so bad about it – this is amazing. I've said it before, I think you should be more of a dickhead, more often.'

'I can probably arrange that quite easily.' Millie smiles, taking the wine out of the cooler bag and offering him a glass with a nod.

'Me? No, I don't drink, and I'm extremely judgemental of people who do,' he replies, sitting down and chucking his bag by his feet.

Millie pauses and stares at him.

'Kidding. Fill me up to the brim, please. If I see so much as a sliver of empty glass around the top, I'm sending it back.'

Millie giggles and pours them two large glasses.

'So, you said you wanted to talk—'

'Ben, I *am* in love with you,' Millie blurts out.

'Sorry?' He frowns.

'I'm in love with you, Ben. I'm sorry I couldn't admit it out loud before, to you or to myself. I was confused, and I was scared. I'm new to all this, and I didn't know what these feelings were. I didn't know what love was until you left me. I know I said I wanted space from you, but I hated it as soon as I had it. I hated you being in Australia. You might have been thousands of miles away, but you were never out of my mind. Not for a minute. And look, if you've moved on, if what I've done in the past has ruined any chance of us being together, I'll understand. If I've blown it, I have no one to blame but myself and my infuriating obsession with sticking to what I know. I've always felt like my life was a hamster wheel, when in fact it was a hamster *ball*. I was trapped. I've been scared of anything different. Terrified of *being* different, and of what people think. When you left, it's like everything became clear. That I want you. I want *us*.'

She pauses to catch her breath, and, for an agonising few minutes they say nothing. She has blown it. Maybe he met up with Sarah in Australia. Perhaps they're back together. Or maybe having space has made him realise that he wants to be single. That he isn't in love with Millie at all, and it was just a passing crush. Millie's insides burn as she waits for him to say something. Anything.

'I hated being in Australia too,' Ben comments. 'It was their winter, for a start. And, on the plane out there, I kept on watching the map. Watching the plane take me further and further away from you. Feeling relieved to get everything off my chest, but wretched at the same time about how we left things. It was a weird goodbye, wasn't it?'

'The weirdest.' Millie nods, imagining them staring at their maps at the same time.

'Maybe it was wishful thinking, but it didn't feel like things were over between us. It didn't feel like goodbye. When Ruth called to offer me the job, I was sitting on Manly Beach on my own, wondering what the hell I'd done. Missing home. Missing you. Missing us. I felt lost.'

'You missed me?' Millie asks slowly.

'Well, of course I did. I don't think I could ever get over you. Unless, I don't know, I . . . took Oxytoxin.'

Millie still hasn't told him she took it. Or, what she thought was it. Should she? What's the point? What if it scares him off? If Millie was *that* determined not to be with him a month ago, how can he trust her feelings now?

'Millie, are you sure you really want this? Because three weeks ago you were sure of the complete opposite. What happened to the Millie who hates change, loves routine, thinks I'm going to spoil her sixteen-year-old dreams? The Millie who cares so much about what people think? Are you going to hide me away? When we're together, are you going to dive into a bush if you see someone you know? What if we went for it, and you changed your mind? Decided you were right to have those fears and doubts. Millie, of course I still love you, but I also love myself. And I need to protect myself. Because if we're a couple, I'm all in. Then if you decide you're out, I'll be left with my heart broken, and my heartbreaker sitting opposite me all day.'

'I will struggle to adapt. But after being with you, and then without you, I know that I'm going to struggle to adapt to life without you more.'

'Good answer.'

'But there is one thing I have to tell you.' She sighs.

'Uh-oh,' Ben says.

'The night you left my flat, I took my first Oxytoxin. And the night you left for Australia, I took my second. I was feeling so, I guess you'd call it lovesick, that I was desperate.'

'I know the feeling,' Ben comments, looking taken aback at her admission. 'But then, what are we doing here? Didn't they work?'

'They were fake. I nicked a prop from Sasha's pop-up shop. Turns out they were filled with flour.'

Ben purses his lips, hiding a giggle.

'Yeah, I know.' Millie half laughs. 'Muppet.'

'OK, I should be mad at you for taking the devil's "medicine",' Ben says, 'but I almost did it too. That's what's so evil about it. Imagine if they had been real? There'd be no going back.'

'I don't want to think about it,' Millie replies. 'I felt hideous afterwards.'

'Bit of bloating?' Ben titters.

'Very funny. No, I felt like the entire world had been dumped on me. I was tired, sore stomach, moody, miserable, and I couldn't stop thinking of you. I knew something was wrong. I thought it was a sham.'

'I wish it was,' Ben replies.

'Look, Ben, you don't have to give me an answer right now. I know I might be a bit of a risk,' Millie says.

'Makes a change from me being one,' Ben says, and smiles.

'Maybe take some time to think things through. Write a pros and cons list or something. But just know that I'm here. And I'm all in.'

Her declaration hangs in the still air between them for a few minutes as they sip their wine, before Ben turns to her.

'You want me to go away and write a pros and cons list, huh?' Ben teases gently. 'Well, as the seasoned expert in relationships, I think the proper thing to do in a situation like this is to start with a first date. Don't you?' he says, nodding behind him at the seats.

Millie grins and nods.

Ben holds her gaze as he clinks her wine glass with his.

'I mean, it feels like a first date,' Ben says. 'Between you and me, I thought our first date was the night before the pitch on the roof terrace, but I guess it's not a date if the other person doesn't know it's a date. Then it's just creepy, isn't it? I've warned you before, I'm a creep. And thanks for one-upping me. All I ever did was steal a coffee and fetch a couple of beers. This is next level. I feel like I'm at a ski resort. Bet the ducks are loving it. They're suckers for romance. And the goose, well, he's proper gooey.'

Suddenly Millie realises something: Ben is as nervous as she is. That's why he hasn't stopped talking for the last few minutes, not even to catch his breath. When it strikes her that they've both got first-date jitters, her heart slows down.

'Ben?' she says.

'Yes?' he replies, finally pressing the pause button.

'Can we play a game?' she says, reaching into her bag to retrieve a piece of white paper and a pen, and unfolding the paper on the table between them.

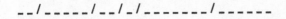

'What's this?' Ben frowns, taking the paper and holding it under the light.

'It's the hangman puzzle from the first messages you ever sent me. I've spent weeks desperate to know the answer, and I'd like you to put me out of my misery.'

Ben pauses and looks hard at the paper before glancing up at her with amused eyes. 'Lucky for you that I remember,' he says, and smiles.

'E,' Millie says.

Ben nods and takes the pen.

_ e / _ _ _ _ _ / _ e / _ / _ e _ _ e _ _ / _ _ _ _ _ e

'O.'

_ e / _ o _ _ _ / _ e / _ / _ e _ _ e _ _ / _ o _ _ e

'U.'

_ e / _ o u _ _ / _ e / _ / _ e _ _ e _ _ / _ o u _ _ e

'I.'

Ben shakes his head and draws the first line of the gallows.

'A.'

_ e / _ o u _ _ / _ e / a / _ e _ _ e _ _ / _ o u _ _ e

Millie takes the piece of paper, holds it under the light for a few seconds and then smiles.

'P.'

_e/_ou__/_e/a/pe__e__/_oup_e

'L.'

_e/_oul_/_e/a/pe__e__/_ouple

'W.'

we/woul_/_e/a/pe__e__/_ouple

'D.'

we/would/_e/a/pe__e__/_ouple

'R.'

we/would/_e/a/per_e__/_ouple

Ben starts to giggle.
'C.'

we/would/_e/a/per_ec_/couple

'B, F, T,' Millie states quickly.

we/would/be/a/perfect/couple

'Very well played, Belle.' Ben smiles at her.

They stare across the pond, watching the surface ripple under a soft breeze. She pulls her blanket over her shoulders and scrapes her chair closer to his, wishing it was a chair built for two.

'So, Millie Jones, can I ask you a question?' Ben says.

'What is it, Ben Evans?' Millie replies.

'Are we a couple?' he asks.

'I think we are,' Millie says.

'Yikes,' Ben whispers. 'Should we get matching tattoos?'

'I mean, I have promised my mum we will. But no,' Millie says.

'Haircuts?'

'Definitely not,' Millie says.

'OK, don't say no immediately. What about matching Christmas jumpers? Wait, no, what about one giant Christmas jumper that fits us both?'

'Well, it'll certainly help fend off the *Are you still in a couple?* question.'

'OK, one last suggestion. Should our couple name be Billie or Men?' Ben says.

'We're breaking up.'

Ben laughs softly, lifting his head up from hers and kissing her on the temple.

Millie tilts her head towards Ben – her boyfriend – and smiles. Then she turns round, leans over to him and presses her lips hard against his, inhaling the scent of eucalyptus that surrounds them.

Acknowledgements

I couldn't have written *The Couple* without the wisdom, talent and infinite patience of my editor, Sarah Bauer, who – apart from her questionable taste in confectionery – is always right about everything and is far funnier than me. Thank you, Sarah, and thank you to the rest of the team at Bonnier: Katie Lumsden, Jessica Tackie and Clare Kelly. Clare made *Slide* happen and, for that, I am forever grateful. Thank you also to my wonderful agent/agony aunt Hayley Steed. Writing this second novel gave me the jitters at times, and Hayley was a voice of calm, reason and reassurance.

To my husband Chris, my family and my friends who read my horrible first draft, sorry for wasting your time and please delete the evidence. Thanks for the kind words of encouragement anyway (even though you had to say that).

I'd also like to thank the entire book community that has welcomed me since I joined it in 2020 with my debut,

The Shelf. Thank you to the bloggers who've read, reviewed, commented and shared – your enthusiasm gives me the confidence to continue. To the authors who have done the same, thank you for finding the time. As a writer, I know how precious that time is.

Finally, thank you to Arlo. For being such a clever boy at feeding, not toooo bad at sleeping and ten days overdue so I could hand my second draft in on time.*

*OK, only a month late.

Dear reader,

A huge thank you for picking up *The Couple*, my second novel. Wearing my heart on my sleeve, I'll confess that my relationship with this novel – like all relationships – has had its ups and downs. Some days, I was head over heels for it. Some days, I wanted to lob my heels at it.

When I wrote *The Couple*, I was feeling uncomfortably pregnant, there was a global pandemic, and I was abandoning my beloved London to start a strange new life in rural Berkshire, where I'm pretty sure the air is 95% horse poo. But, thanks to the encouragement of my incredibly talented editing team at Bonnier Books, *The Couple* and I went the distance, I reached The End, and I couldn't be happier to share Millie and Ben's story.

What inspired *The Couple* wasn't a single moment. It was a series of *being single* moments.

At thirty, I found myself divorced and wondering what had happened to the Disney-sponsored dreams of my youth? Where were the husband, kids, and castle? I was single, childfree and living alone in a tiny rental. I was watching what I wanted on TV, eating what I wanted to eat, travelling to places I wanted to go . . . and feeling happier than I had done in ages. After years of serial monogamy, I realised I loved single life. For the first time in forever, I felt free and in charge of my own life.

What I wasn't free from was having to explain my happily

single status to the smug couples around me. My singleness was a source of fascination to them. One husband would ask me – every time – if I was 'getting any'. So, I'd ask him right back. Still, I preferred being probed to being pitied, which is what his wife would do with a gentle tilt of her head.

I wrote *The Couple* to shut down the single pity party and put relationship attitudes into reverse. I wanted to imagine an alternative world, where we're taught that being single isn't something to be embarrassed of, it's something to embrace. I wanted to create a society that doesn't constantly question why women are single, it questions why women aren't single. And I wanted to convince those who doubt it that women don't need a husband or kids to feel complete – no one does. Most of all, I wanted to show how ridiculous it is to assume that being single makes you 'abnormal' and that being in a relationship is the route to all happiness.

Good relationships are wonderful. I'm lucky enough to be in one now. But I'd love to return and tell my twenty-something, single-shaming self to ditch all the duds. And to stop pursuing the couple status at any cost to my personal dreams, freedom and happiness. I hope to persuade people that being single is a pleasure not a plight, that being in a relationship should feel like a choice, not a necessity. And I hope to silence those smug couples everywhere when they ask that dreaded: *why are you still single?*

Thank you again for choosing *The Couple*. Every show

of support for my writing, whether it's a pre-order, purchase or simply a like, share or kind comment, means the world to me. It gives me the confidence to think – *hell yeah, I can do this*! I *love* telling stories, and I'd love to continue telling stories until my imagination runs dry. Hopefully, that's never.

If you would like to hear more about *The Couple* and my other books, you can visit **www.bit.ly/HellyActon** where you can become part of the **Helly Acton Readers' Club**. It only takes a few moments to sign up, and there are no hidden catches or costs.

Bonnier Books UK will keep your data private and confidential, and it will never be passed on to a third party. Nor will we spam you with loads of emails. We'll just keep in touch now and again with news about my books, and you can unsubscribe any time you want.

If you would like to get involved in a wider conversation about my books, please do review *The Couple* on Amazon, on GoodReads, on any other e-store, on your own blog and social media accounts, or talk about it with friends, family or reading groups! Sharing your thoughts helps other readers, and I always enjoy hearing about what people experience from my writing.

Thank you again for reading *The Couple*.

All the best,
Helly xxx

Reading Group Questions

1. What differences did you notice about Millie's society beyond its attitude towards relationships? How does that shift in attitude affect other aspects of life?

2. Why do you think Millie feels such pressure to succeed at work?

3. Families operate very differently in Millie's world. How does this novel explore family?

4. Who was your favourite character?

5. This novel uses different media to tell its story – text messages, hangman puzzles, work notes. How did this change the reading experience for you?

6. *The Couple* is a love story, but it's also very much a book about friendship. How do Millie's friendships affect her life?

7. How do you think gender and sexuality might be viewed differently in a world not orientated around couples?

8. The 'couple-shaming' in this novel is in part a commentary on 'single-shaming' in our own society. Can you think of examples from your everyday life where being in a couple was presented as the norm and being single was not? Do you think you'll change your behaviour at all, after reading this novel?

9. Have you ever felt like you've been 'single-shamed'? How did it make you feel?

10. Were you aware of some of the advantages that couples experience in our world, such as the tax breaks?

11. Several of the milestones we celebrate in our world are based around being in a conventional couple – engagements, weddings, having children, wedding anniversaries, etc. What other milestones could we be celebrating?

12. *The Couple* references the notion of bringing up children with friends, rather than romantic partners. Is this something society should be more open to? Would you ever consider it?

13. In our society single people are often categorised as 'married to their work' or 'career women'. How does the author explore, and challenge, this idea in the novel?

14. Do you think younger generations are more confidently

single? Do they feel as much pressure to be in a relationship as older generations once did at the same age, or are younger generations more 'pro-single' than previous ones?

15. What do you think would be different about your life if you lived in Millie's world? Would you, like her, risk it all for love?

16. If Oxytoxin existed, would you take it?

If you enjoyed *The Couple*, why not try
Helly Acton's debut novel, *The Shelf*?

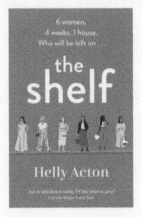

Everyone in Amy's life seems to be getting married,
having children and settling down (or so Instagram tells
her), and she feels like she's falling behind. So, when her
long-term boyfriend surprises her with a dream holiday,
she thinks he's going to *finally* pop the Big Question.
But the dream turns into a nightmare when, instead,
she finds herself on the set of a *Big Brother*-style
reality television show, *The Shelf*.

Along with five other women, Amy is brutally
dumped live on TV and must compete in a series
of humiliating and obnoxious tasks in the hope
of being crowned 'The Keeper'.

**While inside the house, will Amy learn that there
are worse things than being 'left on the shelf'?**